pink clay

JENNIFER LUCIC

UNDERGROUND
HOUSE

Pink Clay

Copyright 2024 Underground House Publishing

www.jenniferlucic.com

Thank you for purchasing an authorized copy of this book. Supporting authors means creating a space for artists to breathe light into an otherwise dark world.

The publisher reserves all copyrights. No part of this book may be reproduced in any form, stored in any retrieval system, or transmitted by any means without permission from the publisher. To request special permission to duplicate any part of this book for purposes protected under copyright law, please contact the publisher directly.

This book is a work of fiction. Any characters, places, and incidents are products of the author's imagination or used fictitiously, and any resemblance to any persons, living or dead, businesses, events, or otherwise is entirely coincidental.

ISBN: 978-1-7368383-7-2 (paperback) | ISBN: 978-1-7368383-8-9 (hardcover)

ISBN: 978-1-7368383-9-6 (eBook)

Library of Congress Control Number: 2024911313

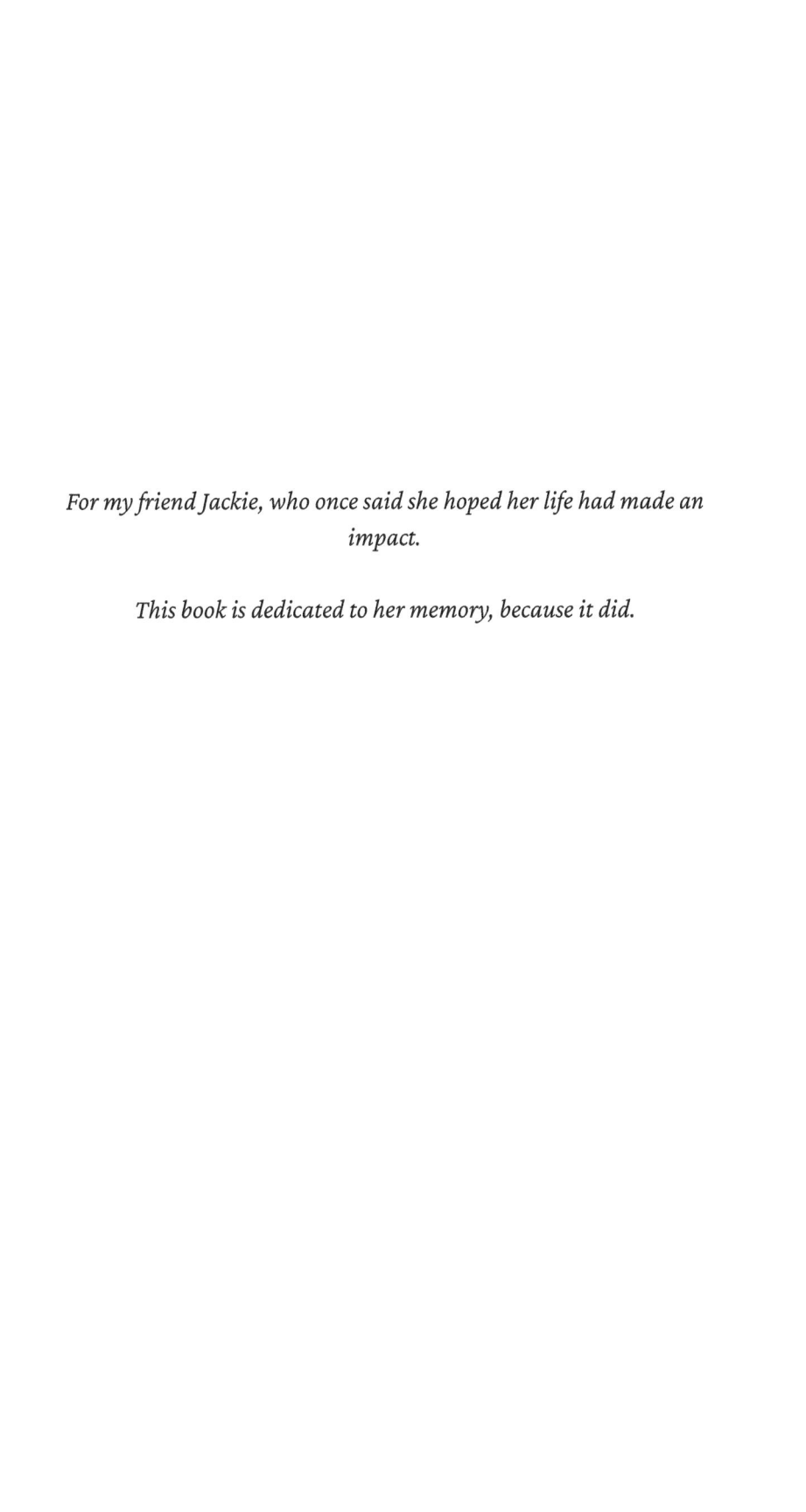

For my friend Jackie, who once said she hoped her life had made an impact.

This book is dedicated to her memory, because it did.

one

A FANCIFUL BRUNCH display adorned by coffee-colored and coordinated balloon bouquets decorates a cold corporate meeting space in the grand ballroom of the Los Angeles Convention Center. Eight-top round tables draped in white linen host gilded floral centerpieces and polished tableware circled with standard-issue stackable chairs. A stock photo banner brands the event: *Welcome to The Daily Grind Coffee House, Shareholder's New Product Summit!*

Decorated vendor booths line the outside perimeter stocked with coffee-themed knick-knacks, coffee table books, and *The Daily Grind* branded merchandise. Small-business owners smile and wave as they stand behind their tables and showcase their for-sale items. The women, accessorized with fancy hats and jeweled broaches, scan the tables and make small talk as they peruse the venue's offerings. The men flaunt bespoke tailored suits and gather in small groups as they pass the time, waiting for the event to begin. Intermittently, the attendees shuffle about the ballroom between the vendors and the buffet station while they gab in polite conversation, before taking their seats.

The backdrop of the stage is a slideshow presentation; images of happy people laughing over their *The Daily Grind* coffee cups. Life is grand with *The Daily Grind* subliminally drilled into the attendees' minds with aesthetic marketing and thematic attention cues.

Hidden from the pleasant gathering, employees with anxious eyes and furrowed brows meticulously inspect the arrangements. They hold crystal glasses up to the light—ensuring perfect cleanliness, jot notes on their clipboards, communicate with one another through walkie talkies, and wipe nervous beads of sweat from their foreheads.

"Please refill the fruit tray!" Samantha says to a uniformed catering server. The server complies and hurries off toward the kitchen.

Samantha huffs. "Ridiculous..." she mutters, before her anxious gait takes her away to continue on her route around the ballroom. Her walkie talkie beeps.

"Samantha, Emily needs you backstage." Without hesitation, Samantha's legs burst into a sprint.

"I'm coming!" Samantha says with heavy breaths into the walkie talkie. She exits the ballroom through double doors and runs down a long corridor.

* * *

Emily Cassius sits behind a lit vanity at the center of a vibrant backstage room. Surrounded by employees in various stages of preparatory tasks, Emily holds her shoulders up and back as the unmistakable focus of the flurry of activity. At twenty-five years old, her beauty and youth match the fake smile plastered on her face.

A stylist teases her hair and shapes it into perfect waves with the precision of a trained artist.

"More," Emily says to the stylist in a voice that demands a perfection above perfect. The stylist nods and gulps down her nerves.

A makeup artist applies foundation with a soft and focused hand.

"Don't forget the contour. That's not enough!" Emily says, the bark in her tone even harsher.

The makeup artist whimpers in fear at the command. Her hands quiver and she drops her makeup brush. "Sorry…" she pleads as she bends down to pick up the mistake.

Emily rolls her eyes. "Oh my god, I have to do everything around here." Emily snatches the brush from the makeup artist's hand and finishes the contour herself. "Where the hell is Samantha? Hello!" Her voice rises as she shouts into the ether. The room full of employees stop what they're doing to look around them like a pack of prairie dogs.

"There she is!" the stylist says. She points toward the entrance door as Samantha jogs in.

"Ugh, there you are, my god. What took you so long?" Emily says.

Samantha takes a beat to breathe, catches her breath. The room of employees go back to their assignments.

"Sorry, I uh…"

"Is the buffet table being restocked? What about the demo?" Emily says as stress bubbles in her voice and she grits her teeth. She straightens in her chair, twists to face Samantha, and stares daggers into her eyes, waiting, without patience, for an answer.

Samantha's shoulders tense at the attention. "Yes. I had a server restock the fruit tray and Adrian has the dem…"

"Adrian! Adrian!" Emily shouts, cutting Samantha off. She waves her away with a condescending hand and reverts her eyes toward her reflection in the vanity. She relaxes back into her chair and waits for Adrian.

Samantha releases a deep breath. A heaving chest shows her relief. Emily rolls her eyes at the theatrics.

Adrian, an assistant, decorated in his own coffee-colored and tailored suit, enthusiastically walks toward Emily with a tablet. His response is respectful, yet relaxed. He approaches with a smile and a calm confidence missing from the rest of the employees in the room.

"Did you finalize the PowerPoint? The numbers have to be perfect!" Emily says with a bite.

"Yes, Miss Emily," Adrian says. "Everything is set and ready to go."

"Ugh! I don't believe you." Emily rolls her eyes, annoyed. "Show it to me."

Adrian whips through several screens on his tablet. He pulls up a slideshow presentation and adjusts so that Emily can see it. Not good enough. She snatches the tablet from his arms and swipes through the slides herself.

"Is my mother here yet?" Emily says when she finds no mistakes or excuses to yell at her employees more.

Adrian opens his mouth to respond, but the click of heels behind them answers before his words escape. Heads turn as Helen Cassius, CEO and the indomitable force of *The Daily Grind Coffee House*, enters. The room quiets as the bustle slows, stops, like they need permission to continue in her presence. She strides in; her muted mocha pants suit immaculate, a testament to her impeccable taste. An entourage fans out behind her, a satellite of aids orbiting the planet of her influence. Adrian stands up taller, stiffer. His calm confidence falls away as the atmosphere of the room shifts. Helen's gaze sweeps the room, like a queen surveying her court. The wide-eyed employees wait for her to speak, move, anything to slice through the thick air of tension.

"Good morning," Helen declares, her voice resonant. "Wonderful job, everyone! The setup looks marvelous. Give yourselves a round of applause."

The room erupts in a collective relief of captured air and grand applause. Helen claps along with her employees. It doesn't last long; the celebration falls away, and employees release themselves back to the chorus of activity. Helen approaches Emily's vanity.

"Emily, darling," Helen says.

"Mother!" Emily rises from her chair and rushes to greet her.

Mother and daughter come together in a warm embrace—people are watching, after all. A silent beat passes as the room holds a collective breath, a reverence for the moment. Emily melts into Helen's arms as a smile relaxes into her face.

"You've done a wonderful job, dear," Helen says as she pulls away in a harsh break. A silent communication to her daughter. Emily's face flushes red and turns away, admitting her shame—like she should have known this was an act, and she'd missed her mark, allowing herself to take a reprieve in her mother's arms. Stupid, stupid girl. Helen's lips curl into a micro-smile, an understanding that Emily has received the message.

Emily must shake off her shock as Helen's quick movement reminds her who she is, and that hugs, in this family at least, are only for show. The room snaps back into action. The spell breaks and again activity rises into the background.

"You're fulfilling your role as I always expected you would." Helen's words are disjointed from the stern look on her face, and the stiff hold of her shoulders, up and back.

"We have a charcoal coffee demo." Emily's nerves grip her throat and her voice comes out in a high-pitched squeak. Triggered by Helen's stiff posture, she feels forced to grovel for her mother's acceptance. She'll say anything, all in pursuit of even the most subtle smile. She continued, "A performance by the Bean King Band, and goodie bags for everyone. I tried to make everything perfect, just like you wanted." Emily no longer sounds like the domineering boss-lady she was before. Under the eye of her mother, she's as soft and scared as a child scorned for getting caught in the cookie jar.

"As you should..." Helen nods her approval. She surveys the room again with a hawk's precision, her lips curling into a smile that doesn't quite reach her eyes.

Emily reacts to the assent like she's won a secret prize—Helen's smile belongs to her. Eyes wide, a spark ignites in their depths as an invisible chorus sings triumph. The hint of a grin plays at the corners of her mouth, her chest lifts in a silent, prideful inhale. She gives a subtle bow of her head, as if to acknowledge an ovation from an imaginary crowd only she can see, a muted celebration of her personal victory. "Thank you, Mother! I'm so happy you're pleased."

An alarm on Emily's phone blares. Emily jolts to attention. "Places everyone!"

A horde of bodies rushes through the space in an attempt to organize. The hair stylist finishes a final shape with a brush through Emily's hair. The makeup artist blots Emily's lip, her own lips copying the shape of Emily's as she perfects the final color. Samantha hops off with her clipboard, and darts to the stage entrance. Adrian takes his place behind Helen, head buried into his tablet. After Adrian, the rest of Helen's entourage take second, third, and fourth place behind Helen in V formation. The choreography of her followers is ceremonial, or instinctual, or well-trained. In unison the group moves to the stage entrance. Emily holds her breath.

two

HELEN WALKS out onto the professionally dressed stage. Behind her, an immaculate display of coffee beans, cups, products, shelving, and balloons of complementing colors placed in strategic fashion to look like the inside of a The Daily Grind Coffee House shop. A podium and microphone await her arrival. Bright stage lights illuminate the shine on her pants suit as the clink of her high heels is drowned away by the applause of an eager audience. She reaches the podium, waves, smiles, and allows the applause to naturally wane.

"Welcome shareholders!" Helen raises her arms high, egging on a reignite of applause. The audience complies with a polite resurgence of cheer. She waits another moment and allows the audience to concede. "I am Helen Cassius, and your presence honors us as we at The Daily Grind introduce our slate of new products for the upcoming quarter." She holds—more applause. "Some of the exciting new products we've developed include a lavender rice milk latte, and a golden turmeric tea. We've brewed up a fresh pot of ideas to ensure the steady growth and dividend payout you've all come to enjoy," she pauses again, an exhibition of a steady thirst for her own accolade.

* * *

Emily rushes through an empty back hallway. The audience's cheers and her mother's speech emanate through the walls. Emily chokes down the thud of her own heartbeat as she runs to her entrance point. Distracted, Emily doesn't see a server holding a restock tray for the buffet. A near miss as the two almost collide. Emily huffs at the inconvenience that could have ruined her perfect look.

"Watch it!" she grumbles.

"Excuse me, miss."

Emily contemplates a rebuke but makes do with an eye roll as she continues on her path.

* * *

Sarah Kenneth smiles brightly and twirls her bohemian dreadlocks through her fingers. The 27-year-old artist, proofed by her clay-stained clothing, hosts a booth of bold colors in her hand-painted, carved, and kilned coffee cups, bowls, plates, and vases. A product of social media culture, the designs display etchings in the clay of funny sayings and cute phrases. "I'd slay for a cup of coffee" or "This is my girl dinner."

Sarah yawns out her boredom as her body sways and listens to the drone of Helen's speech. She turns to her neighbor, another vendor seeming to be as uninterested in the downtime.

"Oh yum, a lavender latte? That sounds amazing. Doesn't that sound amazing?" she whispers, thinking a little small talk will help pass the time.

"Yeah, sure. Kinda hoity-toity, if you ask me, but I guess if it justifies a six-dollar cup of coffee..." her neighbor responds with a nod and a polite smile.

"Pfft! Six dollars! For purple coffee?" Emily laughs out loud. An audience member sitting at a table not too far away hears and turns toward her with a micro-scowl. Sarah clinches her jaw in embarrassment as she mouths an apology.

"Yeah, I'm with ya… selling knick-knacks ain't exactly purple coffee money," the neighbor says.

Emily nods agreement. "Hey, do they have free coffee here?"

The vendor nods and points to the buffet station.

"Oh, thank god. All this coffee talk and suddenly I can't help myself. Hooray for subliminal marketing. Haha! You want one?"

"Yeah, thanks."

"Oh sure! Cream and sugar?"

The vendor shakes their head, "Black."

Sarah nods and jets off.

* * *

The audience tires of gifting Helen ovations as they sink in their chairs, play on their phones, or chat in whispers to one another. Helen, a woman ever self-aware and socially competent, sees it all. She staves off an annoyed eye roll. The bright lights of the stage remind her they're all still watching. She cuts her speech short and moves on to the main event, the reason they're all here.

"Without further ado," Helen says, "please welcome my daughter, newest member of The Daily Grind board, and Chief Marketing Officer Emily Cassius."

The audience finds the enthusiasm to revive their energy. Applause for a fresh voice erupts from the ballroom.

Emily hears her cue and enters from behind a closed door at the back of the room, giving the audience plenty of time to continue their admiration as she struts toward the stage.

The walk, in heels, takes her into the audience where her stakeholders wait with smiles to greet her. Their eyes follow and invite her approach. If there were babies here, she would kiss them. The rehearsed entrance, set to music, tells the audience it's time to party! With her swagger, Emily runs through a repetitive routine of plastered smiles and princess hello waves, mixed with one-sided-hug greetings with her audience. In her head, she counts herself down. From the onset of the music, she knows she's got 45 seconds to shake hands and say hello on her way to the stage.

"*36, 35, 34.*" She shakes hands.

"*22, 20, 19.*" Hello waves, big smiles.

At the buffet station, Sarah fills two coffee cups.

"Thank you for coming. Hello. Welcome." Emily smiles through gritted teeth as she continues her rush to the stage. "*13, 12, 11...*"

Sarah sips from a cup and grimaces. "Ouch! Hot!" Cautious now, she turns back to her booth. Her careful movement carries her in a glide back through the ballroom as she balances the two cups full to the top of scalding coffee.

Emily's inner monologue spirals with anxiety as she counts down faster, and her feet move quicker. "*8, 7, 6...*" The music is almost over. Tunnel vision sets in. She *must* make it to the stage!

Sarah's crossing back into her booth...

Emily's not paying attention to where she's going, expecting her path to be clear. She makes a turn around a table, blind of what's directly in front of her, and CRASHES into Sarah!

Hot coffee scalds both of them as they collide, and the audience collectively gasps!

The room falls silent as both women process what's happened. Emily's gaze soaks in her coffee-stained, coffee-colored satin minidress.

Sarah lets out a nervous laugh, "Ooopsie! Guess you didn't see me there. Sorry about..."

"THIS IS A COCO CHANEL!" Emily screams at the top of where her voice allows. "My Coco Chanel!" she yells, screaming, shaking, stomping as she cycles through a toddler-style meltdown.

Sarah takes a moment longer to process. Her face contorts into a surprised confusion. As she watches Emily, the tantrum reminds her of her son and a giggle slips out.

Emily stops in shock. She looks from the woman to the booth

and makes the connection. *Woman, booth, this is that woman's booth.* Without further hesitation, she grabs one of Sarah's pieces from the booth and smashes it on the floor in front of her. The audience gasps, coordinated like they're being cued, only they're not. This doesn't deter her. She continues to rip plates, cups, and delicate works of art off the display and hurls them to the floor, into the audience, and at the wall. The sound of ceramic pottery smashing into pieces, over and over, mixed with the audience's dread, fills the space.

three

BACK ON STAGE, Helen holds her composure. A seasoned businesswoman, painfully aware of the importance of public perception and image, she maintains her posture—tall back and upturned nose as she watches her daughter destroy their cumulative lives. As Emily runs out of breath and things to break all at once, and her body slows to a stop. The audience turns away from the disgrace of Emily's performance and back to center stage. Their faces silently beg for Helen to react.

Her entourage waits, searching her face for a silent command. Helen tilts her neck toward Emily in a gesture to act.

Message received. Backstage, Adrian, leader of the court, whispers, "Get Kyle!" No one moves. He says again, "Where's Kyle?" this time in a panic. The swarm dissipates and searches the backstage area for Kyle.

"I found him!" Samantha says, still holding her clipboard and dragging behind her a big-ol-hunk-a-man in a popped collar and khaki slacks, pretentious if an outfit could say so. Kyle releases himself from Samantha's grip, ready to heed his call. He jogs onto the stage. Passing Helen, he nods and smiles, as if to offer confidence to her. He jets toward the commotion.

He shoulder checks Sarah in his pursuit of Emily. The encounter takes Sarah by surprise, and looks at him like she's preparing herself to receive an apology, but there is none. Kyle doesn't acknowledge her existence. She's otherwise invisible to him in his relentless focus on the task. He grabs Emily by the arm, and with a calm but firm hand, leads her backstage. Emily huffs and puffs, continuing her tantrum, but follows unopposed to Kyle's force.

"You'll never work in coffee cups again! You hear me! Never!" Emily shouts at a bewildered Sarah.

Kyle jerks at her arm harder, losing patience. "Come on, honey, let's get you cleaned up." The pair make it onto the stage and disappear into the blackness of stage-right.

Separate from the moment, Sarah looks around at the shattered bits of her life's work scattered around her feet. Devastation seeps into her face as she inventories the loss. Her booth is destroyed.

"Apologies everyone," Helen says onstage as she smiles wide and attempts to redirect. "The stress of the day has gotten the best of us. I would like to thank all our vendors for participating. We will, of course, reimburse, uh... excuse me miss, what is your name?" Helen says to Sarah.

The audience looks back at Sarah, some with curiosity, others with mouths agape. A long beat passes while Sarah wipes tears from her eyes.

"Sarah." Her voice cracks.

"Sarah," Helen says. Her face softens as she performs a show of empathy. "We are very sorry for this misunderstanding. We will cover the cost of your items and offer an additional stipend for the trouble this has caused you."

Sarah is not paying attention. She's on her knees gathering pieces of her brightly colored ceramics. Other vendors come to her aid and help her collect sharp-edged pieces into a pile on the floor. The fancy audience sit and watch—a play.

"If you would please focus your attention on the screen. We have a performance presentation for you all. You'll see our growth last quarter far outpaced the competition. Please." Helen points upward and directs her audience's eyes toward a screen as it glides down from the ceiling.

The lights dim. Helen's fake smile disappears from her face as she exits the stage with grace and unwavering dignity.

* * *

Emily's shoulders shiver and her chest heaves with adrenaline as she waits in front of her vanity. Her staff titters around her and attempts to clean up the evidence of her outburst. The stylist tussles her hair with anxious eyes. The makeup artist blots the beads of sweat on her brow and the coffee stains on her dress with fervent pace. Kyle consoles her, rubbing her back. The staff surround and point curious ears toward their conversation.

"I can't believe this! Did you see that woman? She ruined everything!" Emily whines to the response of validating nods and *poor you* coos.

"Honey," Kyle says, "you're ovulating. We can't have you stressed. Take some deep breaths with me..."

"I don't need a breath, Kyle. I need..."

"What in the god-forsaken-hell was that?" Helen shouts as she bursts into the space. Emily straightens up and falls silent. The entire room halts all activity.

"What is the matter with you?"

"Mother, I was... It's not my fault... I..."

"Enough! Do you have no sense?" Helen's arms flail in anger and her face contorts by her gritting teeth.

Emily drops her head in shame.

Helen takes in a breath and composes herself. She lifts her head high and straightens out her blazer. Calm now, she continues. "This was your coming out! Our chance to showcase you to the shareholders. Our investors have been with us since the beginning, Emily. The beginning! They've watched you grow, marry, and have been waiting for you to follow in my footsteps. How could they ever trust The Daily Grind again after this? They'll pull out, we're finished. You've ruined everything!"

Tears streak Emily's face.

"Take her home, Kyle…"

"Yes, Ms. Helen." Kyle all but takes a bow as he pulls Emily up and leads her away.

four

EMILY SITS cross armed in the passenger seat. With her nerves calmed, she reflects on her behavior. Her shoulders sink in on themselves as her stomach twists itself in knots. What has she done? How will her mother ever forgive her? Why would she even bother?

"I think I'm gonna…" Emily says as she dry heaves. "Oh god…" She covers her mouth with one hand and wipes the sweat from her face with the other. "Please…" Her labored breaths fight to hold in the contents of her stomach—bile and acid. She's not eaten anything today. "Can you pull over?"

Kyle drives with a stone-face and ignores her request. He opens his mouth as though he wants to say something. Emily looks at him, her eyes beg for his words, but he closes his mouth. He takes a long beat, like he's jumbled in his own thoughts. His mouth opens again. Emily's face brightens and a subtle gasp escapes her throat as she anticipates his words. Again, only silence leaves him. Emily's shoulders slump when she realizes he's got nothing to say. He lets out a heavy and lamented sigh.

"Whatever…" Kyle says out loud as he settles into his own indifference. Emily searches his face for a sign, any sign for a clue of what he's thinking. Kyle shakes his head, and his disappointment hits

Emily. She suffocates in a feeling of dread, of ending, of not finding a way back from this.

"Whatever?" Emily says with a quiver in her voice. "Whatever, what? What do you mean?" She clears her throat, straightens up in her seat, and forces herself to project her voice—a manufactured confidence and attempt to give herself the upper-hand. "How could you not defend me? You embarrassed me in front of my whole team!"

"What was I supposed to do, Emily? You were acting like a complete psychopath." He chuckles. "Nope, not this time. This is yours to own..."

A silent moment passes between them as Emily soaks in his response.

"I mean, I don't even understand how you could..." he continues. "You worked on this event for months. We missed three ovulation cycles for this! And now it's all for nothing because you spilled coffee on yourself?" He scoffs. "Your mother was right. You weren't ready for this. This was your moment to prove yourself and instead, you destroyed a poor woman's life's work and got us canceled at the same time. Good job."

"SO? So, what! I don't care anymore!"

Kyle's eyes about pop out of his head as he jerks the steering wheel. A startled driver in the next lane over slams on their brakes and angry honks as Kyle swerves into their lane. Emily shrieks and puts a hand on the dashboard to brace against the impact as she's tussled in her seat despite the belt. Kyle's shoulders tense and his teeth grit down on themselves as he reestablishes control of the vehicle.

"Don't care? About what? Your life? Mine? You can't just decide you don't want it anymore, Emily. This is what it is. On camera and behind the curtain. This is how it's always been, and how it always will be. You don't get to have the things we have without a positive public perception. If the surfs don't love us, THEY'LL EAT US!"

Kyle takes a breath, composes himself. "We toe the line, we

exceed expectations. You know better than I what happens if we don't."

Emily groans and drops her head in her hands and covers her eyes. She knows what he says is true, yet she wishes it didn't have to be. She sinks into her seat, and submits, like she always does, like she's been raised to do, as is expected of her, and always will be. "But... it's all a lie..." Her voice comes out as a soft whisper.

"Don't pretend like that matters. You know there's only one thing that does. Say it."

Emily's eyes dart away in defiance.

"Say it, Emily. What matters? Say it!"

"Protect the money!" Emily shouts as she blubbers through tears. In full sobs, she repeats a mantra burned into her like a nursery rhyme. "Just do what you're told and you'll always protect the money."

Kyle relaxes, a look of satisfaction rests on his face.

* * *

The mantra carries Emily out of the car and into her memory, where it becomes a lullaby.

"Just do what you're told, and you'll always protect the money. This life isn't easy to hold, but thank god, it's filled with honey..."

* * *

Emily is five years old, in a blue silk dress with matching stockings and gloves. Her shiny black shoes reveal a painted red sole. Surrounding her are several other children, all dressed like their overtly wealthy parents and dripping in class. The children sit in silence and play with expensive toys. They're gathered in a living room trapped in luxury inside an exquisite mansion home. The gilded walls have gold accent and hand carved moldings. The furniture is sturdy, traditional, and clad in deep brown leathers or jewel-toned velvets. Thick fabric drapes the windows and reaches from the floor to the ceiling. Fancy ropes tie a single layer back, only to reveal more layers of lace and velvet that keep them cloaked from the outside world.

Several young adult women, at least one per child, tend to their wards at play. They offer toys, read books, or play quiet games, but never interact with one another—only the children.

Little Emily plays with her F.A.O. Schwarts train set, but is bored by it, and her nanny is unable to entertain her with anything else. Emily lets her eyes wander from the borders of the living room and down a wide-open corridor where a black-tie party takes place. All the children's parents and more fill the ballroom with sparkling designer-dresses and obnoxiously expensive tuxedos. Among them, Emily finds her mother, Helen, 20 years younger, holding the same stern confidence. She speaks to a man, Tom VonMarr, just as posh in his luxury attire and commanding posture. The two sip champagne while they speak. Emily watches with longing eyes as she wishes to be among them. Why can't she dance in the ballroom with the adults? These toys are for babies. She's not a baby, she's a big girl and has just as much to offer as anyone else. Little Emily turns back to her nanny. "I want to go with mother. Take me to her."

The nanny chuckles and shakes her head with a soft smile.

Emily protests with a sadistic glare as she stomps her feet and balls her fists. The nanny giggles at her, as if her angry were cute or something. Emily looks back at her mother, only to find her and Tom have left the ballroom and are walking down the corridor, toward the very living room where she waits! Emily gasps.

"Mother's coming! She's coming now!" Emily shrieks back to her nanny, who jumps into action. The nanny pulls and fusses at Emily's outfit, dusts off her dress skirt, straightens her collar, fixes her hair, and gives her a once over. Done and satisfied, the nanny steps aside and stands behind little Emily, who flashes a bright smile in her mother's direction.

"Emily!" A chipper and eager young Helen calls for her daughter as she enters the play area. Emily stands half an inch taller and pulls her smile a tad bit tighter. She's trained for moments like this, and she wants to impress.

"Hello sweet pea," Helen says without acknowledging the nanny.

Emily holds her smile tight on her face, so much so that the corners of her mouth flush white as her muscles fight against fatigue.

"This is Mr. VonMarr. He and his family are going to become a very special part of our lives someday." Helen's eyes dig deep into Emily's and deliver to Emily a silent message.

"Oh!" Emily says as she receives the message and remembers something important. She curtsies and says, "Hello, Mr. Von. Pleased to meet you." She looks to her mother for approval.

Helen releases the demand in her eyes and nods a smile. Emily knows she's done well.

"Mr. VonMarr, Emily," Helen says with a stern voice. Emily's smile dissipates under the weight of the criticism. "He wants to introduce you to someone."

"Hello, dear. You can call me Von. I like that name." Tom smiles, bending half an inch to greet Emily.

Emily allows her smile to seep back onto her face.

"How wonderful. Aww yes, there he is..." Tom says as he looks up.

Another nanny across the room gathers a little boy away from his pile of magnetic blocks. She straightens his clothing and bow tie with a once over to perfect his presentation. The nanny pushes the little boy forward with gentle encouragement. He fights against her with feet that stick to the floor and a head that thrashes side to side with an aggressive no. Stronger than him, the nanny yanks at his arm until he complies. The little boy drops his head back and lets out a cry. He's vanquished, and all he can do now is make noise.

"No! I don't wanna!" The nanny grips his arm tighter as she pulls. "Ouch! You're hurting me!"

This doesn't deter her until she brings him over and drops him off next to Emily.

In the presence of his father, the boy gives up his protest and settles. Tom's face relaxes into a subtle smile as his boy quiets.

"Emily," says Tom, "I want you to meet my son, Kyle. He's your age. Your mother and I think the two of you could be the best of friends."

Emily's eyes gauge, and her nose makes a scrunch—eww. Helen snaps her fingers. Emily corrects herself within a millisecond of the command. Her face reverts to the tight smile and her eyes focus on the boy's face.

"Pleased to meet you, Kyle. My name's Emily," Emily says as she performs another curtsy.

Helen beams as she wins the invisible competition of whose child is best behaved.

Little Kyle runs off, screams, and falls into his nanny's arms.

Tom gives a slight shake of his head, a gesture to the ever-watchful nanny. She nods and yanks little Kyle out of the room and away from his father's sight. Kyle screams and cries like he knows what's coming for him.

Tom flashes a face of shame, but never relents his confidence as he clears his throat and pulls his shoulders up and back. "Ha! Boys will be boys! No matter, they're still young," he says.

"Yes, of course..." Helen says with a subtle smirk. "Now, please tell me more about your upcoming book release. I'm so interested to hear what self-help mastery you've..." Helen's voice trails off as the two adults venture back toward the party and leave Emily.

The smile drops from Emily's face as she watches her mother leave her, once again, without even an atta girl or an approving wink. She'd done well, or so she thought, but still not good enough. Her head drops to the ground as she wonders how she can be better next time, if only to earn a coveted accolade.

Emily's nanny watches her face. As Emily's head drops, the nanny's face sighs with empathy. The nanny pulls Emily into her chest and squeezes her into a hug. Emily receives it as a consolation, but it's not the hug she longs for because it's not a hug from the only person left in her life who's supposed to love her. It's not a hug from mother. The nanny sings Emily a song and tries to get her back to playing with the train set.

"Just do what you're told, and you'll always protect the money. This life isn't easy to hold, but thank god it's filled with honey…"

five

SARAH SHUFFLES through a kitchen hardly bigger than a life-size Barbie play set in her one-bedroom, weathered apartment. The cluttered space is filled with clay artwork, mismatched photos on paint chipped walls, and dishes that live on countertops. The top of the refrigerator hosts boxes of cereal and processed food snacks. A two-burner stove holds a clean saucepan and a mid-sized skillet. The two pots touch each other by lack of space. Inside the accompanying oven, cookie sheets rest on racks—nowhere else for them to go. The space is clean. There're no dirty dishes in the sink, no trash or leftover food on the wobbly kitchenette table, yet lackluster storage makes the space appear lived in and cluttered.

She empties a brown paper bag of leftover buffet food on to the kitchenette table next to a neat pile of old mail. A white envelope falls out with the food. She opens it and leaves through the cash contents.

"Just paid my rent! Yaaay!" Sarah says to herself as she celebrates the silver lining.

Her arm reaches for the refrigerator door. The shelves are bare except for a few juice boxes and half-consumed condiment bottles.

The emptiness brings her to sigh. She tosses cake pops, muffins, and sandwiches into the cold storage.

"Momma!" Her son, seven-year-old Liam, prances in from the other room. He squeezes Sarah into a bear hug.

"Hi baby boy. How'd you sleep?" She says, relishing in his affection.

"You were gone when I woke up." Liam's face frowns and his eyes puppy-dog as he leans hard into a sulk.

Sarah tussles his hair with a soft smile. "I told you I had to work, baby. Remember?"

"You mean you didn't leave me?"

Sarah laughs out a scoff with a playful eye roll. "Leave you!? Never ever!"

Liam and Sarah fall back into a deep hug, his head buried deep in her shoulder and her arms wrapped around his little body.

"You hungry?" Sarah asks as she pulls out of their embrace. "I got your favorite. Chocolate cake pop!"

Liam screeches with excitement as Sarah goes back into the fridge for the treat.

*** * * ***

Sarah and Liam cuddle on a hand-me-down couch behind the glow of a small television. Tapestries partitioning off the space into a makeshift bedroom for Liam divide the living room in half. Shoes and clothes scatter the walkways. It's not dirty, but also not tidy.

Cartoons blare on the TV as Liam's head rests in Sarah's lap. His mouth falls open and his weight subtly deepens. Liam's eyes flutter and close. He falls asleep.

A buzz alerts Sarah to her phone as she receives a text message. She opens the notification to a screen that reads a message from Drew.

"You up?"

Sarah's curious eyes study Liam's sleep state. She wriggles a bit, but he doesn't move.

"Yeah, come through."

* * *

Under the moonlit window of her bedroom, Sarah's bare body straddles her naked companion. Every nerve ending ignites as she thrusts herself up and down. Drew's muscles tense beneath her touch, his tattoos sweat, and a groan of pleasure escapes his lips. The pair ride through their lovemaking like time has stopped and the world's fallen away, connected in a passion that emits in sound from their throats and flushes red on their skin. Their eyes meet and hold one another with a deep and idling gaze.

Drew's stare breaks away and wanders down Sarah's body. His hands follow. Sarah's body responds with an enthusiasm that tells him, without words, she wants more. He reaches to grab her left breast and squeezes. Sarah lets out a soft moan that hints at a wince of pain.

"What?" Drew says with concern. "That hurt?"

Sarah stops. "I don't know, a little."

Drew repeats the action, but harder.

"Aaarrrgghh!" Sarah falls from his hips, pulls herself away, and crumbles into the fetal position on the bed. She seethes from a pain that pulsates in her breast.

"What?" Drew says with arms raised in alarm.

Sarah shakes her head, squinting as she rises and tries to mount him again. "Nothing. It's nothing. Come on."

Drew pushes her away. "Stop!" He shakes his head.

She complies but her face reads annoyed. "What, Drew?"

"Was that a... lump?"

Sarah scoffs. "No."

"That's a lump!" Drew's voice rises in volume, almost too much.

"Shhhh! Liam's sleeping."

Drew rolls over toward the edge of the bed, searches for a bedside light, finds it, and flicks it on. Sarah hides under sheets, as if a thin fabric shield could change the direction the conversation is taking.

"Are you for real, Sar?" He tries to pull down the sheet, but Sarah keeps a firm hold and remains hidden.

"You're making a huge deal out of nothing. It's nothing. Stop it. Stop pulling."

"It's something!"

Drew pulls harder now. He uses both his hands and yanks, ripping the sheet away from her body—her strength no match to his.

"Keep your voice down," Sarah says through gritted teeth, not reacting to her exposed nakedness or his aggressive insistence of it, only the volume of his voice.

"Did you get it checked?" Drew says in a whisper.

Sarah pulls the sheets up again and tucks her chin underneath while her fingers grip its edge in a wad.

Drew groans and this time sits up in bed and positions himself in a pose of power over her. He removes the sheet in one swift movement and throws it to the floor where Sarah can't reach it. "Answer me, Sar?" he says with aggressive hand movements and a quickened breath.

"Ugh! What is your problem?" Sarah says in a heated whisper.

"Did you get it checked?" Drew repeats himself.

"Ugh! I'm only twenty-seven. It's probably just a muscle knot or cyst or something. I feel fine."

Sarah sits up in bed and folds her knees, pulling herself into an even position with his, a move that seems to neutralize him as his shoulders relax and his breath slows.

"You still got state insurance?"

Sarah nods in quick succession. "Of course, I do."

"Get it checked now, Sar. You already know how I feel about this type of stuff."

Sarah sucks her teeth and rolls her eyes. She doesn't speak, but picks her nails, trying anything to avoid Drew's stare.

six

THE PRIMARY BATHROOM in Emily's house is bright with skylights that rest in vaulted ceilings, open with square footage that makes space for movement and excess, rich with spa-like amenities like the sauna she never uses or the black-light skin rejuvenation station that collects dust in the corner. The bathroom alone is bigger than Sarah's entire apartment, and a stark contrast to its overlain layers of paint and worn carpets. Emily's home boasts like a picturesque magazine spread of luxury amenities and expensive trims.

Standing rigid over her Italian marble bathroom counter, Emily looks down at a pregnancy test. Negative. *Of course...* She thinks to herself. Her face gleans a mix of disappointment and a somehow expected outcome. She picks up the test, turns around, and readies herself to face Kyle, who leans with arms crossed up against the bathroom wall.

"Well?" says Kyle.

Emily shrugs, shakes her head, and pulls her gaze away.

A subtle expression of irritation releases from Kyle's body as he rolls his eyes and relieves a sigh. "Seriously, Emily?"

His disappointment in her triggers a nerve deep within in her psyche. A wound from long ago and never healed. Emily reacts not to the words, but to her own internal turmoil. She throws her arms up in the air, and shouts, "How is this my fault?"

Kyle sighs again. He runs his hands through his hair, a feeble attempt to self-soothe. "Calm down."

"I AM CALM!" she yells back. Her face is flushed red and her fists reveal white knuckles.

Kyle ignores her overtly emotional reaction, instead focusing on himself. "Why is this so hard? You're supposed to give me a baby. This is what we're supposed to do, Emily. What's expected of us!"

Emily's head casts down as it becomes heavy from his words. The pent-up anger bubbling inside her releases itself in a cascade of tears. Her body becomes weighted like she's soaking in a pool of responsibility, of failure, for this moment. "I know... I'm sorry..."

Kyle takes a breath. "Just... fix it." As Kyle turns to leave, he smashes his fist against a cabinet.

Emily recoils at the surprise, causing her to jump, drop the pregnancy test, and gasp with fear. She takes in a quick breath, and holds it, trying to be perfectly still until he leaves. He's gone. Her captured breath releases and her body trembles through a reignite of her tears.

She holds herself as she cries, and allows herself to feel her pain, until she doesn't remember what she's crying about it, and feels childish for even feeling anything at all. She rolls her eyes at herself and calls herself stupid as she turns back toward the mirror to assess her face. Runoff makeup stains her cheeks, her eyes are puffy-red, and the blue veins on her temples pop up with stress. She shakes her head.

"We're not doing this, Emily. No, we're not," she says as she wipes her tears, sniffles, trying to curb her emotions, and stands up tall. With a fresh coat of lipstick, she plasters back on her Stepford smile and, with a last glance in the mirror, where Emily admires her own resilience, she walks out just as her phone pings.

An Instagram pop-up tells her: *Tiffany has tagged you in a story.*

Like a trigger, Emily's eyes follow the phone screen as it opens to

Instagram and to the post. Tiffany, too young for it, but botoxed and cake-faced anyway, like her Insta-feed tells her she has to be, is wearing a fire engine red silk blouse, and smiling over a mimosa at brunch with a group of gals, all carbon copies of each other with stone faces in real life just as they are in the photo. The caption reads *@EmilyCassius Wish you were here! The Gal Pals miss you! #TheDailyGrind #Mimosas #BestFriendsForever*

A smile creeps onto her face. She hearts the post and types, *Love my gals! Let's catch up soon!*

* * *

In the living room, decorated in the traditional luxury of the type of designer furniture an average person wouldn't even know the name of or where to find, marble floors, oversized and aesthetically placed decor and color palates courtesy of a professional interior designer, and high-priced electronics, Kyle relaxes on a sprawling sectional and watches a football game on TV. In front of him sits a streak-free glass coffee table with a display of various bottles of expensive whiskey and clean crystal cups. Kyle leans forward, grabs a cup, and pours himself a round. He savors the first sip and lets out a soft hum that says, *this is the good stuff.*

Emily watches him, assessing his mood and deciding how to approach, before she assumes the proper posture—shoulders back and chin up. Ready, she steps forward. Her heels click across the Lux Touch tiles in the adjacent foyer beneath the designer imported chandelier she loves to point out when guests arrive. She stops before taking a first step onto the hardwood of the living room floor. A space for him, another for her. Before she announces herself, she cocks her head to the side, smiles wide, and holds her hands together in front of her chest, elbows out. The pose is akin to an early Sears catalog advertisement of a 1950s housewife pleading with her hardworking husband for the newest, latest, and greatest model vacuum from GE. An ungenuine and purposefully manipulative expression that's got her through this marriage thus far. It's how she was trained to address her husband, and so far, it's not failed.

"Darling?" Emily asks for his attention. She speaks loud enough so he might hear her over the square footage and the game announcer's calls, yet sweet enough to maintain her presentation of submission.

He glances in her direction, and takes another sip from his drink, not putting his glass down or inviting her to join him.

"I've made an appointment at the fertility clinic. Would you please be the supportive husband you always are and come with me?"

A moment passes as Kyle ruminates. Resolved, he installs his own fake smile to match her enthusiastic request. "Course, honey. Can't wait."

seven

EMILY AND KYLE sit in oversized leather chairs that line the lobby of the fertility clinic, waiting to be called back for their appointment. Emily fidgets in her seat, trying not to, but her nerves fail her. She looks over at Kyle and watches him scroll on his phone, seemingly disinterested in his surroundings, but she knows this. He's only there because he must be playing his part as the supportive husband, albeit poorly.

To distract herself, she looks around the room and follows her gaze to the corner where a small child-size table hosts a box of building blocks, several coloring books, crayons, and a little girl in a floral sundress that matches that of the woman's who is sitting in her chair next to her. The woman flips through a magazine while the little girl colors. Emily smiles sweetly at the little girl, but her nerves take her back into the escape of her phone.

"Mommy?" Emily hears the little girl say to the woman in the matching dress. "Wanna color with me?"

"Not right now, sweetie," the woman says with a smile. Emily reacts to the statement with silent empathy. It's a phrase she herself hardly heard as a child, not because mother always wanted to color with her, but because mother was never around to even ask. Mother was busy building her coffee-business empire, and Emily was left to color alone. In that moment, Emily's throat clenches with a contradiction of jealousy. *At least her mom's there, and smiled at her, she thinks,* twisted up in the empathetic understanding that both of them are just little girls whose mothers are too busy for them.

At the subtle rejection, the little girl looks around the room and notices Emily. The two lock eyes. Emily smiles at her, but looks back down at her phone, the interaction feeling complete.

Emily hears shuffling feet approach as she scrolls her phone, but pays no attention.

"Would you like to color with me?"

Emily looks up to find the little girl is right in front of her, holding up her coloring book, a fistful of crayons, and a wide smile with two empty spaces where baby teeth have fallen and adult teeth are coming through her gumline. Emily is taken aback by the question. Unsure, she looks at the mother before answering.

"Sorry! Hahaha, she's very friendly," the woman says with a friendly reassurance that tells Emily she's unalarmed by her daughter's likeness to a stranger.

Emily relaxes and addresses the girl, "Um, sure! What colors do you have?"

The little girl opens her fist to present her collection. "I have green, and pink, and red, and orange. Would you like pink and green and I'll take red and orange?"

"Oh, yes, please. Thank you." Emily picks the pink and green crayon from the girl's palm.

"Okay, so we're coloring a cat in a bubble bath. You can color the bubbles pink and I'll make the cat orange," the little girl says as her head bobbles side to side and her fingers point at the coloring page.

"Oh! Pink bubbles! I love that!" Emily says as she brings her hand and pink crayon down to meet the paper.

The little girl nods with a genuine smile. "Pink's my favorite color." She says as she gets to work coloring the cat orange. She moves her elbow out of the way so Emily can better reach the bubbles.

* * *

Emily lies on an exam table dressed in a paper gown in a private exam room. The room sports the typical medical decor—plastic babies inside wombs and posters of placentas and their disorders. The table is cold. Her body shivers, both from the chill of the room and her own anxious nerves.

Doctor Roberts, the obstetrician, sits on a rickety rolling stool opposite Emily's wide-open knees and performs a pelvis exam.

"Everything okay?" Doctor Roberts says, raising his head a couple of inches above her legs.

"Hmm?" Emily bends her neck forward to meet Doctor Roberts' gaze. "Yeah. Fine. Thank you." Her head falls back on the tiny plastic pillow strapped to the exam table. She twists her neck uncomfortably to see behind her—Kyle standing against the wall, still buried in his phone, oblivious to Emily's discomfort. She wonders if he even remembers she's there at all.

"You'll feel a small pressure," Doctor Roberts says as he inserts the speculum into her vagina.

"Oh!" Emily gasps. She squints through the sensation. She turns her head back again toward Kyle, who still hasn't looked up from his phone. Emily's face resolves to show a hint of sadness, rejected once again. Confirmation that in this room, at her most vulnerable, and in the company of the only person who should care, he couldn't care less about her. A feeling that was all too ordinary and familiar.

Doctor Roberts clicks off his headlamp and pulls away. Emily shuts her legs and moves to sit up.

"One moment," the doctor says. "I still have to do your breast exam." Doctor Roberts gestures for her to lie back down. She hesitates but complies.

The doctor snaps off his gloves and tosses them into the trash. He moves up toward her chest, presses his fingers around her breast in a clockwise movement, and manipulates the tissue. His face contorts, and his fingers stop. Something's wrong.

Emily recognizes his expression. Her heartbeat quickens as cortisol pours into her bloodstream. She tries to pull herself up, "What?" but the doctor's hands hold her down. She doesn't fight him, but submits, and falls back down to the exam table.

"Hmmm…" the doctor says with discontent.

The doctor's voice pulls Kyle's attention from his phone. He looks up at the doctor with wide eyes.

"Ms. Cassius," the doctor says, "have you ever had a mammogram?"

eight

THE DOUBLE GLASS doors of the Breast Health Center are opaque. Across the front, vivid black type reads, *Your Journey Defines You, Not Your Diagnosis.* Emily stands with arms crossed and reads the words to herself. She scoffs—the message of hope offends her. *This is such a complete waste of time...* she thinks as she pushes through the door and walks in.

In the lobby, cold faux leather chairs line the perimeter and make partitions out of themselves in the open space. Old magazines rest on end tables. Hung portraits of doctors and their smiling patients color the walls.

Emily makes her way toward the reception, but someone else is already there. Emily frowns with a furrowed brow as she listens in on the conversation and wonders where she's heard this voice before.

Oh. She realizes it's...

"Sarah. Sarah Kenneth... Hold on," Sarah says as she rifles through her boho shoulder bag and whips out a Medi-Cal insurance card. The receptionist reads the card, and types on her computer. Emily notices the same contorted face on the receptionist that she had witnessed on her obstetrician before he asked her to come here.

Uh oh.

"And how old did you say you were?" the receptionist asks, holding the face.

"Twenty-seven. Why?"

Here it comes...

"This card was issued to you through the Former Foster Care Youth insurance program offered by Medi-Cal. Unfortunately, it expires at age twenty-six. See here?" The receptionist points to an expiration date on the card.

"What? No, that's not possible," Sarah says, pained with anxiety.

Emily signs out of the conversation. Money had never been an issue for her and she can't relate to the panic in Sarah's voice. Rather than bother herself with it further, she resolves to scrolling on her phone while she waits for her turn to check in.

* * *

"Depending on your income," the receptionist continues, "you may still qualify for Medi-Cal, but you'd have to go through the application process."

Sarah lets out a lamented sigh. She can't believe this is happening right now.

"The good news, however, is you can still see us today. We accept cash or credit card. Medi-Cal can reimburse you for any treatments up to three months, if you're approved."

"Oh. Uh..." Sarah chews on her bottom lip as her anxious foot taps the ground. "But what happens if I'm not approved?"

"In that event, we have social workers here who can help with resources for any treatment plan you may need..."

"No, no, no," Sarah says, cutting the receptionist off with a firm shake of her head and flailing arms that compliment her panic. "No social worker. I don't need treatment. I'm just here cause my... whatever... is freaking out about nothing."

"Your whatever?"

"Uhh... nothing. It's probably nothing... whatever. It's whatever..." Sarah rambles through her nerves.

"Um, okay! I think I understand. Would you like to keep your appointment today?"

"How much would it cost?" Sarah bites down harder on her bottom lip, too hard, and winces with pain. "Ouch."

"Today's visit with screening is two-hundred and fifty dollars."

Sarah's eyes widen as she processes the information. A streak on her lip turns red as blood bubbles up through the tiny cut.

"Oh, my god... Um..." Sarah's tongue flicks out of her mouth and over the laceration on her lip. Her eyes open wide like they're reacting to her tongue that must have tasted blood. Her finger comes up, touches her lip, and pulls back into her eyeline. Bright red blood outlines the grooves of her fingerprint. "Uh..." she says, distracted. She holds her thumb over the wound and shakes her head to refocus. "Can't you just hold a tab for me or something? I'm gonna get the Medi-Cal. I swear!" Sarah says with a nervous chuckle.

"Well, I have seen some of our patients work out financing plans, but you'd have to speak to a founding doctor about that, which means you'd have to keep your first appointment."

"Uh..." Sarah's mind spirals, knowing she doesn't have the money, but also that she doesn't have options. It's nothing, sure, fine, but also, what if it's not? "Okay... hold on." Sarah rummages in her bag and finds several loose notes scattered among her ChapStick, keys, and old McDonald's receipts. "20, 40," she says out loud as she counts the bills on the counter, "140, 240, 5... 250," Sarah gasps in pleasant surprise! "Yes! I do have it!" Sarah whispers.

"You got it?" the receptionist says.

"Yes!" Sarah says with a child-like delight, like she found the surprise toy in the cereal box on the first pour. "Cash, please. Thanks," and hands over the stack of bills.

* * *

Emily listens back in to the conversation as she watched both Sarah and the receptionist celebrate the small win with their bright smiles. The scowl drops from her face as the realization of her own privilege humbles her. There's never been a time in Emily's life she had struggled to come up with money, or even a time she cared about a price tag. Money is always available to her. Often, she receives things for free, because she has value coursing through her veins. People with things to give would exchange them for the chance to access her. Her relationship with money was about power. Not having enough of it had never been an afterthought. With this woman before her, she considers, for the first time, what this kind of struggle might feel like.

Sarah settles her bill, turns around, and startles in Emily's presence.

"Sorry! I didn't mean to scare you," Emily says with a wide but sheepish smile. She wants to say more, but can't find any words that might be... appropriate.

Sarah offers a polite smile, but no words. She looks at the ground, hurries out of Emily's sightline, and collapses into a waiting room seat. Emily's gaze follows her, hoping for a moment of opening. She watches as Sarah disappears into her phone as if it were a cloak of invisibility. Emily breathes out and shakes it off. She takes her turn at the reception.

"Hello, Emily Cassius, 10:45."

nine

THE LOBBY IS QUIET, with only Sarah and Emily waiting for their names to be called. Emily's eyes catch Sarah's looking at her, just before they dart away. Sarah squirms at the catch until she can hide behind her phone again. Emily respects Sarah's need for distance and forces her attention to any other corner of the room, then back to her phone, the safe refuge.

The door that separates the medical unit from the lobby creaks on its hinges as it's pushed open. A woman in scrubs and holding a clipboard presses her foot up against the base, holding it open for her next patient. Nurse Jackie, a gray-haired woman with a soft face who has worked in hospital halls longer than these twenty-somethings have been alive, calls out "Sarah Kenneth?"

***

Nurse Jackie leads Sarah down a hallway and makes polite conversation as she rolls through her script.

"You ever come see us before?"

"No."

Nurse Jackie smiles at her like an adult smiles at a child still discovering the world around them. She leads Sarah into a locker room, and points to a locker.

"Okay, dear. You're gonna change out of your top and wear with this gown. Are you wearing any lotion or deodorant?"

"No... Uh, I mean, yeah..."

"Okay, no problem. Use one of these alcohol wipes," she hands over a plastic basket of wipes, "and make sure you remove all that. The aluminum in those products sometimes interferes with the machine."

Sarah nods, but her wide eyes, tense shoulders, and gulp in her throat give away her nerves. Nurse Jackie notices.

"Aww, don't worry 'bout a thing. We're gonna get you all squared away." Nurse Jackie rubs her shoulder and exits the room.

Sarah stands inside the small changing room and stays still for a moment, giving herself a chance to understand what's about to happen. Her mind reels with possibilities. Could she have... it, could she not? If she leaves right now could this all just go away? Would she wake up tomorrow and this all be a dream? Please? Her thoughts consume her until she feels a tightness in her chest, and realizes, she's forgotten to breathe.

GASP! Sarah sucks in air, coughs, and breathes deep until she's caught up with her racing heart. A few more calm breaths in, and she's okay.

Settled, she removes her shirt.

* * *

It's dark inside the mammogram room. The space is wide and empty, except for the elephant-sized machine in the center and an imaging computer in the corner. Sarah stands up against the machine, full of discomfort, fear. Nurse Jackie guides her as she speaks.

"Okay, now we're gonna get you all the way up close." Nurse Jackie nudges Sarah forward. "I'm just gonna use my hands to position your breast on the plate." Nurse Jackie cups the bottom of

Sarah's breast and places it onto a small plastic plate. Another plastic plate above tells Sarah what's about to happen next.

"Okay, now, I'm just gonna step over here." Nurse Jackie steps aside. Over at a monitor, she clicks on buttons. The machine whirs awake and the plates contract.

Sarah watches the two plastic plates come together, sandwiching her breast tissue. Her breaths quicken as she sees her breast flatten into an unnatural state. She's unnerved by the sight of it. The pain makes her panic, and she imagines her breast popping like a pimple—blood, fatty tissue, and ripping skin all within the confines of the machine's plastic breast plates.

"Look forward, please," Nurse Jackie says.

Sarah looks up and away from the imaginary carnage her brain invents.

The plates contract further. Sarah winces, the pain's more intense. The plates go tighter, it's too much, and she yelps!

"Ow! Aww! Oww!"

Sarah yanks herself away. The whole machine rattles.

Backed against the wall, Sarah hides her face behind her hands and sobs.

"Oh, dear. I'm so sorry. You alright?" Nurse Jackie says as she approaches to offer comfort. Nurse Jackie's gentle touch on her shoulder tells her it's going to be okay.

Sarah wipes tears from her face and sniffles back more.

"I remember the first time I did one of these. I was a little older than you. But not much."

"You were?" Sarah can't imagine Nurse Jackie being as young as her. She was so maternal, more like an eternal grandma.

"I was in my thirties. My husband found a lump and begged me to get checked out. We had kids. It was scary. Do you have kids?"

"A son. He's almost 8."

"Well, all this is, is a test, but we're gonna get you through it. For you and your boy. As for these machines, first time's the worst. But you get used to 'um." Nurse Jackie offers a reassuring smile.

"I have to come back?" Sarah's voice cracks.

"Let's not get ahead of ourselves. Today, we're just gonna see. That's all. And I know you can do it."

Sarah nods with a surge of energy; she can do this.

"Can we try again?" Nurse Jackie asks with a kind voice.

Sarah takes in a deep breath and feels herself fill with strength. She steps forward, toward the machine.

Nurse Jackie helps her reset. "Okay, we're gonna go nice and slow this time. Don't worry, I gotcha."

* * *

Back in the changing room, Sarah blubbers as she pulls her shirt back on. She wipes away tears and tries to silence her cries.

Dressed, but not ready to face the waiting room again, she takes a breath and lets her body slide down the wall until her bottom reaches the ground where she hugs her knees, and cries.

* * *

Sarah barges through the office door and back out into the lobby. Emily, still waiting, startles at the unexpected commotion. Sarah pays no attention to Emily while she storms out of the center with sniffles and tears hidden behind crossed arms.

Emily stands like she's going to chase Sarah when...

"Emily Cassius?" Nurse Jackie says as she reappears and calls back her next patient.

Emily lets Sarah go and instead turns back toward Nurse Jackie. "Hi. Yes. That's me. Thank you."

* * *

Inside the darkness of the mammogram room, Emily goes through the motions, led by Nurse Jackie. The exam goes quick, and with little discomfort.

"You alright?" Nurse Jackie asks.

Emily smiles and nods.

After the exam, Emily stands in her robe next to Nurse Jackie at the computer. Nurse Jackie reviews the images while Emily watches. She points to a pea-sized white dot on the screen.

"What's that? Is that... cancer?" Emily asks, her voice drowning in anxiety.

Nurse Jackie offers a sullen smile. "Oh, it could be a lot of things. I've been doing this for a long time and if there's one thing I've learned, it's not to get ahead of yourself. Your doctor will get these results and call you real soon, alright?"

"What about that other girl? Why was she so upset?"

Nurse Jackie shakes her head and frowns. "Sorry, dear. Not allowed to discuss other patient cases... But you're sweet for asking. You look out for a call from your doctor, okay?"

* * *

Emily walks out into the parking lot and climbs in her G-Wagon. She presses on the ignition.

"Call Kyle," she addresses the car's entertainment system, and the cabin erupts in a trill.

"How'd it go?" Kyle offers no pleasantries or affection.

"Small white dot. Know nothing for sure yet."

"Urrrggghhhhh."

Emily's chin quivers in the weight of his disappointment. "I'm trying to do everything right, Kyle," she says as her eyes fill with water.

"This just... was never part of the plan, Emily. What are we supposed to do now? Add a supplemental addendum for breast cancer?" Kyle's voice hints at sarcasm, but Emily knows he's not kidding.

A scowl builds on her face. She agrees with what he's saying, but wishes she didn't have to. "Yeah, well... most people don't start a life with the love of their life just to submit to some predetermined contractual agreement!"

"How dare you throw that in my face again! Your mother was the one who insisted on the prenup. I'm just trying to make this work, Emily. Cancer doesn't make this work!"

Emily shudders at the sound of Kyle's shouts. She knows as well as him what's expected of them and in this marriage—and he was right. As it all sinks in, Emily soaks in the shame of her shortcomings. Every moment of her life is predetermined for her. She follows the rules; she does as she is told. But this wasn't part of the plan. No one ever prepared her on how to handle... cancer.

Defeated, silent tears fall on her cheeks. "Yeah... Um... I just... What do we do now?"

Kyle sighs. "No idea, call your mother. She'll figure something out," he says and clicks off.

ten

SARAH JIGGLES the lock on the front door of her apartment. It sticks. It always has. She fights against it today with a strong arm and a short temper.

"Come on…" she says with a groan as she grips the knob. It's supposed to work. If she jiggles it just right, it's supposed to… "Come on! Why aren't you…" She pulls the key out of its hole. With gritted teeth she goes to jam it back in, but misses. Her hand jams into the doorknob instead. "Oww!" She cries. It hurts. The pulse of pain in her hand triggers her to break. She screams out, the heaviness in her heart mixed with injury now too much to bear. She screams again, this time with force and anger. A release that sucks away her energy and leaves her a gasping puddle of tears when her phone rings.

"Ugh! Seriously?" She rolls her eyes as the door finally gives. Inside and the battle won, she closes the door, and finds her phone in her bag.

"Oh!" she says, surprised to get a call from the Women's Breast Health Center. "Hello?" she says. "Hello?" Anxious nerves make her repeat herself.

"Yes, may I speak to Ms. Sarah Kenneth?"

"She's me. I mean… I'm her…" Sarah shakes her head and scoffs at herself. What is she even saying? "Sorry. Yeah. Hi."

"Hi Ms. Kenneth, this is Bre calling from the Breast Health Center."

"Yeah, I was just there. Did I forget something?" Sarah opens her bag and look inside for missing items.

"No, you didn't. We're calling to get you set up for another appointment. The doctor would like to see you in as soon as possible."

Sarah's brow furrows with confusion. "What… what do you mean? Can't he just call me?"

"Unfortunately, no, we'll need to see you in person. Can you come tomorrow?"

Sarah gulps at a lump growing in her throat. "Um, why does this seem so urgent? Do I have cancer or something?" Sarah lets out a nervous chuckle, a silent pleading for confirmation of the opposite.

"Unfortunately, I'm not allowed to discuss results of any scans, but the doctor will go over everything with you at your appointment. He's one of our founding doctors, you'll be in the very best of hands."

"Uh…" Sarah freezes in her own shock. Her body stops moving, her face turns to stone—she can't process.

"Ms. Kenneth? Are you there?"

She snaps back. "Yeah, Hi. Um… I'm gonna have to call you back. Thanks," Sarah says. Her arm drops to her side as she stands in stillness. She darts her eyes around the room like she's looking for *anything else* to focus on, and finds Liam's clothes on the floor, his shoes in her way. Her head shakes left and right in a show of exaggerated disappointment.

"Liam! Ugh! If you weren't so cute, I swear to god!" There's no Liam, who's still at school. But the shoes and clothes present an opportunity of distraction from the thing she doesn't want to face. She marches up to the shoes, moves them to the wall by the door. She picks up the clothes and brings them to a laundry hamper in the corner. Her movement through the space is accompanied by the annoyance she always has when she cleans up after Liam. The why-is-he-so messy thoughts and how-many-times-do-I-have-to-tell him mantras run through her head like they always do. It's a normality she needs right now.

* * *

Despite its interior being small and cluttered, Sarah's apartment includes within in it a secret getaway. A Zen-style, backyard balcony where she keeps her most precious things. A single clay turntable, its original color covered in the gray air-dried clay accumulated from many sessions of use, takes center stage among its accessories—a damp cardboard box of pliable clay, a mini firing kiln, various piles and boxes of art supplies, paint, etching tools, and box cutters. Scattered around the yard and placed under bits of sunlight are pieces of finished and fired ceramic artwork. The aesthetic of organized mess matches the vibe of her art, her life.

Sarah sits behind the turntable. Eyes closed, she inhales deep. Several times. In, out. She stretches her neck left, right, down, up—a ritual. Her arm reaches toward the box of wet clay, muscle memory guides her. A full scoop of sticky gray mass comes back out with her hand. She plops it down on the surface of the turntable and opens her eyes. A soft smile comes into her face when she looks down to see the large blob of raw clay. She imagines it's waiting for her to shape it into something beautiful. Hunched over in its current blob-like state, she visualizes what it could be, what's inside of it.

"I see you clay. I will make you beautiful, and funny, and bright." She says, personifying the material. Internally she promises to bring out its true form, one the clay can feel proud of. It's a process that puts her in the right mind state to start the mold, and love the outcome.

She moves through the movements, almost a meditation. Pedal the wheel, shape the clay, wet the hands, spin the clay. Again, again. Her body and soul puppet the clay as she guides it through a dance on the turntable. Every other thought she pushes away. This is her time to escape from responsibility and doctors' office appointments, from bills, mammograms, and impending uncertainty. She relishes in the freedom of her hands wet with clay.

The experience is short-lived. Intrusive thoughts about a diagnosis she can't afford find their way inside. She breathes them out and shakes her head... *no.* As the clay takes form, tears well in her eyes until she's overcome by them. It doesn't matter how hard she tries to deny; the thoughts are there; the mammogram is true, and she could have cancer. A future she's never spent more than a moment wondering about, because she'd always assumed herself entitled to it, could be no longer available to her.

She weeps on the clay shaping up to become a coffee mug. Silent tears drop into the bowl. Her hands smooth and blend them into the clay. But rage bubbles inside her. Soft hands turn violent and she destroys the piece back to a blob. The table stops, and her head drops. She takes a deep breath in, an attempt to calm herself before she crumbles, but it doesn't work. Her inhale escapes in a whimper that breathes out into full tears.

eleven

SARAH'S CAR, a sun-spotted and rusted Toyota that still gets from A to B, pulls into a parking lot. An attendant wearing a bright orange traffic vest stands in front of a sign that reads "Vendor Parking Only." The attendant waves her in with a smile. Sarah smiles back. From the backseat Liam waves with enthusiasm as Sarah pulls into an empty parking space. She looks at Liam in the rear-view mirror.

"You ready, Freddy?" Sarah says.

"Ready!"

"Alright! Let's make some mon-ay!"

"Mon-ay! Mon-ay! Yeah!" Liam hops out of the car with vigor while Sarah trails close behind.

The parking lot is full of vendors unloading their vehicles—tents, equipment, generators, boxes.

"Morning!" A pleasant old farmer in a straw hat and cowboy boots shouts over to Sarah as he unpacks boxes from the back of his truck. "Got a fresh harvest today. Come get um!"

"Hey, Ted. Avocados finally came in?" Sarah says.

"Yes, ma'am! Peaches, apricots, nectarines, too. Send the chief over when y'all get setup."

"Will do! Thanks!" Sarah says while she loads up a cart with supplies from the car.

"Thanks, Ted!" Liam says like a tiny adult as his mother hands him items to carry. With a full load Liam marches off to the local farmer's market.

Sarah and Liam set up for the day's sales among a sea of white vendor tents, food trucks, and the smell of deep-fried wonderful. Under their raised canopy, the two organize a display of Sarah's ceramic pieces. Liam reads the etchings on each piece as he sets them out.

"Not adulting until I've had my coffee," he says aloud and places a coffee cup next to several others. "My spirit animal is a coffee bean." He sets another next to the last. "Therapy is more expensive than coffee." Again. He chuckles. "These are some good ones, Mom."

"Thanks, baby." Sarah beams as she relishes in the glory of her son thinking she's funny. A moment she'll get to carry with her, that reminds her why she loves being his mom.

* * *

The afternoon sun beats down on the canopies. The walkways bustle with patrons. Sarah makes a few sales waving goodbyes to her customers as they walk away with pieces of her art.

* * *

Sarah looks down at her phone for the time. 2:00pm. She scans the aisles between the tents. The crowd is dwindling and slowing down after the hustle of the morning.

"Alright. I think that's it. Go see Mr. Ted before he packs up,"

"Oh, yeah!" Liam says with excitement as he bolts out of the tent and down a wide-open aisle. He approaches a large booth, three tents wide that houses mostly empty tables—the morning's take been good for them.

"Hi, Ted!" Liam says to announce himself.

"Hey there, chief! How's you and your mom?" Ted says as he pulls a plastic bag from under a table, and loads it with leftover fruits and vegetables.

"We're good."

"Sales good today?"

"Eh, mom's inventory's low. She got a bunch of her pots smashed by some crazy lady."

"Uh oh! Here? Today?"

"Naa... she went to some coffee meeting thing."

Ted takes a beat while he looks around his farm stand. "Here. Why don't you take this..." Ted hands over the plastic bag, now full of fresh produce. "And, hold on..." he reaches for another plastic bag. "Let me set you up for another." He fills a second bag and hands it over to Liam.

"Ahhh, this is too heavy! I can barely hold it!" Liam plays with the bags, pretends to curl them like they were gym weights and he's a strong man.

Ted laughs. "Ya'll enjoy the rest of your weekend. See you next Saturday."

"Thanks, Ted. Bye!" Liam says, already running back to his mother.

* * *

Back at the tent, Liam wraps the unsold pieces while Sarah accounts for the day's take. She mumbles the count to herself.

"120, 40, 5, 6, 7, 8, 9. One-hundred and forty-nine dollars." The scowl on her face makes it clear she's not hit a comfortable number. "No!" she groans.

Liam alerts. "What's wrong, momma?"

"Nothing baby... Come on. Let's finish up." Sarah says as she moves, ready to take on the next task.

"Can we go to McDonalds on the way home?"

Sarah chews on a thought. "I don't know, baby. We got all this stuff from Ted. Doesn't that sound yummy?"

Liam lets out a lamented sigh. "Mom, we can't just eat avocados!"

"Um, excuse you, Mr. Attitude, there's peaches in there too." Sarah tussles his hair, waves him off, and refocuses him on their task. "Come on, let's finish up."

* * *

Sarah stands in line at Market Vendor Services behind farmers and cottage food permitters. She pays her booth rental, $149 becomes $124. Sarah looks down at the rest and thinks through what each dollar should go to. It's a mental flex she does each time money comes in as she attempts to control how quickly it goes out. $25 for booth rental, then she must pay her cell phone, and light bill, no. That can wait. The car needs gas instead. Then there was food for the week. The gift from Ted would help to bulk out her grocery haul. She was lucky to have friends like Ted. Maybe Drew would help with the light bill? She hopes.

Inside a cell phone store, Sarah stands at a kiosk to pay her phone bill. She inserts $90 into the bill slot, and recounts her earnings, $34 remain. Her brow sweats. Gas. Food? She questions whether she can do both. Maybe less gas and a little food? That could work. Drew would come through for her. She was counting on it now.

Liam sits inside the car while Sarah runs into a gas station.

"Hi, uh..." Sarah says to the station attendant. She studies her cash in hand. "Fifteen on pump 7, please." She slides $15 across the counter, the day's winnings now cut to $19.

Gas pumped, and back in the driver's seat, Sarah turns on her car and observes the gas meter with fixated eyes. The orange needle ticks up from Empty to just over a quarter tank. A smile creeps onto her face. It's enough.

"Does somebody want McDonalds for lunch?!"

"Yay! Yay! Yay! McDonalds!"

Sarah smiles. At least she can do this for him.

"Welcome to McDonalds, what can I get for you today?" The drive-thru attendant says through the menu speaker.

"Hi, yeah. Let's do a chicken nugget Happy Meal?"

"Gotcha. What else for you?"

"That's all. Thank you."

"That'll be $6.70 at the first window."

Sarah pulls the car forward.

"You're not getting anything, momma?"

"Uh... I'm not hungry." Sarah is hungry, but with only $12.30 to make it through the rest of the week, she'll stay hungry.

At the window, Sarah counts out six singles. Before she counts out a seventh, she scratches through her cup holders for seventy cents. "Yes!" she says out loud as she finds the exact coins to make the change.

With her errands complete, Sarah ends the day with a grand total of $13, one bill paid, and a Happy Meal in Liam's lap. Today is a good day.

* * *

Sarah and Drew lie in bed, wrapped in each other's arms. What should be intimate and sweet is off. Sarah's eyes tear up. Drew doesn't make any efforts to hide his discomfort, his disturbed frown a heavy weight on Sarah.

"It doesn't matter what the X-ray looked like," Drew says.

"Mammogram. Not an X-ray."

"Man, whatever. What'd the doctor say?"

"I haven't been to a doctor yet."

"Why not?"

"I didn't have enough money! Just the screening was $250. I only got $149 from the market. I had to pay my cell phone, gas, food. Next market isn't until next week. I don't have anything left for another doctor visit."

"But we have Medi-Cal."

"It expires at twenty-six."

"Wait. Really?"

"Yup... When's the last time you went to the doctor?"

"Man. I don't need no doctor." Drew says and sucks his teeth.

Sarah scoffs, but says nothing. The two sit in silence while Sarah chews on her nails and Drew stares up at the ceiling with his mouth agape.

"Anyway, I have to reapply." Sarah says, her fingers still between the bite of her teeth. "The lady said I could still qualify based on low income."

"Okay, so did you?"

Sarah stops biting her nails to shake her head.

"What you doin, Sar? This is for real! You can't be playin around and wastin time. You gotta think about your son."

Sarah's mouth falls open, and her eyes figuratively bug out of her skull. "My son? Really, Drew? Why don't you tell me what you know about *my son?*"

Drew sighs hard. His hand comes over his face and he massages out his stress. "How much for the doctor?"

"I dunno. I didn't even ask. Probably another $200, at least."

Drew reaches over the side of the bed and into his pants pocket. He pulls out a wad of bills and counts.

"100, 20, 40, 50, 60, 70, 90." The bills run out. "I got $190. You got $10?"

Sarah smiles and nods appreciation. Drew puts the money in her palm.

"Make that appointment tomorrow," he says as he kisses her neck.

"Okay, okay." Sarah chuckles.

"I got something else for you too." Drew pulls Sarah on top of him.

twelve

UNDER THE NATURAL light of a small kitchen window, Sarah sits with her laptop and scrolls through an online Medi-Cal application. She sips on a steamy cup of coffee when her phone alarm blares. LIAM SCHOOL, the screen reads. Sarah dismisses her alarm and takes one last fast gulp of her coffee before she pops up from her seat and hurries into the living room area.

Inside the sectioned-off makeshift bedroom, Liam sleeps on his floor mattress. Sarah pushes aside the tapestry door to let herself in. Her movement is so slow, it's almost creeping. A smile on her face reveals a plan in her head. Like a lioness stalking prey, she inches closer to Liam's bedside. Rolled opposite her. What she can't see is that his eyes are closed, but the smile on his face proves he's awake.

Sarah makes her move to pounce, but Liam's too fast for her! In one swift jolt, he turns over, jumps up and ROARS!

"Ahhhh!" Sarah screams with delight. The both of them collapse into a puddle of tickles and laughter. "You got me!"

"I always hear you coming, Mom. I have powers."

"Oh, you do, do you?" Sarah says with a chuckle.

Liam nods, his shoulders straight, nose turned up, and chest puffed out.

"Alright, power-man, come on. School."

"Arrrgghhh!" Liam says in protest as he falls back on the bed. "I'm still sleepy..." he whines.

"Oh, come on..." Sarah falls on top of him, cuddles him close. "I'll make you strawberry yogurt with fruit loops," she says as she gives him one last squeeze.

"Okay!" Liam pops up. He scoots to the corner of the bed and in front of a small dresser where he searches for the day's outfit.

*　*　*

Back at the kitchenette and sitting at her computer, Sarah continues her scroll through the Medi-Cal application. Her fingers click against the keyboard as she completes the form.

Liam enters, his backpack strapped and ready for school.

"Mommmaaaaaa! My strawberry yogurt!"

"Okay. Hold on," Sarah says as she jumps up and rushes toward the fridge. She searches the storage shelves. Her eyes dart left, right, up, down. "Uh..." She panics. "Looks like we're out, baby. How about..." She searches the shelves for any available food and finds a half carton of eggs, deli meat, a tub of sour cream, coffee creamer.... "Eggs? I can make eggs. And we still have an avocado from Tim."

"Ugh." Liam slaps his forehead. "We're gonna be late!"

"Okay, okay." Sarah slams the refrigerator door closed and reaches up. She grabs a box of fruit loops cereal. "Here." She tosses the full box at him and looks at her phone clock. "We're late!" In a hurry now, she rushes back to her laptop. A few more clicks follow anxious finger pecks on the keyboard. She looks at Liam, his hand stuffed into the cereal box, then into his mouth with a full scoop of brightly colored and frosted cereal rings. A smile brightens her face.

"Come on, Mom!" Liam says with a full mouth that sprays sweet cereal powder as he talks.

"Okay. Okay," she says and clicks submit. The laptop screen

reveals a message: *Thank you for applying. Please check your email for updates.*

"Yes! Okay. Come on, baby boy. Time for school."

"Yeah, I know, Mom."

Sarah cocks her head back but laughs away his attitude.

* * *

Sarah and Liam drive fast through the streets of their poverty-stricken neighborhood. Liam plays on Sarah's phone in the backseat. The phone rings, interrupting his game.

"Ugh! I was gonna beat my high score!" Liam says with a sigh. The phone continues to ring. He reads the caller's name. "Women's Breast Health Center?" Liam's face cycles from confusion to worry as the phone continues to ring. "Mom?" Anxiety blossoms in his voice.

Sarah reaches back and snatches the phone from his hands. She silences the call and tosses the phone to the floor of the front passenger seat.

"Why... why were *they* calling you?" Liam says as he gulps down a lump in his throat. "Did they need something from when Ms. Linda died?" Liam sniffles back tears.

Sarah lets out a deep sigh. "No, baby." She stares into the rear-view mirror, not stopping, still in a hurry to school. "That was a long time ago. And Ms. Linda was an old woman. Remember, we talked about how sometimes people get sick and there's nothing we can do?"

Liam shifts his gaze down to pick at his fingernails. "Yeah..."

"I know you loved Ms. Linda. We both miss her very much, but she wouldn't want you to be sad still, baby."

Liam's eyes meet hers in the mirror. "But... why are they calling you? Are you sick? Mom?" Liam's lip quivers.

Sarah looks away, back at the road. Her heart breaks, and she can feel the sharp edges of its broken pieces scrape her insides as they fall into the pit of her stomach. "No." She gulps. "I'm okay. No."

* * *

The vast front lawn of Liam's elementary school hosts loitering children of varied ages, all waiting for the day to begin. A string of cars line the street as passenger doors open to let out more children, who shuffle out and into the crowd on the lawn. A bell rings. Children move to head the call. All at once, they run, skip, and hop toward the entrance, two tall and thick metal double doors with chipped paint and a push bar handle, mortared into the outdated and cracked, carved façade of an old brick building that's been painted over more than enough times to justify a renovation, but still goes without. Campus aids push the kids along and encourage the less enthusiastic stragglers behind the crowd.

As the front yard empties and the last school aid heads inside, Sarah's car pulls up, its old and overtired engine announcing their presence. The aid alerts to the sound and waits with her hip on the heavy push bar door to hold it open.

Liam scurries out of the car, urgency fueling his pursuit.

"Hey! Hey hey! Where's my kiss, mister?" Sarah shouts.

Liam stops dead in his pursuit, rolls his eyes, and obeys his mother. He leans back in the car for his kiss.

"Have a good day, baby."

"Bye, Mom."

Liam darts back out, faster this time.

"I'm coming! Sorry!" Liam shouts to the patient school aid like a polite little gentleman who respects the time of others. "It was my mom's fault," he says, throwing Mom under the bus.

* * *

Sarah stares at her phone screen, worry filling her face. She knows she can't keep avoiding them. She takes a deep breath, presses the call button, and brings the phone up to her ear.

"Hello, thank you for calling the Breast Health Center. How can I help you?"

"Hi, yeah. I'm returning a missed call. This is Sarah Kenneth."

"Oh, okay. You need an appointment with our oncologist... and you still don't have insurance, correct?"

"I mean, yeah. But I submitted my application today, so maybe it'll come through soon."

"No problem. Can you come in today?"

"Wait... How much for the appointment?"

"The initial consult is $185."

"Oh!" Sarah breathes out in relief at the first sign of good news. She can do $185. She's got that much. But the feeling is fleeting. This means she's running short on excuses. On the other side of this phone call is finding out a truth she knows she's not ready for. "Uh... today? I mean, I have... stuff to do..." Her mind reels as she grabs at any excuse, even though her eyes roll at herself—laundry? Really?

"The doctor has requested to have you in as soon as possible."

"Yeah, yeah. I... I know. Um..." Tears well in her eyes. A feeling of dread sets in and becomes overwhelming. She mutes the phone to suck in big breaths as her chest barrels her into a panic attack. Her body hyperventilates and shakes, her eyes cry, and her teeth chatter. In her mind, she replays the vision of Liam's sad face in the backseat when he asked if she was sick. Over and over, she hears his voice. *Momma? Are you sick?* It's too real, it's too much.

"Oh, my god..." she says, thinking words might distract and calm her down. If nothing else, they might drown out the sad little voice in her head. "It's okay. It's okay. You got this. Not a big deal. Just a consult." She takes in more deep breaths.

"Ms. Kenneth?" The receptionist is still on the phone and brings her out of her private moment.

Sarah shakes her head, her hands, an attempt to shake out the panic. One last deep and slow breath brings her back to center. She clicks off the mute button.

"Yes," Sarah says. "Yes, hello. I'm here. Uh… Thank you. Yeah. I'll be there today."

thirteen

HELEN STANDS in Emily's gilded living room and holds a Breast Cancer Support Group pamphlet. Emily is a ball of tears in her husband's arms, cuddled on the couch. Although receptive, Kyle's eyes are blank. His body fulfills an expectation, but his emotional empathy is void.

"Oh, Emily. Pull yourself together," Helen says. "You heard the doctor. Stage one. A single round of chemo will put this all behind us. We have far more important matters to tend."

"This isn't fair! I'm only 25!"

"Emily. Enough." The stern tone of Helen's voice makes Emily snuff up her tears.

"You forget who you are. With every privilege in life, you really think a little cancer is meant to slow you down? Please! I had my first chemo in '96. Melanoma. That god damned baby oil marketed for suntanning. My god, the mistakes we make when we're young." Helen sits down, eye level with Emily. "People like us don't have to worry about things like cancer. You'll be set up right here at the house, your treatment and doctor will come to you. It's already been arranged."

"What!" Kyle shouts, finally making his presence known.

"Yes," Sarah says. "Yes, hello. I'm here. Uh… Thank you. Yeah. I'll be there today."

thirteen

HELEN STANDS in Emily's gilded living room and holds a Breast Cancer Support Group pamphlet. Emily is a ball of tears in her husband's arms, cuddled on the couch. Although receptive, Kyle's eyes are blank. His body fulfills an expectation, but his emotional empathy is void.

"Oh, Emily. Pull yourself together," Helen says. "You heard the doctor. Stage one. A single round of chemo will put this all behind us. We have far more important matters to tend."

"This isn't fair! I'm only 25!"

"Emily. Enough." The stern tone of Helen's voice makes Emily snuff up her tears.

"You forget who you are. With every privilege in life, you really think a little cancer is meant to slow you down? Please! I had my first chemo in '96. Melanoma. That god damned baby oil marketed for suntanning. My god, the mistakes we make when we're young." Helen sits down, eye level with Emily. "People like us don't have to worry about things like cancer. You'll be set up right here at the house, your treatment and doctor will come to you. It's already been arranged."

"What!" Kyle shouts, finally making his presence known.

Emily jumps away, startled at his reaction.

"I'm not living in a cancer house!"

Helen rolls her eyes and waves him off.

"Cancer house?" Emily's jaw drops. "What does that mean?"

Kyle opens his mouth to respond, but it is silenced.

"Both of you! Enough. I have enough of a PR nightmare dealing with your little outburst at the shareholder meeting, Emily. And you, Kyle, will not worsen the problem by showing even an OUNCE of neglect to your now cancer-ridden wife."

Emily cowers like a scorned child.

Kyle crosses his arms and shuts up.

"Now. We have to do something. It's all-over social media. #TheDailyMeltdown is trending. And don't even get me started with the memes."

Kyle lets out a chuckle. "They were pretty funny."

Helen waves the pamphlet back in Emily's face. "This is a perfect opportunity."

"What are you talking about? What opportunity?" Emily asks.

"Oh Emily, please tell me I didn't pay half-a-million dollars for an Ivy League education in marketing for you to miss the ball on this?"

Emily balks. "You want... me to..."

Helen gestures for her to catch up and make a point.

"Play the cancer card for public sympathy?" Emily resolves into an expression of understanding and submission. She knows her place.

"Finally, Emily. Thank you. Yes. You go to this support group, show face, a few photo ops. Poor Emily Cassius, breast cancer, she must be under so much stress, she's so young, blah, blah, blah. We sponsor the meeting, coffee, and treats for everyone. The world sees you again as the compassionate leader we've trained you to be."

"Another reason she should go to the regular hospital for treatments, like everyone else, instead of getting special treatment with a home hospital setup! Right, Ms. Helen?" Kyle tries.

Helen thinks on it. "He's right, Emily. As part of the campaign, receiving treatment at the hospital is best for optics. It's only three months. You'll survive."

Emily nods along, dejected. "Yes, mother. Whatever you think is best."

"Good. It's settled then."

Kyle mumbles under his breath. "It's not though."

Helen waves him off again.

He speaks a little louder. "What about what this does to her body? There could be surgery, radiation. Scar tissue?" His shoulders shudder and his face squelches. "Not to mention she'll be sick all the time. She can't have a baby now. Who's gonna take care of the house? What about my needs? How am I supposed to deal with this?"

"Your mask is slipping," Emily says to Kyle with a scowl. Kyle returns the disdain. The two of them stare each other down like children standing in front of an angry mother trying to pass the blame for the broken cookie jar on to one another.

"Oh, for Christ's sake, Kyle, find a hobby!" Helen scowls. "We don't have time for your needs."

Kyle holds up his arms in surrender. "I... I need a minute. Excuse me." Kyle stands and, with a fast and wide gait, leaves the room.

Emily, stunned to silence, follows his exit. The gesture feels more personal than him needing space. It's feels like utter abandonment, and the feeling comes with a twinge of pain in her chest as her heart breaks.

Helen rolls her eyes as he goes. "We need you back in working order, quickly now. Before that one runs off with the secretary. Ha!"

"He wouldn't. Right?" Emily asks, looking for reassurance where she knows she'll find none.

Helen reaches out and holds her daughter's chin with a soft hand. "Aww, to be young again. So naïve, but adorable." She pats Emily's knee, and stands.

"Now, you need rest. You're going to that support group. I'll have

Marco write up the press release. And maybe call a friend or something? No sense in staying locked in here with that barbarian." Helen scoffs.

"Yes, mother." Emily relents on the command with a heavy head and a sullen heart.

Helen leaves with a proud beam stretched across her face.

fourteen

SARAH SITS in a cold office chair across the desk from her oncologist, Doctor Evan, His face sporting a somber smile, says that even after an entire career delivering this news, it never gets easier.

Sarah returns a protective smile as tears stream down her cheeks. A defense mechanism that stops her from falling into a puddle on the floor.

"Hmm..." Doctor Evan pulls on the back of his neck, unsure what to say next. "The good news is, you're young, and we have several treatment options available."

Sarah nods vigorously as water from her eyes continues to rain on the carpet below.

"Based on your results, I think we should start treatment right away."

"I don't have insurance yet..." Sarah's voice is so soft, it's difficult to hear her.

Doctor Evan leans in and squints to hear better. "Yes. Bre, our receptionist, made me aware of that." His eyes and mouth curl down with empathy for her. He opens his desk drawer, pulls out a pamphlet, and hands it to Sarah across the desk. *Breast Cancer Support Group.*

Sarah raises her eyebrows in question but accepts the pamphlet, reads it, and scoffs. "I don't have time for…" Sarah shakes her head. "I have a kid to take a care of. I can't do therapy."

"Uh… I don't want you to think of it as therapy," Doctor Evan says. "I know you're busy, but studies show support groups are effective in reducing anxiety and sometimes even symptoms associated with treatment. You're going to need support through this, and I believe this could help."

Sarah's mind races into anger. She swipes her hands across her eyes, pulling the rest of her tears out. "It doesn't matter." Her voice matches the anger in her heart. "I can't afford treatment. Not right now. I can't do anything until the stupid—"

Doctor Evan raises his arms and presents his palms in a calm surrender. Sarah takes a deep breath and catches herself. *Stop yelling at the doctor, Sarah.* She tells herself.

"Ms. Kenneth. I've been doing this for a lot of years. I want you to get treatment, because I want to help you. So, I'm gonna make a deal with you."

Sarah's interest peaks as her eyes focus with anticipation for his next words.

"If you promise to go to this support group, we will promise to tab your treatment for one month, one billing cycle. That should be plenty of time for your insurance to kick in."

"What?" Sarah lets out a fast breath that brings back tears. "Are you serious?" She brings her hands up to cover her mouth, an attempt to stop herself from crying that doesn't work.

Doctor Evan lets out a quiet laugh. "Yes, I'm serious."

Sarah sucks in and breathes out as she tries to gather herself together again. "And all I have to do is go to this dumb group?"

Doctor Evan chuckles a little more. "All you have to do. We got a deal?" He reaches out his right arm to shake on it.

Sarah accepts his hand, and a handshake solidifies the deal. "Thank you. Thank you so much."

fifteen

SARAH SITS in her car in the parking lot of the Breast Health Center. Her face is stoned, stoic, and all cried out. She turns the engine. The car sputters. She cranks it over again.

"Come on... please," she pleads. The engine turns, and it starts. Relief. She clocks the gas tank. It's low again. "Damn it." She's got a few bucks left for gas, but Liam needs his strawberry yogurt. A trip to the gas station or the grocery store? She chews on her bottom lip as she thinks. Yogurt, gotta be yogurt. Settled in her choice, she runs through the logistics of how it'll all work. A distraction that pushes out the immediacy of the appointment she's just had with Doctor Evan. A needed reprieve.

She's still got a few hours before Liam's off school. Her mind calculates—the gas tank, in relation to her location now, to the yogurt, and car line pickup, tells her she'd better just stay put if she's going to make it to the store, to Liam's school, and back home. But it still doesn't solve her problems. It doesn't put gas in her car or cure her cancer. It doesn't get her to this support group she's supposed to go to, and it doesn't get her back here for her first treatment. But those are problems for another day. She turns the engine off, and sets a new alarm on her phone for 2:30pm, Grocery Store. She drops the phone in a cupholder and releases the seat adjuster to position her seat as far back as it will go. Laying back almost flat, she rests there, in silence, and with a single goal in mind—strawberry yogurt.

The sun shines through her windshield as it moves in the sky from its place in the morning east, too overhead, and settles in the afternoon west. Her phone alarm pings, waking her from a restless sleep. Time to go. Sarah fights to start her car again. After a good three cranks, the engine starts. She wipes the sleep off her face, and drives off.

* * *

Sarah and Liam enter their apartment. He's going a mile a minute as he blabbers about his day—his friend made a fart joke and got sent to detention, the lunch lady gave out free leftover juice boxes from a fundraiser, he helped a new kid find the restroom—it's been a good day. Sarah lets him talk but doesn't respond. She's distracted by the shopping bag in her hand—gotta get the yogurt into the fridge. Liam's voice turns to a piercing pitch in her ear. It hurts! Her head spins, her eyes close.

"Stop!" Sarah shouts.

Liam's face turns to shock and slowly melts into sadness as his eyes pool with tears.

Sarah takes a deep breath as she rubs her temples, immediately regretting her outburst. "Sorry... sorry, honey. I just... your yogurt... I need to put this in the fridge." Sarah tosses her shoulder bag to the side of the room and takes the plastic shopping bag into the kitchen, where she completes her task—yogurt in the fridge. She moves back into the living room and over to the couch, where she plops herself down. Liam squints at her.

"Momma? Can I have chicken nuggets?"

Sarah straightens up. She wipes her eyes and rubs her face like she's washing away anxiety with invisible water. She smiles at him, another opportunity to busy her mind with anything else.

"Yes... Nuggets." Sarah stands up and walks back into the kitchen. "You get goin on that homework, baby boy. I'll get your nuggets."

Liam trots into the kitchen behind her and sets himself up at the table.

* * *

Behind the light glow of their television, Sarah cuddles Liam on the couch. She smiles at him while cartoons blare on the TV and she thinks about what all this means for him—to be a young boy with a mom who has cancer. Tears well in her eyes as the thoughts she's tried pushing away all day flood her. She thinks about how she can't even speak the words to tell him about her diagnosis. About ways around telling him at all. She fantasizes about waking up tomorrow and it all being a dream. How she'd get to laugh this all away. Either way, this would not be another Ms. Linda situation. No. Doctor Evan told her she was young and resilient, and it was all going to work out. She wipes her face and refocuses on the cartoons when there's a knock at the door.

Liam jumps up in overzealous excitement as he runs to answer.

"Drew's here! Drew's here!" Liam shouts.

Drew enters the cluttered space with a pizza box.

"Sup little man." Drew kneels down to Liam's level and opens his arms wide for a hug.

"Mom! Drew brought pizza!" Liam runs through the small space like a kitten with evening zoomies, ignores the gesture for a hug, and goes straight for the pizza box.

"Pizza!" Sarah chuckles.

"Extra cheese and pepperoni?" Liam asks, the box now in his grasp.

"My man!" Drew holds out his hand—secret handshake.

Liam responds and drops the pizza box. The two snap through an intricate dance of their hands—left to left, grip, snap the fingers, right to right, snap with the left, and suave slide through the hair as their mouths and lips *hissssssss*. Too hot! Done, Liam snatches the pizza box from the floor and steals it into the kitchen.

Sarah rises from the couch, on her way to greet Drew. The two meet in the center of the living room and collide in a long embrace.

"I called you earlier. Why didn't you answer your phone?"

"Huh? Sorry, it's been a long day..."

"You make that appointment?" Drew asks, his expression eager for an answer.

Sarah nods. "I saw the doctor today." Her shoulders slump and her gaze turns away. She can't look at him.

"You good?"

Sarah's lip quivers. She shakes her head. Drew holds out his hand, pulling Sarah into a hug, directing her head to his shoulder and holds her as she sobs.

"Shhhhh..." he says softly. "I gotchu." He rocks her in his arms, like a dance, like a father coddling his infant, like a man who doesn't know what else to do, except be there.

sixteen

SARAH, Liam, and Drew sit at the kitchenette, an empty pizza box between them. Liam swallows his last bite, lays back in his chair, and rubs his full belly.

"Oh man, I love pepperoni."

Sarah and Drew chuckle.

"Go on, get ready for bed," Sarah says.

Liam peels away from the chair to comply. Sarah and Drew exchange a glance—they're ready to talk.

"So? It's not nothing, but it's not bad, right?" Drew asks as he starts the difficult conversation.

Sarah shakes her head as her face puffs with red flushed cheeks and worried eyes. "It's kinda bad."

"What do you mean? What did the doctor say?"

Sarah stays silent, but her tears roll forward.

"Sar. Why you cryin? You know I can't deal."

"Deal with what? *My cancer?* Are you for real right now?" Sarah's anxiety bubbles into anger. She's a rollercoaster as she rips through various emotional states. Her sadness brings more tears, but anger makes her rage as she waves her hands in the air and raises her voice.

"What am I supposed to do now? How am I supposed to take care of Liam? You can't deal because you don't have to. But I do! I don't get to just walk away from this! That's your move, not mine!"

Drew sucks his teeth. He grabs at his hair and pulls, releasing his frustration onto himself. "Naaa, girl. You don't need to be doin all that. Calm down." Drew moves his hands and arms in a gesture that presses down an invisible bar—a message of stop, calm down, and be quiet.

Sarah doesn't appreciate being invalidated and brings her face an inch away from his, sizes him up and pushes. Drew pulls back, but only a little, standing his ground.

In an aggressive whisper, and with a finger pointing at him, Sarah digs into him. "You're no better than your father."

"Ay!" Drew shouts, triggered. He reasserts his position of dominance and rises, the two of them close enough to smell the pepperoni on their breath. He points a finger back at her. "Don't you talk to me like that!" he says through gritted teeth. "Don't you say that to me!"

Sarah's face lights up. She's got him now. A smile creeps onto her face. "Your mom died, your dad bolted, and grandma turned you over to state services. Is that what you want for OUR SON TOO? To grow up an orphan like us? Huh?"

Drew's eyes reveal a deep pain behind them, and Sarah knows she got him where he hurts the most. She knows his darkest secrets, and where his pain hides. It's the exact pain she's looking for, poking at, and woke up. His face turns red and the veins that line his temples pop off the surface of his skin. His body shakes as he tries, so hard, to hold himself back, until... "Arrrrrgggghhhh!" Drew screams, steps away, and smashes a floppy kitchenette chair against the wall with a crash!

Sarah laughs at Drew's rage with arms crossed against her body and a smirk on her face. "There he goes. Watch out for the big guy, everyone." She mocks him.

With a deep inhale, Drew regains his composure. He picks up the chair and sits back down, but his knee taps wildly against the floor with anxious energy.

Sarah waits for Drew to speak. She's frozen, her arms still crossed in a show of no fear, but the air catches in her chest. She can't breathe, terrified of how he'll react next. Her posture and presence of control are a façade.

"So, what now?" Drew whispers.

Sarah's shoulders relax as she releases her breath. It's over. She shrugs and pulls out the pamphlet for the Breast Cancer Support Group. With an aura of condescension, she tosses it to Drew.

"Pfft. Bunch a whiney old ladies ain't gonna do nuthin for you," he says, his breath full of fire.

"Oh, and you are?"

"You know I do what I can for you, and for *our* son. Whatchu need, light bill?" Drew digs through his pockets, tosses a wad of cash at the table. "I gotchu. Food?" He points to the empty pizza box. "Got that too. And you know I come through as much as I can."

"Yeah, great. Thanks for the pizza, Drew."

Defeated, Drew throws up his arms in protest.

"Whatever, man. I'm out!" He slams the door in his huff out of the apartment.

Sarah picks up the wad of bills left on the table, leafs through them as she counts. "20, 30, 40, 50." She lets out a breath of relief. "Gas."

* * *

Sarah tucks Liam into the floor mattress of his makeshift bedroom.

"Momma, Drew got angry again tonight?"

"Yeah, baby boy. He did. Did that scare you?"

"No, not really," Liam says, a lie Sarah recognizes in looking at his eyes. "But every time he gets mad, he goes away for a long time. Is Drew going away for a long time again?"

"Ummm..." Sarah fights to force a smile against a tight throat and eyes brimming with water. "Sometimes it's good to take a little break when you're angry. But it's okay. He'll be back. Now, get some sleep."

Sarah completes the tuck, tickles, and gives Liam his goodnight kiss.

seventeen

EMILY SITS at an outdoor bar of a fancy restaurant built on a cliff-hang that overlooks the Malibu coast. A chilled white sangria in a clear wine glass keeps her company. She watches the sunset over the water. For the first time in her California-Sunset life, she notices, and takes in the breadth of its majesty. Bright yellow, pink, and orange sparkles over the surface of the ocean while various hues of purple and navy-blue hang over the top like a halo. It's a vision she must have seen a thousand times before, but only now can she appreciate its beauty. Life had always moved so fast before. With all its issues and disagreements and meaningless redundancies. But now, in the clarity of her diagnosis, something was different.

Everything about her life turns small in comparison as she moves her field of vision to explore how vast the colors stretch, and all they encompass and cover. A tiny, white pea-sized image on a mammogram is insignificant in the grand scheme of this sunset. It's like she can feel her problems seep out of her skin and diffuse into the surrounding openness. Her shoulders turn light. She soaks in the peace.

"Oh, my GAWD!" A squeaky girl's voice from behind breaks into Emily's moment with herself and nature.

Emily turns back in toward the restaurant, the hardened walls, and rigid expectations of her life.

"You made it!" Emily jumps, her movements a little slow and jerky, to greet her friend Tiffany. The two women hug and pretend-kiss each other on the cheek. Pleasantries over, they take their seats.

"So, oh my god, I'm like, so glad you called. It's been forever!" Tiffany's voice holds its squeak.

"Oh, I know. I've been so busy with the new product summit, and just…" Emily nervous laughs. She knows it's coming, and she'll have to address it. Tiffany will ask about her trending hashtag, and Emily won't be able to escape the embarrassment.

"Oh yes, #TheDailyMeltdown! Not a great look, babe…" Tiffany's voice rises with a mean-girl overtone. "Is your team working on that? Gotta protect that image!" Tiffany says as she snaps her fingers at the bartender.

"Yes. Actually," Emily says, and hopes to change the subject.

The bartender approaches. Emily mouths, 'I'm sorry' to him as Tiffany reads a menu.

"What do you want to drink?" Emily says. "My treat."

"Oh! You're so sweet, thank you!" Tiffany tosses the menu aside and orders from her heart. "I'll have the gold-plated sidecar, please! Thanks."

The bartender nods, and moves to make the top-shelf drink.

"You've always been such a big supporter of me and the company," Emily says and restarts their conversation.

"Aww, love ya, girl!"

"Anyway, we have a campaign starting soon. But I wanted to tell you about the specifics before you find out on social media."

"Yeah, okay… what's going on?"

"So…" Emily smiles to keep from crying. "I have breast cancer."

Tiffany gasps! "Oh, no!" She covers her red lips with her hands in a performance of shock.

"Yes…"

"Emily! Did they tell you how long you have to live?"

The brash response strikes Emily like a whip as her head and neck jolt back. She shakes the surprise away so she can respond. "Um, well... it's not exactly..."

"Oh no, Emily! This is... I can't even." Tiffany crumbles, speaking out of turn. "How's Kyle dealing with this? Is Kyle okay? Does he need someone to talk to?"

"Pardon?" Emily raises an eyebrow and narrows her eyes at Tiffany.

Tiffany stammers and backpedals. "Oh, no. I just mean, like, you know, sometimes talking to someone else is helpful. Like a shrink or something?"

"It's only stage one. Kyle's gonna be fine. I'm not dying."

The bartender returns with Tiffany's drink, a crystal glass rimmed with gold leaf.

Tiffany bursts into an anxious laugh. "Oh! Thank god! Emily, you scared me for a second... Phew!" Tiffany sips her drink. "Have you announced on Insta yet?"

Emily turns her head away to roll her eyes. Remaining calm in the face of ignorance—another trait her mother taught her. She breathes out her frustration, and plasters back on a smile. "No. Not yet. The campaign starts with a breast cancer support group, but I might do something..."

"Oh! Me! Me! Let's take a photo! We can #BreastCancerAwareness! We'll do like a sad face, but like, look serious. Think humble." Tiffany moves herself into position next to Emily and practices the sad/humble face.

Emily takes a moment to process—is this really happening? What had she come here for? What was she expecting out of this? Oh, that's right. Mommy told her to. Emily inwardly rolls her own eyes at herself. "Oh... kay... But before you post anything, I have to run it by my mother."

"Yeah, sure thing!" Tiffany smiles wide before going back into a pose.

Emily follows Tiffany's lead, eyes into the camera, then drops her gaze down—sexy-humble. The selfie camera flashes over their faces.

eighteen

FOLDING chairs face each other to form a circle in a small room at the recreation center connected to the Breast Health Center. Close to the door, an art easel holds a presentation pad with a handwritten message: "Welcome to the Breast Cancer Support Group. Your journey defines you, not your diagnosis."

Women enter the room and fill the space. In various stages of disease or recovery, some saunter in sporting sunken eyes, ports under the skin, headscarves, and gaunt expressions. Fewer enter with pep, a rosy smile, or a vibrant face.

Emily walks in, all smiles, and designer shoes, followed by her very own photographer. Click, flash, click, flash. She walks with a permanent pose as her cameraman documents her arrival. She takes a seat in an open chair next to the meeting moderator, Cheryl, a 45-year-old nurse and volunteer—identified by a badge clipped to her scrub top—"Hi, I'm Cheryl", and a healthy smile.

The back of the room boasts a decorated and filled buffet table of coffees, specialty drinks, and bakery treats. A large banner above reads, "From your family at The Daily Grind."

"Welcome, welcome, everyone. I see a few new faces here today," Cheryl says as she nods at Emily.

Emily fake smiles at the mention and points her eyes straight into the camera. Click, flash.

"Uh... I'm not sure..." Cheryl says with a side eye at the cameraman.

Emily cuts her off. "We're so grateful you allowed us at The Daily Grind to sponsor the group. We hope everyone enjoys the goodies." Emily gestures toward the buffet table.

Cheryl smiles. "Well, yes, we appreciate the beautiful spread, but I'm not sure about the camera. Support groups are an opportunity for us women to feel both vulnerable and safe."

"Of course!" Emily says with a smile. "We've brought release forms. We want to respect everyone's privacy. Would you hand them out, please?" Emily hands Cheryl a stack of release forms and continues with instructions. "Please make sure anyone who'd rather not be photographed sits opposite me, and please, don't be shy." Emily offers a warm smile, like a friendly gesture could compensate for the disrespect.

Cheryl's shock propels her hands to move on autopilot as she accepts the stack of forms. A woman sitting in the seat next to Emily's stands up to move across the circle. Emily hides a scowl with a toothy-smile.

Slam! The heavy double doors open as a latecomer joins the group.

"Sorry! I'm late. Sorry," Sarah says.

Emily scoffs at the stolen attention, all eyes now on *her*.

"No problem, more fresh faces. Welcome!" Cheryl shakes it off and moves on. She gestures for Sarah to take a seat in the only one left open. As Sarah passes by, Cheryl offers her a release form. Sarah accepts without looking at it.

"Thanks," Sarah says before slinking into the chair right next to Emily. Both women adjust themselves to lean away from one another and create distance. Click, Flash.

"Well, now that we're all settled. Who'd like to share and show our newbies here how it's done?" Cheryl says as she walks the circle, passing out release forms. As the women accept, and realize what they are, they gaffe, curl their noses, or simply don't have enough energy to react at all.

A frail old woman raises her arm. White peach-fuzz hair carpets her head and scars on her skin tells the story of her treatment. Despite a tired and a thin face, a glimmer of hope brightens her eyes.

"Anna, thank you. Please," Cheryl says with a gesture to proceed.

"Hello, girls. Welcome," Anna says, more to Sarah and Emily than the others. "This week was a wonderful one! My granddaughter had her spring recital. So, I asked Doctor Ron if we could fudge just a little on my scheduling, so I wouldn't miss it. He coordinated with Nurse Jackie, and they kept the infusion center open after hours so I wouldn't miss the recital."

The audience oohs and awws at the story, comforted by life's simple pleasures.

"I know that Nurse Jackie is such a sweetheart," Anna continues. "Any-hoo, this round hasn't been so bad. Only kept me down for three days! Haha!" She holds her hands up over her head with clenched fists, like she's celebrating a victory. The audience cheers for her and relates to the sentiment.

Emily wears a forced smile as one after the next. Patients and survivors regale their stories, offer hope, and sometimes tears. Sarah's eyes glaze over as she disconnects from the event.

"Sarah?" Cheryl says.

Sarah doesn't respond.

"Sarah?" Cheryl raises her volume.

Sarah snaps back. "Yes. Hi," Sarah responds.

"We have a tradition of giving our newcomers a chance to talk about their prognosis as an official welcome. If you're comfortable, would you like to share?"

Sarah's eyes dart around the room as she stammers out a response. "I... uh... I... well... uh..."

"I'll go first!" Emily interjects. Sarah sighs in relief. Click, flash.

"Hi. I'm Emily. I'm from The Daily Grind. Maybe you've heard of us? I'd love to get some feedback on our new product line. We brought lots of yummy stuff! Does everyone love a lavender latte?"

Click, flash. Click, flash.

"Emily..." Cheryl interrupts.

"Yes?"

"We try to keep the conversation focused..."

"Yes, sorry. Sorry, sorry. I'm 25, newlywed. My husband and I and trying for a baby. We're so excited. Busy, busy, busy!"

"Emily..." Cheryl, again.

Her camera-ready smile masks the annoyance in Emily's eyes as she reminds herself why she's here—to campaign for her reintroduction to the stockholders.

"Can you speak about your prognosis?" Cheryl says, also aggravated. None of them are here to listen to Emily babble about how wonderful her life is *outside* of cancer.

Emily laughs, stalling for the right word. "Um, prognosis. Sorry, I guess I didn't realize I'd have to talk about..." Emily gulps. A marathon of thoughts competes in her head. How is she supposed to talk about this while keeping it Insta-worthy? Is she going for the poor me sentiment? The strong-warrior persona? All her mother told her was to smile at the camera and bring treats. She didn't want to *actually* talk about...

"Cancer?" Cheryl says. "You didn't think you'd have to talk about cancer in a cancer support group?"

"Uh..." Emily shakes her head as her brain scrambles her words. She wasn't hadn't prepared her for this. No etiquette school had ever taught a class on tactful ways to present your cancer diagnosis. Even in the presence of the one room of people who would understand, she couldn't bring herself to remove the mask. "It's uh. I..."

Click. Flash.

The camera brings her back to focus. She gathers herself. "Has everyone visited the goodies table?" Her words sound confident, but her face gives her away. Her eyes point at the floor and her shoulders slump inward as she sinks into her own embarrassment. No one speaks. But it doesn't help. Her chest tightens and her throat closes. She knows the tears are coming, and she's failing her mission, miserably.

"Sorry," she says, ashamed. "I'm much better at speaking than this..." She lets out a nervous laugh as her attempt to earn a chuckle through self-deprecation, but fails, and is met with her audience's silence.

Sarah's eyes seep with sympathy as she watches Emily. Sarah too knows struggle. A different kind, but a lifetime of it gives her enough experience to see it happening in front of her.

Two almost strangers, and no hard feelings, Sarah reaches over and grabs Emily's hand as if to say, it's okay. The gesture takes Emily by surprise, but she doesn't fight it. She grips Sarah's hand back, not understanding why she feels the urge to.

"I'll go," Sarah says.

Emily and Sarah share a look of gratitude that speaks louder than words ever could.

"Hi, I'm Sarah. I'm here because... I have cancer. Duh. The doctor says H.E.R. 2, which, I guess, means it's kinda serious, cause my age, or something? My sex hormones, I guess? Whatever that means. Chemo and estrogen blockers first. Then probably surgery cause it's like *huge*, like Cutie tangerine size huge."

Emily's face turns back to Sarah with an intense but slow growing shock as Sarah continues to speak. Click, flash.

"Yeah, so, um, prognosis? The doctor says as long as it doesn't meta-size? Metasta...? Whatever that word is... he hasn't really said much other than he wants to start treatment as soon as possible. But that's kinda why I'm here. I don't have insurance, so he said as long as I come to group, he'll start a tab for me and hold the bill for up to three months, until Medi-Cal starts up. But like, whatever. Even if I don't end up qualifying for Medi-Cal, at least this gives me some time to pick up a few extra markets and earn the cash to cover it."

The rest of the group reacts with bug eyes, shook by the young woman's naivety at her own situation. A few of the women sitting within ear shot whisper to each other.

"Did she just say cash?" one woman says.

"What's an extra market?" someone says.

"Does she even understand what she's saying?" the woman says back.

"Cash? For chemo?" another woman says.

Cheryl moves her arms in an up and down motion to signal the women to silence. Sarah's eyes dart around the room like she doesn't understand the reaction.

"What?" Sarah says.

Emily holds her silence and doesn't react. Paying cash for expensive things doesn't seem outlandish to her, but she also knows Sarah is not a person who could cover such an expense, understanding now, her life could very well be at the mercy of a Medi-Cal claims adjuster.

"Thank you for sharing, Sarah. Do you have family that can support you through this?" Cheryl asks.

"My parents died when I was little. I haven't spoken to my foster family since they kicked me out when I turned eighteen. It's just me and my son, Liam," Sarah says with a nonchalant disregard for her own misfortune.

"Oh, my god! You have a kid?" One woman from the audience speaks out of turn, almost shouting. She covers her mouth at her mistake.

"Well, I mean..." Sarah tries hard to make them understand, but a lifetime of adversity hasn't jaded them. "It's not all bad. His dad's somewhat in the picture. He helps sometimes."

"Have you spoken to someone at the hospital about treatment costs?" Cheryl asks.

"Eh, no, but like I said, I can always scrounge up a couple extra hundred bucks until my coverage kicks in."

Her audience gasps and shakes their heads. The room falls into a heavy silence charged with an all too familiar and burdening empathy. They all watch her with sad eyes but have no solutions to offer. Sarah squirms in her seat like the energy is eating her alive.

Cheryl lets out a deep sigh. "Oh dear… Well, keep coming. If nothing else, talking helps."

"Yeah, I do feel better now. Thank you." Sarah sits back in her seat, a sign she's done.

* * *

Near the meeting's end, Cheryl walks around the circle with offerings to her attendees.

"Thank you, Emily, for the catered donation. Both of you, please keep coming," Cheryl says to Emily and Sarah. She hands them each a sticker of the muted pink breast cancer awareness ribbon.

Sarah studies it with intention as Cheryl walks away.

"Hmmm…kinda dull, don't ya think?" Sarah says, partly addressing Emily and partly talking to no one.

Emily turns to Sarah, smiles her acknowledgment, but doesn't understand what she's asking.

"The color. Light pink," Sarah says.

"Oh! Yes. You'd think they'd brighten it up a bit, right? Isn't it supposed to represent femininity and fighting back?" Emily says.

"Right?" Sarah laughs.

Emily offers a light chuckle.

Click, flash. Click, flash.

"Sorry about him, too. It's this… never mind. I just… I don't know if you remember me…"

"I do. Oh, I do." Sarah drags on the tails of her words, not afraid of being a little sarcastic. Emily deserves it, she thinks.

Emily titters and looks at the floor. "Yeah, I wanted to apologize for…"

"Smashing my inventory?"

"… yes. I'm so sorry about that. I'd like to pay you for the damages. How much?"

Sarah pulls back. "Don't worry about it. Your people took care of me at the event."

Emily nods, searching for something more to say. "Uh... your prognosis. That sounds like a lot to juggle with your art, and... your son."

"Yeah, well... we're both here aren't wet we. Can't be a walk in the park for your either?"

Emily shy smiles. Her arms cross in front of her body and the hand not holding her phone squeezes herself in a half hug. "Uh, I'm sorry if this is too forward, but would you maybe wanna exchange numbers? Maybe we could like... I don't know..."

"Sure!" Sarah grabs Emily's phone from her hand.

"Really?" Emily asks as her eyes squint in question of what's happening.

Sarah types her phone number into the contacts on Emily's phone, saves it, and hands the phone back.

"Great," Emily says as her arms throw themselves up with pleasant surprise. "Uh, here's mine." Emily sends a text message to the new contact.

"See you next week," Sarah says.

Click, flash...

nineteen

EMILY DRIVES HOME from the support group wrestling with mixed emotions as her head swirls with thoughts. How could she have gotten off so... easily? Not only with her pea-sized cancer tumor and trivial prognosis, but life? Born with every privilege, she'd had her whole life handed to her, and she felt the reality of it sitting in front of those women listening to them talk through their struggles like they were walking through a park. She had never known struggle in the way these women had. All she had to do was follow her mother's directions, and she's guaranteed an easy ride. Before and after her impending chemo treatment, life was, and would again, be, perfect.

Then there was Sarah. The struggling single mother who'd lost her parents, grew up in a broken foster care system, providing single-handedly for her and her son, and hasn't a clue about the cash price for a single treatment of chemo drugs, yet still found the motivation to wear a smile? Emily fills with disgust at her own behavior and an urge to make amends.

* * *

Emily enters through the front door of her luxury home to find Kyle snatching items from the wet bar. Without a greeting to his wife, items in tow, he stomps through the house on his way to the bedroom.

"Honey?" Emily asks in a calm tone, not wanting Kyle to feel like a deer caught in the headlight of her scrutiny.

"Yeah?" he says, his lackluster response out of sync with his aggressive movements.

"What's going on?"

Emily walks back toward the bedroom, led by her curious eyes, and finds the information she's looking for. Kyle is packing a messy suitcase with clothing, shoes, and his prized alcohol from the bar. Emily's eyes go wide as she processes.

"Wh... wh... what are you doing?"

"I can't do this."

"Do what?" Her tone shifts into a surprised anger.

Kyle packs faster, taking no attention off his task.

"Would you, please!" Emily demands his attention. She runs to the bed, and sits *in his suitcase.*

"Emily, please, what are you doing?" Kyle sighs. He throws his head back and stomps his feet, both of them acting like children.

"So what? You're just gonna leave your cancer-ridden wife behind to die?"

"This wasn't part of the plan, and you know it."

"I know it wasn't part of the plan, Kyle. Cancer doesn't have a playbook! But please, don't you..." Emily's words tangle up in their own desperation. "At least some of this was love, right? You had to love me at least a little bit... to marry me? Right?" Her voice cracks with anxiety, not sure she'll get the answer she's hoping for.

Kyle looks deep into her eyes. He makes a motion with his hand across his face like he's removing an invisible mask. "No," he says with a sour grin.

"What?" Emily says, her heart breaking. "But what about the first time you told me you loved me at the Vineyard in Napa? Or that trip to Mykonos where we sat on the beach drinking mimosas and planning our future children's names? Or... on our wedding night when you promised to be a better husband to me than my father was to my mother? You promised to love me!" Emily pleads and grabs at Kyles's shirt. She pulls him to her, but he resists and pushes her away. Kyle scoops Emily up in his arms, removes her from his suitcase, and... sets her back down and out of his way.

"Please! Kyle. Don't do this!" Emily pleads while she stands still in the spot he placed her. The instinct to please taking over as fear grips her.

Kyle zips his suitcase closed. "Cancer was unforeseeable, so it's not my fault."

"Does that make it mine?" she says, collapsing on the floor, as the fight leaves her body.

"I'll be at my father's." Kyle carries his suitcase out of the bedroom. Emily gets up and follows close behind.

"Oh, of course! Go, run back to daddy and the comfort of his wallet!" Emily screams, stopping only once Kyle reaches the front door.

"Well, cancer kinda removes the comfort of yours..." he says as he opens the door, steps outside, and slams it shut.

"Mooooooooooommmmmmm!" Emily screams to an empty house.

twenty

EMILY CUDDLES herself on her living room couch. She's not bothered to wipe away the disheveled makeup this time, or worried about what her ugly swollen cried out face looks like. There's no husband here to perform as his picturesque perfect housewife. The house is cold and empty. She picks up her phone, presses the call button. The line trills.

"Emily," Helen answers. "Marco just sent over the photos. Wonderful job, dear."

"Hi, Mom." Emily sniffles.

"You sound ill. What's the matter?"

"Mom… Mom! He left! He's gone! Kyle left me." Emily breaks down into sobs.

Helen lets out an audible scoff. "My god. Men and their hissy fits. So exhausting. Women should rule the world, you know."

Emily blubbers through deep sobs. "Mom!"

"Oh, calm down, Emily. We'll take care of it. Obviously, I can't have a divorcee daughter with breast cancer running around like an emotional bull in a china shop."

Emily tears are almost cartoonish, so hysterical, it's comical.

"Honestly, Emily, you'll give yourself crow's feet," Helen says—her personal brand of encouragement.

Emily stiffens and grits her teeth to stop herself from crying. It's no use. Her mother never has and never will coddle her, not even in the face of impending divorce by cancer diagnosis. Looking for emotional support from her mother was not even in the same area code of where she might find it.

"When is your first treatment? Hold on..." Helen shouts, "Adrian! Adrian! When is Emily's first chemo treatment?... Yes... Thank you... Emily?" Helen addresses her daughter, back on the line with her. "Still there?"

"Yes, Mother."

"Your first treatment is this Wednesday. I'll send a car, darling. And stop worrying about Kyle. He's most likely taking care of his pent-up angst at the cabaret as we speak. Nothing like a grand serving of guilt and shame to bring a man to his senses."

Where Emily searches for compassion and understanding she finds logic and the beginnings of a guilt laden plan to retrieve her stray husband. Let down once again by the mother who could never offer an emotional reprieve. But at this age, it was probably her fault for expecting anything different.

"I have a meeting. Bye, darling."

Emily sobs, alone and sad, but also relaxed in a sense of peace knowing her mother would fix this. Helen was good at fixing, and on that Emily could rely on. All she has to do is stick to the plan, follow the rules, and always protect the money...

* * *

As the hours pass, Emily moves from sobbing on her bed to sniffling back tears in her bathroom. She cleans her face and reapplies her makeup, preforming now only for herself.

In her cold and half-lit kitchen, Emily cooks a dinner for one. Step-by-step, the meal's preparation distracts her from her misery.

She glazes a hassle-backed chicken breast and sticks it back in the oven for the second round of baking, she kneads a pie crust into an individual size pie tin and stirs a blueberry filling on the stove, she tosses vegetables in a skillet. Her movements are fluid and soft, almost like she's preforming a choreography over the stove. Still enveloped in sadness, a tear escapes her eye and falls into the hot pan. A splatter of garlic oil catches her cheek.

"Ouch!" she says as she finds a dish towel and applies it with pressure to the wound. Like a pinch to wake her from a dream, she takes the shock as her sign to stop crying and move on. "You're done now," she says out loud. "Stop it." A final command to keep herself together.

An opulent dining room meant to host large parties and lavish meals, hosts only her and a steaming plate of chicken breast, broccoli, and quinoa. Her individual blueberry pie adorns the top right corner of her plate. A glass of white wine, her only companion. The scratch of her fork and knife dragging across the plate as she eats is the only sound to break the otherwise deafening silence.

Emily tells herself to stop thinking about him. Her mother's confidence this will all work out the way they want it to is enough to reassure the intrusive thoughts that tell her otherwise. Between commanding herself to hold back tears and forcing down her overcooked chicken, Emily remembers the rare moments with Kyle when life felt sweet, when she felt actual love, and how she thought it was strong enough to stand the tests of life. With each memory of his seldom act of kindness, every gift, and all his smiles, Emily's heart taints with doubts that any of it was ever real. Or maybe it was? Or wasn't it? She can't decide. None of it makes sense anymore. She takes a deep sigh, as rebellious tears track down her cheeks.

Emily dumps leftovers into the trash, the untouched blueberry pie part of the waste. She scours plates and pans, the mechanical motion of cleaning serves as yet another distraction from her reality. With her kitchen reset, she allows herself to rest on the couch. She squirms and fidgets in search of a comfortable spot, but she can't find one. The silence unbearable, Emily clicks through channels on the TV in a daze, looking past it.

She can't shake herself out of this gnawing emptiness that itches her insides. The TV doesn't help. Social media doesn't offer relief either. She scrolls through the comments under Tiffany's photo of the two of them having drinks at The Cliffhanger restaurant. Hundreds of likes and comments of support pour out for Emily and her diagnosis. She wants to smile, but can't.

On her own page, she scrolls through photos of her and Kyle happy, or at least pretending for the camera. These only bring pain. She'd still take that over this giant, open loneliness. Steaks of more of her makeup mark her face.

Drained of her emotional and physical energy, Emily stares at her phone until the screen goes dark. A thumb tap wakes it. There's nothing there, and she can't think of anything else to look at, but something about staring at the clock rids her of her thoughts and calms her nerves when a notification appears. Text message from... Sarah.

"Huh?" Emily says out loud, bewildered by the sudden interruption. She opens the text chain.

"Is it weird that I'm going in for my first chemo tomorrow and all I wanna do is get drunk?" the message says.

Emily erupts in a smile that burns across her whole face. She responds. "Haha! I've got wine!"

Emily waits with a captured breath while she watches the ellipses dance on the screen.

"1124 Kennedy Dr. Apt 27."

Emily jumps off the couch more excited than a puppy who's waited all day for Mom to come home. The prospect of friendship waiting on the other end of her phone.

twenty-one

EMILY'S NERVES tingle with apprehension as she stands in front of apartment number twenty-seven. Her knees wobble, her hands shake. What is she doing here? This was a mistake. She'd never even been inside a multi-family residence before. Not something her private school upper-crust lifestyle made room for. Were her nerves because of what was waiting for her on the other side, or because of the area of town she found herself in was the type of place her mother warned her to stay away from? Her mother would never approve of such a relationship. Yet, here she was, gripping tight to a bottle of Champagne and hoping to experience something real.

"Ugh!" Emily groans out loud as she shakes the negative thoughts out of her head and knocks.

"Coming!" says a muted voice from the other side.

The door swings open with wild enthusiasm. Sarah greets Emily with an eager energy. "Hi! You got the wine?"

Emily laughs a little. "Is Champagne okay?"

"Oh! I love me a little sparkling..."

"No, oh... I did promise wine." Dread befalls Emily. She's made a mistake, promised wine, and delivered not its sparkling cousin, but a class of drink all its own. Her first social faux pas in a world where she's unfamiliar. "I'm so sorry. This is Champagne. From Champagne, France. Is that okay?"

Sarah smiles wide and shrugs like she doesn't know the difference.

Emily mimics the gesture, relieved it doesn't matter and she's averted a made up social crisis. "I also brought some..." Emily holds up a brown paper bag branded with The Daily Grind's logo. "Uh... Does your son like blueberry muffins? Cake pops?"

Sarah laughs. "Loves um! Come on in, girl."

Emily follows Sarah inside with an awkward gait and a nervous smile. She trips over hallway shoes and Liam's backpack, but catches herself against the wall. Rosy red cheeks reveal her embarrassment.

"Ooops, sorry... Kids." Sarah's three words explain something only she understands, that Emily has no concept of.

"Yeah? What about them?" Emily asks with genuine curiosity.

"Huh? Oh, nothing. Just sorry about the mess."

"Oh! Yes. No. I mean, no. I hadn't even noticed." Emily chuckles, feeling like not even a polite conversation between the two of them makes sense. It's like they speak different languages, another reminder that she shouldn't be here.

***

Sarah gestures toward her small and worn-down couch.

"Have a seat! I'll get glasses."

Emily sits, and Sarah heads off toward the kitchen. Emily sees the sectioned-off living room, the tapestries pulled aside like curtains and feels like she's intruding. Like she's already too close, and this is all too intimate. Strewn in the space are the private lives of Sarah and her son. There's no place for hosting, no neutral area for company. She's thrown right into Liam's bedroom and she's only just stepped in from the front door. The feeling shakes her nerves and makes her uneasy.

Inside, the fabric walls of Liam's bedroom, the bed is empty.

Emily searches her brain for an explanation but has no reference to makes sense of the context. The thought makes her eyes bulge like she just walked into the lifestyle of an extraterrestrial. Afraid to point out any more glaring differences between them, she composes herself before Sarah comes back.

"Uh, is your son not home tonight?"

"He's sleeping in my room. Wasn't gonna miss an opportunity for girls' night!"

"You don't have a nanny?"

Sarah laughs out loud and hands Emily a plastic wine glass with its removable stem. "I'm the nanny, the maid, the cook. Multi-talented."

"Uh... how do I?" Emily accepts the cup and the plastic stem with both hands.

Sarah smiles like a mother smiles at her toddler learning something new. She takes her own and attaches the stem to the bottom of the cup. "Voila!"

"Okay..." Emily mimics the process and chuckles.

Sarah grips the head of the Champagne bottle, gritting her teeth as she attempts to pull the cork from the neck, to no avail.

Emily covers her mouth as she giggles. "Here, let me show you." Emily holds out her hand for the bottle. "There's a trick to these." She positions the bottle in her hands like she's holding a baseball bat, her left thumb pressing up against the cork. With her bottom hand she twists, while the top hand and thumb hold the cork in place. "It's all about the twist," Emily says as her mouth tightens, all her strength focused into her hands.

The bottle releases a hiss, and POP! The cork falls to the floor as the sound of bubbles mixes with their laughter.

"It's so nice of you to have me over after I... I just feel so bad for ruining your art. That was completely uncalled for."

Sarah waves her off. "I should be thanking you. I didn't know how I was gonna pay rent this month. Plus, I'm always happy to make more. Molding clay is my escape."

"Escape? Like, what do you mean?"

"It's how I disconnect from life, when I need to. Decompress, reflect, make sense of what's happening around me."

"And you get all that from playing with clay?"

"... and making it pretty!"

The women laugh, at first.

Emily falls into a depth of thought and stares off at nothing. "Wish I had something like that..."

Sarah sits up, the sparkle of an idea in her eye. "You wanna try?"

"Oh no, I couldn't." Emily's shakes her head, a hard no. "I don't wanna mess with your groove, or whatever. I'm already intruding."

Sarah laughs off the formalities. "Oh, stop being a baby. Come on!"

Sarah grabs Emily by the wrist and pulls her up and off the couch. Emily spills a few drops of her drink, unable to adapt to the jarring motion.

* * *

The simple beauty of Sarah's balcony strikes Emily in a way she isn't prepared for. A space made only for Sarah, by Sarah, and filled with all the things Sarah cares for most without compromise or room for the opinions of anyone else. The space tingles with Sarah's personality—the colorful ceramic pieces, random trinkets, bright green plants, scattered art tools, and messy workspace. Without even knowing her all that well, Emily could piece together a perception of her, only by the unique world she had built around her.

"You... you made this? All of this?"

Sarah looks at Emily with narrow eyes and a tilt in her head like the question doesn't make sense. "What do you mean?"

"The way you made this. The decor. The clutter. It's so... specific. Like no one else could have done this for you, or told you what was allowed. It's so... free."

Sarah almost laughs. "I mean, I pay rent here, so, yeah. It's my space to do with whatever I want."

Emily offers a polite smile, seeing Sarah's sweet naivety, but also knowing Sarah can't understand the difference between the two of them. Something that's now crystal clear to Emily.

Sarah is free to make her own choices, live her own life, and even decorate her own space. Emily lives in a cage of opinions, controlled by her mother, her husband, and the standards and exceptions that encircle its boundaries. She couldn't even visualize what a space of her own might look like, because she didn't know her true self well enough to know what she'd put inside it. Sarah was a vibrant artist who loves color and has a sarcastic sense of humor, illustrated by the cheeky sayings etched into her art. Emily hadn't the slightest clue who she was outside of the box she lived in—if she liked color, or even if she could crack a joke.

"Sit!" Sarah says, pointing to the clay-stained stool that rests behind the turntable.

Emily complies. She takes a deep gulp from her glass. Sarah pulls up another stool and sits in front of the turntable, opposite Emily, so close, their knees touch. The women notice each other, and Emily giggles. Nothing funny except the realization that she'd never been this close to a person outside of a romantic context.

"What's so funny?" Sarah asks.

"Nothing, sorry. I just… Your eyes are like, right there."

"You never looked someone in the eyes before?"

Emily thinks about the question. Not that she'd never looked into someone's eyes, certainly there had been a business deal or two where she'd done so—they teach eye contact technique in business school, after all, and she'd practiced. But looking into Sarah's eyes, and watching her look back, she realized no one else had ever looked at her with intimacy and a genuine ask for connection. Her interactions with peers, lovers, colleagues, or her mother all curated, rehearsed, or seeped in power. No one had ever seen her, because no one had ever really cared to know her, only looking for what she offered.

Emily clears her throat and looks down. The intensity of the moment too much. "So, now what?" Emily asks.

Sarah smiles, "Follow me," she says, guiding Emily to shadow as they move through the motions.

"First, we wet our hands." Sarah points to a bowl of gray water on the floor.

Emily turns up her nose. Sarah's giggles soften her eye roll.

"Clay is full of natural minerals. It keeps the water clean enough..." Sarah dips her hands in the bowl.

Emily follows.

With hands dripping wet, Sarah reaches for the wet cardboard box. "Now we grab a hunk of clay."

Emily follows Sarah's movements. Her hands dig into the clay. It fills her palms, embeds her fingernails. The weight is heavy in her grasp. "This enough?" Emily pulls her hands back and looks at the lump of clay she holds.

"Nope!" Sarah adds her own mound to Emily's. "Here."

"Ooopf!" Emily says as her hands jerk down from the added weight.

"I gotcha," Sarah says with reassurance. Her hands guide Emily's away from the box and back toward the turntable, holding her at the wrists. "Okay, now!" Sarah moves Emily's hands apart. The mountain of clay falls from Emily's control and plops onto the turntable.

The women shriek in surprise! Emily wasn't expecting that, and Sarah revels in the fun of it. They chuckle together.

"Cool. Now... see that pedal there?" Sarah says as she points to the floor. "Hit it!"

Emily touches the pedal, her shoulders tense—afraid of new things and unreliable outcomes. The turntable moves three inches, with sloth speed.

"Come on. More! More! More!" Sarah's voice entices the action.

Excited, but still tense, Emily hits it hard, again, again, again. The table spins, faster, faster, harder, until... The clay flies off the surface and splats to the floor.

"Eeek!" Emily screams.

Sarah laughs, hard. "Gotcha again!"

Sarah resets the clay. "You're too easy. I had to... Just relax... It's just clay," Sarah says with a warm smile. "Okay, serious this time."

Sarah uses only gestures to guide Emily. She moves in-sync with her breaths. Emily adopts the choreography and finds her rhythm. Both of them now, in time and tune with a silent pulse that makes them move, work, mold.

* * *

Sarah and Emily both hold wet molded coffee cups in their hands caked with gray. Sarah directs Emily, shows her how to add a handle with a small, snaked piece of clay.

"How has it been for you? Like all of this?" Sarah makes a gesture with her hands that encircle her breasts.

"Oh... um. Honestly, it doesn't feel like anyone actually believes I'm sick. My mother thinks all that matters is how my PR team can spin it to benefit our company. And my husband, well... he... left."

"Left? Like gone?"

Emily nods as her eyes well.

"People that leave aren't worth the fight to keep them around. You should let him go."

Emily stops working on her cup. "Excuse me?"

Sarah shrugs and etches an engraving into the side of her cup with a special tool. "Who cares? You're too young to care so much about what other people think. We gotta take care of ourselves, ya know?"

"Look, it's not that simple, okay?"

"Why not?"

"Because!" The question offends Emily, but she can't explain why or how. Referencing her years of private media training, instead, she pivots. Her shoulders straighten and her chin lifts high. "Kyle is a good man. He's just overwhelmed. He'll be back. He knows he has to come back."

Sarah finishes the etching on her cup, grabs Emily's from her, and etches again. "But do you want him back?"

Emily can't decide if she's more taken by the question, or by Sarah's command of her coffee cup. "Uh... Of course I do. He's my husband."

"Uh-huh. And why'd you want to get married in the first place?"

"What kind of question is that? I don't know. We've known each other since we were kids, that's just... You go to school, get married, have kids. That's what you're supposed to do."

"So, you wanted to get married, because... you're supposed to?"

A familiar melody haunts Emily's memory as she stammers through her response. *Just do what you're told, and you'll always protect the money...* "Uh... I... Uh..." *This life isn't easy to hold, but thank god it's filled with honey...*

"Hey!" Sarah says.

Emily snaps out of the echoes of her own memories.

"I said, how's that working out for you?" Sarah asks, seemingly for the second time.

Dumbfounded, Emily can't believe what she's hearing. This woman is *so* brash, so forward. She can't find the words to respond.

Sarah hands her coffee cup back to her and turns her own around to show both cups and the words etched into their sides. The cups match. "WHO SAYS COFFEE CAN'T CURE CANCER?"

Emily's face relaxes at the message, she forgets the offense. "Cute, but you know, coffee is absolutely not a cure for cancer, right?"

"Yeah, but I still can't live without it, so, if you think about it that way, it kinda is."

twenty-two

OUTSIDE ON THE BALCONY, the women enjoy the evening air. They sit on their stools, their glasses close to empty. Sarah sets their coffee cups on plates and moves them into the yard where she knows they'll receive the early morning sun. Emily takes the last drink of her cup, almost a gulp, like she's working up the courage to something.

"So, in group, you mentioned your son's father isn't really around?"

Sarah doesn't react, doesn't respond, but comes back to sit, and sips her drink.

Emily's drink makes her brave. "I mean, what kind of man doesn't even take care of his kid? And you said he comes around sometimes? Why would you allow that? Don't you have boundaries?"

Sarah takes in a deep breath and a full beat before she speaks. "Drew and I have a long history. I don't think you would understand."

"Okay, but you said yourself—people who walk out aren't worth it. You *just* said that!" Emily says with a tone to emphasize her point.

"Yeah..." Sarah pauses before she continues. "I know. I don't fight for him. He's here when he wants to be, and I don't care to ask for more."

"Does he know about the cancer? Even that isn't making him step up? What a loser."

Sarah double-takes and looks at Emily, taken aback by the insult.

Emily absorbs the misstep and backtracks. "Oh, I just mean…"

"It's okay," Sarah says. "Drew sacrifices a lot for us. He comes around when he can, but he can't stay. He gets… he has anger problems, ya' know? And it's okay, I don't push him, I don't want to."

"Uh, yeah. Ever heard of therapy?" Emily says, mocking the ridiculousness of the excuse she can't accept.

"You mean the super expensive mental health treatment?"

"Oh, my god… I'm so sorry… I… ugh… sorry." Emily is beyond embarrassed at herself. Her face turns red with shame.

"He can't help it. He knows he's not welcome when he's like that. So, that's why he's not around all the time and *that is* my boundary." Sarah shrugs her acceptance. "Liam calls him Drew. Just Drew. We take what we can get and that's good enough."

Emily connects a thought and is… confused. "Good enough?"

"Yeah. Good enough is enough."

"Good enough! You're hilarious." Emily chuckles.

Sarah doesn't laugh. "I don't get what's hilarious about it."

Emily straightens up. She considers Sarah's stance, but can't grasp it. "I mean. It just doesn't make sense. You tell me to let people go. People who don't want to stay. So how can anything less than living up to the expectation be enough? You and your son clearly don't have what you need, and that's his failure, right? So why would you accept anything less? It's just… I'm sorry to stomp on your life, but how could you continue a relationship with someone who's forever falling short?"

Sarah takes a long pause, considering the question. "Expectation? How can someone be expected to live up to some standard, when everything else has been ripped away? We have nothing, except one another. Expectation is something you can strive for when you have support and resources. When you're not just fighting to survive."

"Oh..." The word leaves Emily's throat like a whisper. She'd never considered how privilege entitles her to live a life of expectations and comfortable boundaries. "I... uh..." Emily's face flushes red as she struggles to find words that might save her the embarrassment.

"The point is, we have a relationship of acceptance and understanding of one another. That's something both of us had before, and lost at a young age when our parents died. It's the lack of something in our lives that brought us together. And it's the feeling of unconditional love and acceptance in one another that keeps us together. Everyone deserves compassion. I know what's in his heart. And that's... enough."

Emily's turn to think. She makes another connection, and in doing so, loses more of her confidence. "Um... so do you think because you remember what unconditional love feels like, from when you were a kid that, *that* helps you have compassion and empathy for someone like Drew, even though he can't live up to expectations?" Emily asks like she's in the presence of a guru, someone who knows and has experienced unconditional love not tied to a life of expectation. Something foreign to her experience.

"Love isn't built on expectations. I think because I know and love Drew, I'm not afraid of what he is or what he'll do. To me, love is the absence of fear."

Emily sits with this. *Love is the absence of fear.* Then what was anything in her life? Because she doesn't know any love without fear. Emily nods like she understands, but still struggles with her thoughts. Instead of going deeper, she changes the subject. "And how has your son adapted to the news?"

"What news?"

"Um... that you have cancer..." Emily says matter-of-factly.

"I haven't told him yet. I can't."

"Why?"

Sarah lets out a deep sigh. "I've never had a lot, but I get by because I've always had friends. Drew around or not, there's always been good people in my life to help, the people who live in the slums lean on each other. Anyway, my old neighbor, her name was Ms. Linda. Sweet old lady. I moved in here when I was pregnant. Drew and I were together. We were gonna start our little family, do it right, ya' know?"

"Yeah, sure..." Emily leans in, eager to learn more.

"As you can probably guess, that didn't last too long. Drew was gone again, and I was alone. Ms. Linda stepped in and helped. She was the one who carried in my groceries and tied my shoes when I was so pregnant I couldn't bend over anymore. The one in the delivery room with me. Some nights, she stayed over so I could sleep and recover. She was what I know my mom would have been if she were still alive." Sarah takes a deep breath.

"Anyway, over the next several years Drew would come in and out, and she never judged me. She babysit Liam when I needed to work, or if Drew was around, she'd help him when he hadn't a clue how to take care of Liam. Liam and I got very close to her. Um... then, uh..." Sarah takes her time as it becomes harder to speak. "When Liam was five, she got diagnosed with stage 4. At the same health center. It was already fatal. They did treatment and kept her comfortable. She lasted another two years and we're grateful we got those last couple of years with her." Sarah wipes tears from her face.

Emily feels a pang in her chest as it tightens. This woman's story keeps knocking the wind out of her.

"So, uh... that was less than a year ago. I can't tell Liam yet. It's too much right now. I'll go to the appointments and whatever, but I'm not doing that to him right now. I don't have to. It's not even that serious, I don't think."

"Thank you for sharing that with me. I'm so sorry for your loss."

Sarah waves her away. "Yeah, whatever. Thanks," she says as she wipes her face, hiding her tears in laughs.

twenty-three

SARAH DREAMS of a weathered old building. The front door hosts a wooden cutout sign: Community Group Home for Abandoned Youth. What used to be a community center turned into a home for runaways and overflows from the child welfare system.

She is eleven years old. She sits in the backyard next to a decrepit play area, and a high chain link fence that cozies up to an open field. Opposite the field rests a campus of industrial style buildings, high fences with barbed wire, and guard towers. Young Sarah stares off at the open field and the buildings, and waits.

Miss Ashley approaches Sarah. "Rest 'o the kids are playin' in the yard. What chu doin' ova here?"

Sarah looks up. Innocent and naïve, she answers with honesty. "Waiting for my friend."

"Honey, don't be messin' with them juvie boys. I already done warned ya."

Off in the distance, a loud bell rings out. Automatic locks unlock, and giant steel doors on the distant buildings open. Out pours a flood of young boys wearing matching jumpsuits. Some hold balls and bats, others weights and exercise equipment. Some run into the field, some to the adjacent blacktop basketball court. One boy is empty-handed, but walks into the field, hands in his pockets, and straight to young Sarah.

The sight of him excites her. Sarah gasps with glee and stands ready to receive his greeting.

Miss Ashley watches her, scoffs, laughs, and rolls her eyes. "I don't even know why I try with you kids. Hormones, have you actin' all crazy." The woman walks off and away.

The boy quickens his pace, the closer he comes. Sarah brings herself up to the fence, her fingers mingle into the chain link.

"Hi Sarah!"

He's here. Wide smiles erupt on both sides of the fence as boy and girl meet.

"Hi, Drew." Sarah blushes and looks down to the ground.

Drew, a 13-year-old version of himself, without the tattoos, smiles at her timid greeting. The wear of a stressful life to come doesn't yet hang under his eyes.

"I talked to my social worker today. He said when my sentence is up, I get to choose between two places."

"You're gonna be free! That's awesome, but..." Sarah's eyes yearn, "where are you gonna go?"

"Guess two places right now. Go!"

"Uh... uh, uh... Your mom's and your grandma's."

'Pffftt. Wrong! My mom's dead, stupid!" Drew laughs out loud.

"Oh, yeah. Mine too." Sarah giggles, not because her mother's dead, but because it's a pain she knows she doesn't have to feel alone in.

"Okay, well, yeah, I could go to my grandma's, but the other place I could go is... Drum roll! Community Group Home!" Drew jumps and his arms reach to the sky, an expression to match the joy in his voice.

Sarah's face lights up as she gasps with an equal excitement! "Here! With me! You're coming here?"

"Yup! Only one more week!"

Sarah jumps up and down, clapping, celebrating. "Oh my god, I can't…"

"Puente!" a far-off voice interrupts their interaction. "Andrew Puente! Inmate! Get away from that fence!" A uniformed guard jogs across the open field and toward the two kids.

"One more week, Sarah. Just one."

Drew puts his face up to the fence. He finds a gap in the link for his puckered lips. He squeezes his eyes closed.

"Inmate! Final warning!" The calls get louder.

She's seen movies before, she can guess what this is about, she just can't believe it's happening. Her expression changes to elation. She closes her eyes, puckers her lips, and leans toward the invitation.

"Puente!" The guard is almost right behind…

Their lips meet. A first kiss.

"Arrrgh!" Drew exclaims as he's ripped away from the fence. They're caught.

The guard pulls Drew to the floor, kicks him, tussles him, and shouts. "I warned you, boy!"

"Ahhhhhh!" Sarah screams in horror as she watches Drew get beat down. Blood spews from his nose, his eyebrows.

The guard tires and stops the beating. He bends over, holds himself up on his knees, and tries to catch his breath. "I… warned you… Puente." The guard pants through his words.

Drew cowers in fetal position on the ground. The guard regains himself, grabs Drew by the shoulder, and pulls him to his feet. Drew's swollen and lacerated face trickles blood down his nose and drips into speckles on his jumpsuit. He whispers as he's dragged away, "One more week…"

twenty-four

THE MORNING SUN pokes through a gap in the curtains of Sarah's apartment. A beam shoots through the living room and lands on Emily's eyes, who is asleep on the couch. Emily's face twitches to the exposure as her eyes feather open and search her surroundings. The space is quiet until it's not.

The bedroom door smashes open, and a child's voice screams joy. Liam is ready to start the day.

"You better get in that bathroom and brush your teeth, mister!"

Sarah follows Liam out of her bedroom and chases him to the bathroom. Liam runs and screams, playfully flailing his arms and pretending his mom is a monster. He loves this game. Sarah chases him into the bathroom and shuts the door. Emily smiles at the sound of mother and son giggling behind the closed door.

Emily sits up on the couch and rubs her head like she's trying to rub away her headache, as Sarah comes in.

"Sorry about that. He's full of energy in the morning," Sarah says.

"Oh, no. Not at all. I'm sorry for overstaying. I shouldn't have drunk so much last night."

Emily holds her head, her eyes seething with a hangover.

"You need water," Sarah says with a chuckle and goes to fetch a glass of water.

"Um, I... want to apologize again for prying about you and Drew. It's none of my business. I shouldn't have said anything," she says, grateful for the water.

"You were curious. I'm not offended," Sarah joins Emily on the couch.

Emily nods. "So, what are your plans today?"

"I gotta take Liam to school and then head to the clinic. First chemo today. Yay!"

"Oh! Today? You can't possibly do that alone. Please, let me drive you?"

"No, no. It's cool. You don't gotta do that. I'm good."

"Absolutely not. I insist. Please."

Sarah shrugs and accepts.

Liam bursts out of the bathroom door, full zoom. "Mom! Breakfast!" he shouts as he enters the living room and... "Oh!" He notices Emily. "You're my momma's friend?"

Liam prances up to Emily and holds out his hand for a shake. Emily accepts his hand with a soft touch. Liam uses Superman strength to shake her hand, all while expressing a playful growl.

Emily titters. Her eyes dart over to Sarah. She's unsure of how to proceed—what's the normal response to a child's growl?

Sarah giggles. "Staaaawp! You're freakin' her out."

Liam runs off to the kitchen.

"Sorry... he's... a lot," Sarah says.

From the kitchen, Liam shouts back, "Mom! We have CAKE POPS!"

The women can't help but snicker at the sweetness of a child's excitement.

* * *

Sarah and Emily enter the Breast Health Center together. Sarah walks up to reception while Emily holds back, her attempt to emit the illusion of privacy, but still listens with intent.

"Hi. Sarah Kenneth. I have a 9 am appointment."

"Yes, Mrs. Kenneth. Because you're not using insurance today, we do require full payment upfront. Your total today is four-thousand, three-hundred and seventy-five dollars and thirty-two cents."

"Oh, no Doctor Evan said... wait... WHAT?" Sarah says, putting her hands on the counter.

"Your total?" the receptionist asks. "Is. Four-thousand..."

"No, no, no. That can't be right. That's insane! For medicine?" Sarah scoffs.

"Excuse me..." Emily interrupts and jumps up to the counter. "Hello..." Emily looks at the receptionist, and back to Sarah. "I'd like to help. Please, let me..." Emily reaches for her wallet in the Chanel bag hanging from her shoulder.

"What?" Sarah says, almost offended. "No." she says to Emily and puts her hand on Emily's arm to stop her.

"I just can't believe it really costs that much money. Aren't you guys supposed to be saving lives here?" Sarah asks the receptionist.

The receptionist stays silent.

Emily tries to butt in again. "Really, Sarah. It's no problem."

"NO!" Sarah says and turns back. "Look," she slaps the counter with her hand. "Doctor Evan told me he would hold billing for this cycle as long as I promised to go to the support groups. I went." Sarah stares daggers at the receptionist.

"Oh!" The receptionist smiles wide. "I'm so sorry about that! Yes. I have the group attendance list here. I just hadn't entered it into the system yet. My apologies."

Sarah rolls her eyes and breathes out relief. "Thank you." She says with a thick breath of sarcasm.

Emily smiles and nods. Feeling settled, she lets her bag drape back to its natural position off her arm, no longer needing to pull out her wallet.

"Thanks, but, you shouldn't have done that," Sarah says to Emily with a quiet yet stern voice.

"Sorry, I was just trying to help. I'm happy to help."

"That's an insane amount of money! They should feel ashamed charging patients that much for a single treatment!" Sarah scoffs disgust, still in disbelief at the cost, as she plops into a seat.

Emily sits gracefully next to her and tries to explain. "I'm not sure how much of it is charging exorbitantly and how much of it is cancer being an expensive disease. When you consider all the studies and research dollars and administrative fees that go into it all."

"It doesn't bother you that normal people could never afford this?" Sarah asks, crossing her arms against her body with a scowl on her face.

Emily considers the question before she answers. In being honest with herself, she realized she'd never thought about normal people, and Sarah's questions made her feel callous and cold. "Um… it does seem unfair."

"Yeah! You got that right! There needs to be some kind of fund or… what's the word… scholarship? I dunno. Something for people who need help. How the heck did Ms. Linda do it? Or maybe she didn't, and that's why she…" Sarah goes silent and stares at the white walls across from her.

Emily studies Sarah, intrigued by her reaction to something she'd always assumed to be a common part of how the world worked. "Well, there are lots of ways to donate… there are breast cancer awareness groups and nonprofits."

Sarah breaks free from her blank stare and looks back at Emily. Her eyes are unsettled. "Yeah, but how many people know about those? There should be something out there, reminding people all the time that this is a thing that needs attention, and it needs more money."

"That's an interesting thought," Emily says, not knowing how else to respond.

The conversation ends, unfinished, but stagnant. Sarah opens her phone and scrolls through her social media. Emily lets out a breath and does the same.

twenty-five

A MEDICAL ASSISTANT escorts Sarah and Emily to the infusion room. Sarah stops at the entrance, like her feet are stuck to the floor. Following behind and not expecting the sudden stop, Emily knocks into her.

"Oopph!"

Sarah doesn't respond. She stands still, wide eyed, as she observes the room. A line of leather recliner chairs hooked up to machines and tubes. Side tables with magazines, books, and plastic flowers in decorative vases pretend to offer a home-y aesthetic but are washed out by fluorescent tube lights that keep the room bright, but cold.

The medical assistant leading them looks back at Sarah with curious eyes.

"Can you give us a minute?" Emily says. The assistant nods.

Emily watches Sarah's face and body as she shakes and shivers in the doorway. "You okay?" Emily asks, cautiously putting a hand on her shoulder.

"Uh…" Sarah sucks in a deep breath. "Mm-hmm," she says with a nod and a forced smile.

"It's okay. I'll be right next to you the whole time, okay? We're gonna do this together." She squeezes Sarah's shoulder.

The touch makes Sarah shudder, letting out a sob.

Emily immediately retreats. To comfort another human being with compassion or even sympathy was a skill she'd never learned. In her world, governed by power, to act in such a way was weak. She only knew how to be callous and calculated. Yet, being confronted by a true human need, the ice encircling Emily's heart cracks, and melts.

"Oh no! No, no. no! Don't cry." She pulls Sarah in for a hug. "It's okay. It's okay. I..." But she's at a loss for what to say. No amount of practice in the art of compassion and comfort could prepare a person with the right words, but any would suffice. Yet here, Emily had none.

"This is a good thing! Right? This is how you get better." Emily says as some finally come to her. She fumbles through her statement; each utterance stands out on its own with no connection to the rest. Nothing sounds right. Nothing is good enough.

"I'm so scared!" Sarah says, and sobs into Emily's shoulder.

Emily fights back her own tears, knowing there's nothing she can do to help, but also, that her time isn't far behind. "This is so scary. But I promise I'll be right with you. Okay?"

Nurse Jackie shuffles into the room. "Well, hello, ladies! What in the world are you two doing here together?" Nurse Jackie asks in a gleeful tone until she recognizes the emotional charge of the moment.

Sarah and Emily separate and Nurse Jackie approaches. "Aww, today's a big day, huh?" Nurse Jackie rubs Sarah's back and offers consolation.

"A bit nervous about her first treatment," Emily speaks for Sarah.

"Well, I think I can help with that. Come on, dear. Have a seat over here." Nurse Jackie gestures for Sarah to sit in one of the plush chairs. "How'd you all get together, anyway?" Nurse Jackie asks, using conversation as a distraction.

"We met at group," Sarah says.

"Well, ain't that nice? And you're here together? That's so sweet."

Emily sits in a chair next to Sarah. Nurse Jackie reaches for the apparatus of wires and tubes as she sets up Sarah's infusion like she's done it a million times.

"The first one's always the scariest, but it is so much easier with friends," Nurse Jackie says. "Now, let me just check one little thing and I'll be right with you." Nurse Jackie does a quick search on the computer and says, "Yup! That's what I was hoping for!" She walks back to them. "Ms. Emily, how's about we move up your tomorrow appointment to… right now!"

Sarah and Emily look at each other in shock.

"Uh, what do you think, Sarah? Wanna do this together, together?" Emily studies Sarah's face for any sign of confirmation.

"But… are you ready for that? This is so last minute, I don't wanna force you to…"

Emily's arm goes up to cut her off. "I'm okay. Let's do it."

"But you probably have a plan already set for tomorrow, I can't…"

"Ehhh!" Emily stops her again, with force this time. "Just let me be your friend!" Emily chuckles.

Sarah relents with a smile.

Nurse Jackie smiles, and gestures to the next closest empty infusion chair. "Take a seat."

Nurse Jackie gets to work setting up both infusions. One at a time, she hangs full bags of medicine from their IV stands, pricks their veins to facilitate delivery, runs the tubing from the drip bags into the IV, and makes sure they're comfortable.

"Alrighty, you girls are all set. It'll be a few hours, but holler if you need me. I'll be in and out," Nurse Jackie says before leaving the room.

Emily and Sarah look at each other, smiling warmly. Not that they want to be here, but the trenches feel less cold with one another. Sarah reaches out her arm to Emily. Emily notices, and holds out her own. The two meet in the middle, and grasp each other's hands tight.

* * *

Emily and Sarah squirm in their infusion chairs. The IV drip bags are near empty, hours of a slow drip now ending. They're restless. Emily's cheeks puff out... something's happening.

"Nurse Jackie!" Emily shouts.

Nurse Jackie hustles into the room.

"I'm not feeling so..."

Nurse Jackie grabs a bed pan and slides like a batter into home. She catches Emily's projectile vomit off the side of the chair.

Sarah is horrified! She gasps, gags, then retches.

"Urrrggghhhhh. Oh god!" Emily groans as she dry heaves.

"Oh my god, stop! You're making me barf!" Sarah dry heaves.

Emily can't help but recognize the humor in all this and finds the will to let out a giggle. Sarah recovers and joins her. The women cycle through sweaty heaves and muted chuckles. Nurse Jackie helps them through it, holding back hair and switching out bed pans.

"You girls haven't been drinking alcohol have you?"

Sarah and Emily frown like kids caught disobeying Mom's orders.

"Girls! You know better than that!" Nurse Jackie scolds them. "Drinking alcohol with treatment will worsen your symptoms, cause dizziness, worsening nausea, lightheadedness. We went over all this in the info packets! You better start taking this seriously or next session I'm gonna make you pee in a cup to see if you've been drinking before we start."

The women lean back in their seats, shamed, and ill. Two piles of a pitiful mess.

"You girls got a ride home?" Nurse Jackie asks, hands on her hips.

Sarah looks down and shakes her head.

"I'll call for a car for us," Emily says.

* * *

In the back seat of a black SUV, Emily and Sarah lean on each other, half asleep, fully ill. The girls groan in agony, as the car runs over speed bumps and potholes.

The SUV pulls into the lot at Sarah's apartment complex. The sudden stop tussles the girls awake.

"You sure you're gonna be okay?" Emily asks Sarah.

"I'm okay. Got a couple hours to nap before Liam's off school."

"Call me if you need anything."

Sarah shuffles out of the car and struggles to make it up to her door. Inside, she attempts to navigate through her apartment, but trips through obstacles—shoes, strewn clothing, her own tunnel vision. There's only one thing that'll make her feel better right now. She keeps it moving until she's outside. Her balcony. Her respite.

Sarah walks on the patio and into the sunlight where last night's coffee cups rest in the sun's rays. Cups and plates she allows to dry in the sun, because the thinner the piece is, the less likely it is to crack or warp. Her vases and bowls she dries in shaded spots or indoors, as these pieces take more time and can dry unevenly in the sun.

She crouches down to pick them up and smiles—they've turned out well. As she stands again, her body wobbles, her vision goes black. Beads of sweat roll off her face, her knees almost buckle, but she catches herself and leans against the balcony wall. She should go sit down, but she persists.

Sarah gathers art supplies and turns on the kiln. While it's warming, she sits down at the table and picks through different shades of paint. Red. White. She mixes them together to create a unique hue of pink. Brighter, more… alive than the soft pink of her breast cancer awareness ribbon sticker. Satisfied, she dips her brush into the paint and starts with long strokes on the cup.

With a flash of inspiration, her eyes light up and her mouth lets out a subtle gasp, like a new idea's popped into her mind. She finds a fine tip paint brush and black paint. She dips the brush into the black, and reaches into the coffee mug, painting something on its insides. Covered in sweat and tears, and seething in pain, she persists through the act. One hand holds her paintbrush and the other holds her stomach.

twenty-six

THE BLACK SUV pulls into the driveway at Emily's house. The driver exits the car, walks around to the trunk, and pulls out a wheelchair. He sets the wheelchair up next to the car and climbs in through the back passenger door to help Emily out, and into the chair. Emily's head slumps down as she's wheeled into her home where Helen is waiting for her. Emily's wheelchair crosses the threshold of the front door. The bump makes her groan and Helen harrumphs.

"Anyone?" Helen says to the driver.

"Not that I could see, ma'am. A few press followed us out of the center, but fell off after we dropped off the other." he says as he shuts the front door behind them.

"Ugh, thank god!" Emily says. She pops up from the wheelchair like nothing is wrong. But it's too fast. Her balance wanes and her vision goes black. She falls right back into the chair.

Helen laughs. "Careful, dear. Some of this is for show, yes, but you did just have a drum of toxic chemicals pumped into your body."

Helen sits on the couch. She waves her hand to dismiss the driver. He responds with compliance and exits the home.

"Come!" Helen says to Emily. "Slowly. Come. Sit."

Emily rises again from the wheelchair but takes a beat to be sure of herself. When she finds her confidence, she wobbles to sit next to Helen on the couch.

"Emily, I don't like you spending time with this girl."

Emily whispers under her breath. "Course you don't..."

"She's a low income, single mother. The plan was to show face at a support group and redeem your image, not adopt a special needs pet!"

"Could you not do a background check on every single person I decide to spend time with?"

"It's too much. The support group is the campaign. You need to focus the rest of your energy on getting well and bringing Kyle home..."

"But, Mom, she..."

"I forbid it, Emily! She doesn't..."

"Meet your expectations?" Emily glares at her mother.

"How's your friend... What's her name? Kimberly?" Helen changes the subject.

Emily slumps into the couch. "Tiffany."

"That's it. Tiffany and the Gal Pal group? They're your friends still, right? Stick with them. The tried and true. It's unnecessary seeking outside your established group of friends who we've already determined are of no threat to you."

"Sarah isn't a threat! She's struggling to even feed her kid, and she has cancer!"

"Oh, Emily... You're still so young. Money is power. Surrounding yourself with people who fear that power ensures they won't try to take it from you. Tiffany, your friends, Kyle... They respect power, because they fear it. And their fear will keep you at the top. Talk about expectations. Those who don't rise to meet their own will never fear power. They're content without it and can't be influenced under it. Thus, they don't belong in our world. That's why you married Kyle, and that's why you won't see this woman again. You'll do what you're told, because that's *my expectation*, and you *will* rise to meet it!"

Helen stands up tall, her nose in the air, as she casts her gaze down over Emily. "When's the last time you spoke to Tiffany and the girls? I'm sure they'd love to hear from you now that you've got some time on your hands."

"I don't know. I haven't texted them in a while." Emily's face shows defeat. It's been so long since she's seen the Gal Pals, she didn't even know if they were still friends. She's never had a friendship she could feel certain of.

"Then stop feeling sorry for yourself and call them! My god, I don't know what's wrong with your generation." Helen gathers her purse to leave. "Dana will be by later to prepare your dinner so you can rest. Go to bed."

Emily, almost on instinct, rises from the couch and makes her way into her bedroom.

Helen stands still and watches her daughter hobble off to the bedroom. When the click of the bedroom door closes behind, Helen crumbles. She holds her hand over her mouth, squeezes tight, and tries not to let any sounds escape. Her chest heaves in silence and her eyes fill with tears.

Helen wipes her eyes at the sound of a door opening. A woman almost the same age, but grayer, approaches Helen.

"Hello Ms. Helen," Dana says.

Helen tries to present herself as stoic, but cannot mask her emotions. Not from Dana, a woman who's worked in her personal and intimate spaces for decades. Still, she tries and keeps her mouth closed and tight while she fights to calm herself.

"I'm so sorry for your daughter, Ms. Helen."

Helen sucks in a deep breath, and exhales, "Thank you, Dana. You've always cared..." she pauses as she tries to hide her tears, "so much..."

"Yea, Ms. Helen. I am here." Dana leans in and offers Helen a hug.

Helen surrenders into the warmth but continues to fight against the emotions spilling out of her. "I can't lose her too." Helen fails and sobs.

* * *

Emily lays in bed, restless. She sweats through her sheets, she tosses and turns. No position is comfortable. She can't stop thinking about what her mother said to her, about her friends, about Kyle. *Money is power? Why does that even matter? Did Kyle marry me because he thinks I'm powerful? And my friends, are they even real?*

Unable to relax, she gives up and pulls herself upright in bed. She clutches her stomach, but it's not bad enough to make her vomit, just uncomfortable.

Emily chews on her thoughts. Maybe her mother was right? She leans over her bed toward her nightstand, and grabs her phone. She scrolls through it, just when Dana announces herself.

"Ms. Emily, how are you? Can I get you something?"

"Hi, Dana." Emily smiles at her. "No, thank you."

Dana moves through the room and picks up clothing, picks at bits of dust on the carpet, brushes the comforter with her hands, and approaches the headboard to fluff Emily's pillows.

"Okay, I will prepare your dinner," Dana says as she looks around the room, satisfied with its tidiness.

"Thank you." Emily smiles again and opens up an old group chat to the Gal Pal group. There's been no messages in months. She scrolls up through the chain and finds it's been several more since there was a message from her. She chews her lip, takes a deep breath. Resolved in her thoughts, she opens Tiffany's contact and presses the call button.

* * *

In a tussled bed of luxurious linens and a bedroom of modern decor, Tiffany rests, naked. Her eyes are closed, but a smile on her makeup-caked face shows her wakefulness. She opens her eyes and reaches for the phone.

"Oh, my god! It's… Emily!" Tiffany says out loud. She sits up straight, alert, and fearful. "What do I do?" she says out loud.

Kyle marches out of the ensuite, naked, the toilet flushing in his wake.

"Don't answer it." His collected response calms Tiffany in an instant. She drops her ringing phone back on the nightstand and falls back to the bed. With a seductive pose, she presents her nakedness to Kyle to entice him back to her. Their bodies collide as they twist themselves up in satin sheets.

twenty-seven

LITTLE EMILY IS ten years old. Puberty has hit her sooner than her peers. She is still plump with baby fat, but also finding her shape as a young woman. The school uniform, a thin button-down dress shirt with pleated skirt and stockings sticks to her. She tugs and prods at the fabric, insecure about how tight it fits to her body. The mirrored trophy case hallways of her private school keep her head down toward the ground to avoid her reflection in the glass, unable to stand the sight of her maturing form. None of the other girls show breast buds popping through their shirts, so she slumps her shoulders forward, hoping to make open space beneath the fabric and turn them invisible.

Eleven years old and still shorter than her, Kyle, comes into Emily's sightline. Surrounded by his entourage of even shorter pre-teen boys; the lot of them fall quiet as they notice her, noticing them.

Emily ignores them, and re-averts her gaze down, the buckles on her shoes more interesting to her, until she hears the whispers. She looks up. They're all staring at her. Instinct tells her to smile and wave, to be polite. She does, acknowledging her old friend, Kyle. He ignores her and passes by. Her gaze sinks to the ground again, this time her red face and sorrowed frown shows a deep rejection.

SNAP! Emily jolts surprise! Her back snaps straight. She feels a sting of pain. Someone has snapped her bra strap! She turns back around to find the goggle of boys cackling, pointing, in absolute stitches. One boy turns to high-five Kyle, who reciprocates with a smirk.

"Nice one!" the boy says to Kyle as their hands slap.

"Yeah! Got 'er!" another one says with fist pumps in Kyle's direction.

Emily's cheeks burn red, her vision blurs, too proud to cry, and her fists squish with sweat. Humiliation wells in her throat leaving a bitter taste she's forced to swallow before running away.

* * *

Dejected and broken, Emily enters the mansion where she lives with her mother. Thoughts tumble out of her lips in hushed whispers. "Stupid Kyle," she says to herself. "He's such a jerk… but I probably deserved it." Her shoulders sink deeper as the negative self-talk shrinks her further. "I'm such a fat, stupid fatty! No wonder no one likes me… My stupid fat face…"

Her feet drag behind as she heaves her normal sized but awkward body into the kitchen, weighted down by the invisible chains of her own self-pity. She sets herself up at a barstool on the counter and gets to work pulling out schoolbooks and homework sheets.

A middle-aged Dana enters. "Miss Emily. Welcome home. Can I get you a snack?" she says with a smile.

Emily sniffles back her emotions to respond. "Yes, please. Thank you."

Dana's face shows concern. "Everything okay? How was school?"

Emily breaks down into tears, drops her head on the counter, and lets out the full expression of her feelings. "Kyle snapped my bra strap!" she wails.

Dana's face turns to rage. "He what?" "I'm calling your mother!"

she says with conviction as she marches over to a wall-mounted corded phone. She dials. "Hello, Ms. Helen. Emily's home from school and she's told me she's being bullied by the boy at school... Kyle... Yes, Ma'am... Yes... Okay, would you like to speak to her?"

Emily's head perks up from the counter. She holds her tears and watches with eager eyes as she silently prays for the possibility of her mother's comfort.

"Uh, huh. I understand. Yes, Ma'am, see you this evening." Dana hangs up the phone.

Emily's gaze drops back down to the countertop where it focuses on an old crumb. "Stupid crumb, how long have you been here? Are you from my breakfast?" She says with a quiet voice. The tip of her finger touches it, presses it. She hears a tiny crack as it breaks apart beneath her pressure.

Dana approaches Emily again, softer, with compassion. "Your mother said she's working late tonight. But not to worry. She's going to take care of it. You won't have to worry about Kyle again. He's going to be much nicer to you from now on. Now, how about a nice charcuterie?"

Emily studies the crumbs on the counter. She looks at her fingertip to find a small dent where the crumb buried into her skin. "Okay."

* * *

The next day at school, down that same hallway, Kyle, and his minions saunter into view. Emily holds her breath.

Kyle approaches Emily. Behind him, his boy band snickers and whispers.

"Shut up!" Kyle shouts back at them and the group quiets. Kyle turns his attention back to a frozen Emily.

"Uh... I'm supposed to apologize, about yesterday. That was messed up."

Emily sighs out a smile of relief. "Oh, uh... it's okay."

"Cool…" Kyle offers a lazy smile. "So, my dad said you can come over to play video games, if you want."

"Oh! Uh, okay. Sure!" Emily beams.

"Kay." Kyle lets out a deep breath of hidden disappointment, reigniting his friend's teases and giggles. "Ugh! I said shut up!" he seethes, and sighs. "Whatever." He refocuses his gaze past her, and walks away, followed by the entourage.

Emily continues to smile, but now accompanied by a furrowed brow, not sure what to think, but settled in knowing her mother did, in fact, take care of it, of her.

twenty-eight

LIAM'S elementary school rings its last bell for the day and a rush of school children flood the front lawn, Liam among them. He stands alone and leans against a wall, watching as buses, parents, and older siblings leave with his classmates. His eyes search the streets as far as they can reach for any sign of his mother coming for him.

The late afternoon sun sets lower on the horizon as the sky turns orange. Afterschool programs let out and another round of pickups take away the next crowd of children. Still, no one comes for Liam. Alone again, Liam lets out a sigh, just as a school aid approaches him. Ms. Lucy wears her Tiger Pride school mascot collared Polo shirt and sturdy blue jeans with her silver hair wrapped into a bun. Her walkie talkie beeps and she says, "Alright, I'm bringin' him in." With a click, she releases the talk button.

"Hey buddy," Ms. Lucy says, now addressing a forlorn Liam. "Mom or dad not here to pick you up yet?"

Liam shakes his head.

"Okay. Wanna come into the office with me and we'll give Mom or Dad a call?"

Liam hangs his head low as he follows Ms. Lucy into the administration building.

* * *

It's dark inside Sarah's bedroom, the outline of her body asleep in bed showcased only by a starker darkness. A contrast without light. No moonlight or sunlight seeps in through the bedroom window. It can't, because it's locked out by a full covering of aluminum foil.

On the nightstand, her cell phone buzzes and lights up. She stirs but doesn't wake. The phone continues to buzz, each ring going unanswered.

* * *

Inside the administration office, Ms. Lucy hangs up. Her expression tries hard not to show concern. She shuffles through a manilla file and searches for something to help the situation.

"Hey Liam? It looks like we have someone here named Andrew listed as an emergency contact. Do you know Andrew?"

Liam's face lights up. The first good news he's heard today. "Drew!"

"Phew." Ms. Lucy relaxes, smiling and mock-wiping the sweat off her forehead, before calling Drew.

"Yo!" Drew answers at the fourth ring.

"Hello, is this Mr. Andrew Puente?"

Liam can't contain his excitement. He jumps and shouts, only for Ms. Lucy to shush him. "Drew! Drew! Yay! Yay! Yay!"

"Who is this?" Drew asks. "Little man?"

"Yes, uh, hello. This is Lucy Gibbons from Liam's school. We're calling you today because Liam wasn't picked up after school today and we haven't been able to get hold of his mother. We have you listed as an emergency contact."

Drew sucks his teeth on the other line.

"Are you able to come pick him up?"

"How come? Where's Sarah?"

"Like I said, Mr. Puente, we've been unable to..."

"Yeah, whatever. Keep calling her; she'll pick up," Drew clicks off the phone.

Ms. Lucy looks at a happy Liam as concern floods her face again.

* * *

Back in Sarah's bedroom, still dark, she startles awake to the sound of loud bangs on her apartment door. She takes a moment to collect herself and sits up in bed. More banging makes her jump up to head the call.

"Sar!" Drew's voice permeates the walls as he yells. "Sar! Open up!"

Sarah rushes for the door but trips over as her vision blacks, again. She catches herself and continues.

BANG BANG BANG!

"SAR!"

Sarah makes it to the door and unlocks the deadbolt. Drew sees her, a mess of what she should be—sweating, pale, and slumped over. The sight of her wipes the anger out of his face and replaces it with alarm.

"Oh..."

Sarah tries hard to hold a smile as she greets her son. Liam prances into the apartment and doesn't notice his mother's condition.

"Mom! Did you make my dinner yet?"

"No, baby. Sorry."

"Arrrgghhh! But Mom, I'm starving!" Liam says with a lamented sigh.

"Okay, okay. Geez!" Sarah snaps back.

Sarah plops herself on the couch and sucks in an exhausted breath. Liam cuddles up to her, his body burrows into her space accidentally poking her with an elbow and knee as he tries to get comfortable. Sarah groans and pushes back. Liam looks at her with a furrowed brow and his head cocks to the side like a confused puppy.

"What's wrong, momma?" His voice gets louder with distress.

"Baby, baby, baby. I'm so sorry, but we're not allowed to cuddle for a couple days, okay?"

"Why, momma?"

Drew steps in and tries to play dad. "Listen to your mom, little man."

Sarah waves him off. "Momma took some medicine today, and it's so strong, it seeeeeeepppppps out of my skin!" Sarah says with complementary expressions of silly gestures and movements as she makes it a game. "And we can't let it touch you, because you're not sick, right? And you don't need no medicine, right?"

"Yeah! I don't need no medicine," Liam says puffing his chest and turning up his nose.

"That's right, sweet boy." Sarah smiles at him with all her warmth.

"But, why do you need medicine?" Liam says. His chest collapses back in and his shoulders sink as he questions the uncertainty of his situation.

"Um…" Sarah says as a ball tightens in her throat. She looks at Drew for reassurance, his face gives her nothing but a weeping mess. "Well, I'm glad you asked, because there's something we need to talk about."

"What, Mom?"

Drew covers his eyes with his hands and turns away. Sarah glares at his cowardice. She's on her own.

"Baby. Remember when we got that phone call from the hospital Ms. Linda went to? And you got scared that momma was sick?"

Liam nods, his anxiety growing. "Do you have what Ms. Linda had? Are you gonna die!" Liam says with a shriek as he breaks into tears.

Sarah's heart shatters as she's confronted with not only her reality, but what it would mean for her son. Yes, she has what Ms. Linda had, and she can't guarantee this time will be a different outcome.

Because she loves her son, she does the only thing she knows will bring him a bit of peace. She lies to him.

"No, baby. I'm not gonna die. Momma's got the best doctors and the best medicine. I'm gonna be all better soon, okay?"

"But... can we afford it?" Liam's voice quivers.

Drew turns back around to face them. Tears stain his face and his eyes are red from the pressure of his hands holding them shut. His voice cracks when he speaks. "Yo... little man... Your mom's... gonna be good... You don't need to worry about money. I got it. We got this." Drew grunts like he's trying to pump himself up with a fake-it-till-you-make-it confidence. "Let's go! We got this!" He claps his hands ferociously. "Don't you worry about it, lil man, you hear?"

The show serves as a distraction. Sarah joins in, hoping to get her own version of Drew's fake confidence. "That's right, baby. You don't worry. Momma and Drew will make sure everything is okay. Understand?"

Liam sniffles and nods. "Then, when you're better, we can cuddle?"

"We sure can," Sarah says as a smile breaks through on her face.

Drew's pulls himself into the corner of the room to shadowbox the wall, unable to engage fully in the conversation.

"Okay," Liam says with a sullen agreement. "But I'm still hungry."

"Why don't you go make yourself some chicken nuggets?" Sarah says.

Liam nods and runs off into the kitchen.

Drew rubs his head, an attempt to release his stress the imaginary boxing couldn't achieve either. With Liam out of sight, Drew and Sarah brace for a hard conversation.

"Uh... I didn't know you started treatment today."

"Cause I didn't tell you."

"Why not?"

"Real talk? Because you said you couldn't deal! That's why!"

"Yo, Sar? You can't even text? You left Liam all alone! You can't be doin' that!" Drew says in an aggressive whisper.

"It was an accident, Drew. Obviously, I didn't mean to leave my son stranded at school." Sarah grits her teeth as the conversation excites.

"What if I wasn't there? What if I couldn't get him?" he says, still in a whisper, but with large arm movements to emphasize his point.

Sarah waves the argument off. "I was about to wake up, anyway."

Drew sucks his teeth. "I can't let you do this to my son. He not gonna go through what I went through."

"And what exactly do you plan to do about it, Drew? Huh? What?"

Drew tries to curb his rage with fast breaths. He remains still, except for the heaving in his chest. Sarah waits for him to react. He clasps his fingers together and rests his hands on top of his head. After several deep breaths, his eyes well again. He tries to speak, but stammers, unable to get words out.

"You know... Sarah, I can't..."

Sarah rolls her eyes. "You can't? You literally just told Liam *'I got this, we got this,'* so get it! Help. I am finally asking you for help." Sarah allows her words to sink in, like it might make a difference. "He'll want ketchup with his nuggets. I'm going back to bed."

Sarah peels herself off the couch and drags her feet back to the bedroom. Drew shakes his head, arms, and body, like he's pumping up to enter the playing field of a championship game, and heads into the kitchen after Liam. She pauses at the doorway of her bedroom to watch.

"Okay, little man. Whatchu need, I gotchu... More ketchup?" Drew says as he reaches for the ketchup.

"Yeah, yeah!"

"On it!" Drew squeezes the bottle onto Liam's paper plate of microwaved chicken nuggets.

Sarah lets out a soft sigh with a smile. She knows better than to count on this version of Drew for long, but she allows herself to relish the moment for what it is—fleeting, but at least he's here, for now. Exhaustion overtakes her, and she slinks back into the dark reprieve of her bedroom.

twenty-nine

YOUNG MEN AND WOMEN, dressed in black, fill the pews of a church and weep as a priest gives a solemn address in front of an open casket. Hundreds of candles line the stone walls and shine their light onto stained glass windows. A small bouquet rests on top of the casket. An easel holds an enlarged photo of the young woman who forever sleeps inside. A young Drew, only nine, and the proverbial clone of Liam, sits in the front row in a black tux, holding his gaze on the ground with a still silence, detached from the service and his reality.

Next to young Drew, his grandmother fingers her rosary as she mumbles prayers to herself. Drew alerts at the sound of his name being called from the stage.

"... Andrew."

Drew raises his head and wipes his face.

"Nieto. Nieto," Drew's grandmother says as she nudges him forward.

"Andrew." The priest calls again from the stage. "Would you like to come forward and say a few words for your mother, my son?"

Drew hops off the pew bench. He drags his feet forward and takes the three steps onto the stage. As he passes the open casket, he looks inside. The makeup-painted face of the woman inside is *not* his mother, not the mother he remembers. His face twists into disgust at the sight of her, and anger bubbles up, making it hard to breathe.

"What did you do to her?" Drew says, his eyes piercing, as he directs his aggression toward the priest. "Why is her face like that?"

"My son…"

"No! No! That's not my mom! No!"

Drew rushes for the priest, blind with rage, and not in control of his body. He tackles the priest to the ground and the priest screams. The audience let out a collective gasp, some jumping to their feet, others rushing to the front. Two men in black suits run onto the stage and fight to pull young Drew away from the priest. In the commotion, no one realizes the tussle inching closer to the casket. As more people join in to save the priest, a person knocks into the casket. It teeters on its risers. The flowers slip inside, the lid slams closed, and the whole thing falls to the floor.

Drew's grandmother grips her rosary tight. She wails as the scene unfolds in front of her. The other attendees cross their hearts—the father, son, and Holy Ghost.

"No! No! No!" Drew wails as he's pulled away.

Several church members help the priest back to his feet.

"Father, are you alright?" someone asks. The father nods as he's helped up.

"It's not! My mom!" Drew screams through labored breaths as he continues to fight against his capture.

"Let us pray." The priest says aloud to the congregation as he prays and speaks in tongues. A mumble of prayer becomes a roar as the audience drowns out the sound of Drew's screams as he's dragged out and away.

* * *

Inside a dreary yet fluorescent-lit room, young Drew sits at a circular metal table and chair bolted to the ground. Prison guards stand watch in front of heavy metal doors. Posters on the walls outline Visitation Room Rules. Drew's Youth Detention Center uniform matches that of other young inmates who sit at other tables with visitors. Drew sits with his grandmother, his only visitor.

"When can I come home, grandma?"

"My boy, you assaulted Father Peter! You disturbed your mother! How can you step foot in the church again? Your mother turns in her grave for this! She may never rest!"

Drew turns his look away to guard his shame. "I'm sorry, grandma."

"Three years. You must pay your penance here and pray. Ask God to forgive you."

A tear drops from Drew's eye. He wipes it away fast and darts his gaze around the room to make sure no one saw. Drew clocks a young boy at another table who stares daggers at him, snarls, laughs, and points. *Ugh.*

* * *

In the yard, young Drew walks on the basketball court in his detention center uniform. Maybe he'll try to play with the boys? He approaches, but the boys stare him down, squinting daggers at him and pursing their lips.

"Can I play with you guys?" Drew asks as his voice trembles.

The snickering boy from the visitation room steps up. "Oh? Little cry baby boy wants to play?" The boy laughs, then pushes him hard.

The boys laugh out loud, drawing in a bigger crowd, all taunting and jeering at him.

"I'm not!" Drew says in defense.

"Little Cry Boy! Little Cry Boy!" The bully eggs everyone on. Boys continue to gather as the circle against Drew becomes even larger. Drew's body shakes as rage builds inside him when the boys stop. Drew straightens up, a smirk on his face, believing the boys feared him. A whistle announces a uniformed guard who towers over the adolescent boys, entering the circle.

"Enough," the guard commands. "Alvarez, back to your game. Puente, take a walk."

Drew huffs, but complies. He walks off the court and into the adjacent field. He walks faster, harder, and forces himself into a run. On the open field and away from the rest of them, he screams his frustration.

"Hey!" a soft voice says.

Behind a fence a little further away, a young girl waves to him. His face moves side to side like he's looking around for anyone else she might talk to instead.

The girl giggles and shouts over to him. "Yes, you. Come here!"

Drew takes another survey of his surroundings, this time making sure no guards are watching. Satisfied, he jogs over. Drew makes it to the fence, but stops just short, unsure and out of breath.

"Hi. I'm Sarah. What's your name?" Young Sarah smiles big through the chain link.

Drew pants with his hands on wobbly knees. Spittle flies from his mouth as he huffs, "Drew. I'm Drew."

thirty

YOUNG DREW and Sarah spend time together at every opportunity. After lunch each day, Sarah hurries to clean up and complete her assigned group home chores. She knows the detention center bell lets out for lunch recess at 12:30, and if she hurries through cleanup, she can make it out in time to meet him before it rings.

Sarah rings out the mop, her chores complete. She empties the bucket in the mop closet and rushes outside to the old play yard of the group home where she has a clear view of the detention center and can see Drew coming. None of the other group home kids spend much time in this play yard. The equipment is old, decorated with chipped paint and rusted bolts. All the better for her and her rendezvous with Drew. This space is for them, and she likes it that way.

The 12:30 detention center bell rings. Her heart rate peaks when she spots him. He sees her waiting and jogs to meet her. The two smile at each other and sit on the sandy ground, separated by the diamonds of the chain link fence.

"Oh, no! What happened to your cheek?" Sarah says when she notices a swollen bruise.

"Alvarez. He's always messin' with me."

"Ugh. Again? How come the guards do nothing to help you?"

"No one helps. We have to defend ourselves. No one's coming to save us."

"Aww, Drew. That's not true. We have to believe there are still good people in the world."

Drew scoffs. "You're good. I know that. But everybody else? Naaa. We have each other, and that's all I need."

Sarah blushes. "Pfft! Ewww! You're so dumb." She giggles.

"What?" Drew laughs and makes a face to mimic her words. He pulls the corners of his mouth apart with his index fingers, crosses his eyes, and sticks out his tongue—half adult, but still a child. "Look! I'm a dummy!"

Sarah loses herself in laughter, her hand covers her chest. She laughs so hard she can't catch her breath. Drew releases his face and watches her reaction with a proud beam at making her laugh.

"Oh my god... I can't breathe!" she says through her show.

Drew watches until she calms herself, the glee never leaves his face.

"We should make a pact!" Drew says, his tone grave.

"A pack?"

"A pact! Like a blood pact! We'll slice each other's hands and join the blood. That's the only way to make it real."

"Oh, my god!" Sarah shrieks. "What kind of movies do they let you watch in there?" She laughs. "I'm not doing that. I'll do the spit one, that's it."

"Okay! Spit pact. We promise to always have each other's back, and when we get outta here, it's me and you against the world!" Drew spits in his hand and threads it through the tight openings of the fence. "Deal?"

Sarah hesitates. Her nose scrunches up and she pulls back at the sight of glue-y spit stuck to Drew's begging hand.

"Deal?" He asks again, this time with desperate eyes.

Sarah relents giving him a playful eye roll. She spits on her hand, smiles, and puts her hand in his. "Deal."

Sarah pulls her hand away, their combined spit globs and drips to the ground.

"Ewww!" Sarah screams and laughs. She jumps up and down with excitement and distaste like she's discovered a scurrying kitchen mouse.

"Gross!" Drew shouts with his own laughter. "Hey, at least it's on your side of the fence."

"Drew!" Sarah says with fake outrage and a final stomp of her feet. They laugh together and relax into the moment. An understanding grows and their forever bond forms.

thirty-one

HELEN TAPS HER FOOT, standing at the floor-to-ceiling window of her office, looking out over her reputed queendom—a pleasant view on the upper west side. Her stoic expression hides the intensity of the inner-turmoil that keeps her thoughts focused on Emily, Kyle, the campaign, and how she's going to rescue it all. A smile creeps onto her face, an idea. She grabs her phone and dials.

"Helen..." a voice answers the other end.

"Tom, dear, how are you?"

"Helen, I have nothing else to say about this. Kyle's decided. You can't actually expect him to stay married to a sickly woman. However, because you've been so kind to us, we are happy to keep this private and remain discreet."

Helen lets out a casual chuckle, in control of her emotions and the conversation. "Would you now? Oh yes, I'm sure privacy is of the utmost importance to you, a man who made his fortune selling women a lie of everlasting love and happiness if only they buy your audiobook series and follow the *Ten Steps to Make Him Yours Forever*. Hmmm, seems an infidelity scandal at the crossroads of infertility and breast cancer might disrupt future sales and speaking events, no?"

Tom huffs. "I provide a valuable service to women in need. You keep my name out of this!"

"Now, Tom, you know as well as I do when the investigators discover evidence of an affair, as is required to service the infidelity clause in the prenup, well, there's just no telling what might get leaked to the press."

"Now! You listen here!" Tom says, his voice bubbling in anger as he loses face. "My son is a man of dignity! And... and... my company has nothing to do with this!"

"Please, Tom. You and I both know how this goes. Get him to leave that hussy's house and back home with his sick wife, and quietly, or I... will... ruin you." Confident in her demand, Helen clicks off the line before she receives a response. She revels in her victory with a sneer, only to be interrupted by a knock on the door.

"Come in," Helen shouts.

"The photos you requested from the private investigator," Adrian says and hands over a sealed document envelope.

Helen opens the package and shuffles through the prints. Photos of Kyle's car outside a luxurious beach home, of Kyle exiting the home, of Kyle waving goodbye to the woman in the doorway, Emily's *friend,* Tiffany.

"You were right to be suspicious," Adrian says.

"Of course I was..." Helen scoffs. "He's just a man. Can't expect anything of you creatures."

Adrian chuckles.

Helen stares at Adrian with a look that scares him back to silence. "Fly too close to the sun..." she says as she glares.

Adrian straightens up and clears his throat. "Excuse me," he says and makes a quick exit.

* * *

Emily rests uncomfortably in her bed. Her stomach turns, cramps, and her cheeks puff. Without time to make it to the bathroom, she leans over her bed's side and vomits into a bedpan. Her body shakes as she heaves.

She leans back on her pillows. Her breath is heavy as she tries to catch up to her exhaustion. Sweat beads on her brow and shallow sobs release from her chest.

With a shaky hand, she grabs her phone. She scrolls through text messages. Still no response from Tiffany, or anyone. She opens Sarah's contact, but remembers her mother's warning, and scrolls away. Instead, she types a new message to Mom.

"Mom, please. I don't want to be alone right now."

The text ellipsis appears. Emily waits for the response.

"Kyle will be ready to talk as soon as you're feeling better. I'll have Dana come by again to sit with you."

Emily drops the phone, covers her face with her hands, and breaks down into a sob. The contraction of her belly triggers an urge for another release; again, she falls over the side and heaves into her bedpan.

thirty-two

LIAM ENTERS his mother's room, feeling his way through the dark room with his feet and elbows as he carries a paper plate of toast slathered in peanut butter for Sarah. The only light in the room bleeds in from the open door and hallway. It's morning everywhere, except in here.

"Momma?" Liam's sweet voice calls to a sleeping Sarah.

Sarah lets out a soft moan, a recognition without movement.

"I made you breakfast, momma."

Sarah rolls over with pained groans. She reaches for the bedside lamp and flicks it on. Tired circles engulf her eyes. Her skin is pale and glistens with sweat. The smell of the peanut butter makes her nose twitch. She retches again. Liam panics.

"It's okay..." she tries to reassure Liam but retches again. "Just take it out, baby." She vomits on to a bathroom towel waiting on the floor by her bed.

Liam runs out of the bedroom with the plate. He shakes and cries at the sound of his mother getting sick in bed. He waits for a minute before walking back into the room, a little apprehensive. "I'm sorry, momma, I'm sorry," he cries, going closer to Sarah.

Sarah wipes her mouth and sits up in bed. "No, baby, don't cry."

She opens her arms and beckons Liam to come. "It's okay. Momma's okay."

Liam cries harder as he crawls into bed with her. He tries to hug her, but she stops him.

"Hold on baby…" She reaches to the foot of the bed for a clean blanket, and drapes herself with it to cover her skin. Protected, she pulls her son into a tight embrace. Liam sinks into her.

"I'm sorry. I didn't mean to make you throw up!"

She grasps him tight, and can't help but chuckle at his innocence. "Baby, no. This isn't your fault. Momma just doesn't feel good because the medicine."

"Promise?" Liam blubbers.

"Promise. It's just the medicine, baby. I'll be feeling better soon and *then* you can make me your famous peanut butter toast. Okay?"

"Okay." Liam sniffles and nods.

"Alright, now you go get ready for school!" Sarah says as she tussles Liam's hair, still wrapped in her covered arms.

Liam giggles, all smiles again. The moment is short-lived. As he walks away and finds himself out of her eyeline, his shoulders tighten and his smile fades.

* * *

Liam, now ready for school with socks, shoes, and backpack, re-enters the dark bedroom.

"Momma? I'm ready for school."

The sound of Sarah's snores is the only response.

Liam whispers, "Feel better, momma." On tiptoes, Liam closes the door and slinks away. He opens the front door of the apartment, and clicks it closed behind him.

Liam walks alone down a busy street through an unsavory urban neighborhood as cars whiz past him. At the street corner, he reaches up to push the crosswalk button of the busy intersection with more cars, pedestrians, homeless people, and litter. The light turns red and the walk sign lights up. Drivers stare at Liam as he makes his way across. A gas station employee, sweeping outside, stops to notice him.

Beads of sweat fall down Liam's forehead, but he keeps walking past suburban neighborhood homes. At the end of the street, he sees his elementary school. His pace quickens as he realizes he's made it. He can hear the bell ring, but he's still far away. Afraid of being late, he runs, arriving at the gate, out of breath. The front yard is empty, the students already inside. The school aide, Ms. Lucy, greets him.

"Morning Liam! No Mom or Drew today?"

"Na..." Liam pants. "Mom's sick. I'm taking care of her now. I'm big enough."

Ms. Lucy acts impressed for his sake. "Oh? Okay, well, get in there, big guy."

Liam grins with pride as his shoulders lift, and he struts into the school.

* * *

Liam jogs to his classroom, passing empty play yards and lunch benches. The hallways are wide open and classrooms are full. He finds his door, the wired glass front stuck with rainbow-colored construction paper cutout letters that read, "Mrs. Davis' 3rd Grade Class," and pushes it open.

Liam pants as he enters, bringing the whole class's attention to him.

"Liam, it's after bell," Mrs. Davis says.

"Sorry, Mrs—"

"What's the matter, Liam, can't get to school on time cause your lazy mom?" a back-row bully shouts. "Haha! Loser!" he laughs.

The rest of the children follow like sheep.

"Marcus! Detention at lunch!" Mrs. Davis does her best to nip it, but it's too late. Liam's face contorts to confusion. He doesn't understand what's so funny. His mom's not lazy, she's...

"What? My mom says his mom must be lazy cause she forgot about him at pickup. Loser kid, loser mom. Haha!" Marcus continues. More sniggers erupt from the class.

"Enough!" Mrs. Davis shouts, and the class quiets. "Please, have a seat, Liam."

Shamed, Liam steps to his seat and tries his best to steady his quivering chin.

Mrs. Davis approaches Liam. She puts her hand on his shoulder. "Kids, our friend Liam is going through a difficult time. His mother is not lazy, she's sick. She has a disease known as breast cancer."

"She's got boob cancer!" Marcus shouts.

The classroom loses composure in total guffaw. Liam hides his face under the collar of his shirt.

Mrs. Davis stomps back to her desk and takes out a pink paper pad. She holds it up above her head like a warning. The children gasp. The air in the room changes from silly to a quiet alarm—someone's in trouble.

"Wait… Mrs. Davis, no. I…" Marcus pleads.

Mrs. David scratches her pen against the pink pad and rips off the completed form. She marches toward the back of the room and presents the pink paper to the class' disruptor.

"No! I'm sorry…" Marcus says.

"To the principal's office!" Mrs. Davis holds firm.

Marcus snatches the paper from Mrs. Davis. He collects his books and backpack and makes his way to the front of the classroom. He approaches Liam with an angered glare. The kids whisper as they watch.

"BAAA!!!!" Marcus yelps and fakes a lunge at Liam! Checking him, testing him.

"Ahhh!" Liam screams, jumps backward, and falls out of his chair.

The classroom is a ball of uproar once again as Marcus points and laughs while Liam cries.

"Out!" Mrs. Davis demands.

Marcus makes his way out the door with his nose turned up to the sky.

"Quiet. Quiet down," Mrs. Davis says to regain control of her class. She goes to help Liam off the ground and back into his seat. "Are you alright, Liam?"

Liam nods, not meeting her eye.

"I apologize. I wouldn't have said anything if…" Mrs. Davis shakes her head.

Liam nods again—it's okay.

Mrs. Davis addresses the class. "Please, children! We're moving on."

thirty-three

SARAH WAKES UP IN A FRIGHT! The perfect blackness of her bedroom engulfs her as she holds out her stiff arms toward the nightstand lamp. She finds it and clicks it on.

"We're late." She grabs her phone and clocks the time. "No! Liam! Come on, baby, we gotta go!" Sarah shouts, attempting to get out of bed.

"Liam!"

Silence.

"Baby?"

Sarah peels herself up from the bed. On her feet, she hunches over and clutches her stomach in pain. She looks through the usual hiding spots in her apartment—towel cabinet, behind the shower curtain, behind the couch. She calls out his name, more frantic with every moment she can't find him.

"Liam. Liam! LIAM!"

Sarah shakes her hands, grabs her forehead, panicking. Not knowing what else to do, she picks up her phone and calls Drew. The line trills.

"Yo, message!" Drew's voicemail.

Frustrated, she tries another number.

"Adam's elementary school, go Tigers." A voice answers.

"Hi, this is Sarah Kenneth. Liam Kenneth's mom. Can you tell me if Liam was checked in this morning?"

"One moment."

Sarah bites on her fingernails.

"Yes, ma'am. He's checked in."

"He was?" Sarah sighs relief. "Who dropped him off?"

"Uh.... One moment, please." The line clicks over to an elevator tune as Sarah waits on hold.

The line clicks back over. "Ma'am?"

"Yes, hello."

"Hi, Ms. Kenneth, Liam arrived at school this morning alone. It appears he had walked. Based on your address records, we can see this means he must have walked quite a long way."

"Walked? What?" Sarah says as her eyebrows shoot up to her hair line and her mouth falls agape. She didn't know Liam knew how to walk to school, much less why he would fathom to do such a thing.

"We'll have a child welfare officer call you sometime this afternoon to discuss the details."

"Child welfare?" Sarah shouts. "Please. No. It was one time. It was a mistake. I'm sorry!"

"The officer will have more information for you this afternoon. Have a good day."

"Wait... please. I'm sick. I just..."

The line disconnects and Sarah vomits onto the floor.

* * *

Sarah soaks in the sun's rays on her balcony. Her brow sweats as she sits on her turn stool, behind her turntable. She takes a heavy inhale in and a long exhale out. The weight of her body feels heavy. She sways on the stool, breathing in a rhythm to help her keep balance, and sits in silence, reveling in her favorite escape. But today feels different. Anxiety about Liam, the impending social worker, and treatment, keeps her mind awake, yet her body coursing with poison begs her to sleep. A session behind the clay table is her only remedy against the pulsing angst that travels through her veins.

Uneasy in her thoughts and desperate for someone to share this weight with her, she looks at her phone. She stares at the screen like she knows she has to, but doesn't want to. She presses the call button, and with a troubled brow, brings the phone to her ear.

"Yo, message." Drew's voicemail. BEEEEEEP.

Sarah lets out a long sigh. Not twenty-four hours ago, she had begged him for help, and already he was ignoring her and his responsibilities again. If the birth of his son couldn't change him, her cancer certainly wouldn't. Still lacking other options, she reaches out again.

"Drew..." she speaks into the phone. "I asked you for help." Sarah sobs. "Something happened today... I, uh... I missed morning drop off and..." she sniffles "... the school filed a report." Her sobs intensify. She takes a beat to choke back her tears. "Call me back, Drew. Please."

On the balcony ledge, she glimpses the pink coffee cups she made with Emily. They, too, soak up sunlight in their resting spot. She reaches over, picks one up, and studies it—looks at all its sides and inside. "Arrrggghhhhhh!" she lets out a frustrated groan. Holding the cup tight, she folds over her knees and wails.

thirty-four

SARAH WAITS in the car pickup line outside Liam's school. Her skin is pale, and sweat drips down her face as she fights against the heaviness in her eyes. She's made it, albeit only by the sheer strength and will of her instincts.

The bell rings and children pour out into the yard through the heavy entry doors. She alerts to the sound and looks out for Liam. Spotting him in the crowd made more difficult by a group of children gathering as a commotion breaks out, disrupting the usual routine of school pickup. Children run toward a tussle, shouting, "Fight! Fight! Fight!"

Sarah's lost her sight of Liam in the excitement. She finds Liam's backpack in a whir of motion as it thrashes around with his body and... LIAM'S IN A FIGHT!

Sarah jumps out of the car and her vision goes black as she rushes out to the schoolyard. She stumbles and falls to her knees, blinded and ill.

"LIAM!" she shouts.

Liam and Marcus thrash around in a flurry of arms, legs, and angry shouts inside a ring of children chanting "Fight! Fight! Fight!"

Ms. Lucy arrives, pulling on backpacks and moving children out of the way. Another aid makes their way in, doing the same.

Sarah's vision comes back, and using all her strength, she pulls herself off the ground. "Liam!" she pants as she limps toward him.

The aides pull the boys apart and contain them on separate sides of the ring. They do their best to disperse the crowd, just as parents, too, enter the ring looking for their children, and pull them away.

Sarah hobbles up to Liam, who's held at the collar by Ms. Lucy. "Liam! What are you doing?" she screams.

Liam's rage dissipates into shame. "Momma, he was..."

"I don't care WHAT he did, you NEVER, EVER, fight someone!" Sarah says with a finger pointed in Liam's face.

"But he..."

"Violence is never the answer! Do you hear me?" Sarah shouts, but more controlled. Her breaths become heavy with an ache as a wave of nausea passes through her.

"I'm so sorry we didn't get a hold of them sooner," Ms. Lucy says to Sarah.

Sarah stands up tall, her eyes watering. "No, no. I'm sorry. I had no idea he was having problems at school... I've been..." Sarah stops herself to hold back tears.

"He'll have to deal with this in the principal's office, but why don't we figure that out later? You've got a lot going on." Ms. Lucy holds out a kind hand to Sarah.

"Thank you," Sarah says. She clears her throat. "Let's go, Liam."

Sarah leads Liam back to the car. Her limp is obvious, and she's filled with pain and anger. She holds her stomach. It's all hard.

"Get in this car, right now!" Sarah growls at Liam, who complies without resistance.

* * *

The front door of Sarah's apartment slams open. Sarah and Liam enter with heat, engulfed in an argument.

"But Mom, you were asleep!" Liam pleads.

"I don't care what I was! You never leave this house alone! And you don't start fights!" Sarah takes short and quick breaths to curb the churning in her stomach and the dizziness that threatens her consciousness.

"But he started it!"

"I don't wanna hear it! You never do that to me again, okay? None of it!"

Liam mumbles under his breath, "Maybe if I had a dad, he could teach me…"

Sarah double-takes. Grief overtakes her initial anger for her life's choices that have culminated in this moment, the moment her son blames her for not having a father. It was a conversation she'd dreaded since the day Liam was born. Her words mangle in the tightness of her throat as she speaks.

"What did you say?"

Liam confronts her, head on, "Why don't I have a dad to teach me? I was so angry today but I couldn't do anything, and everyone was laughing at me. Do you even care about me? A dad could help me be stronger and fight!"

Out in the open now, the elephant can't hide any longer. Liam breathes hard through the confrontation as Sarah's mouth drops open in shock.

She takes a deep breath as she prepares for the conversation she hoped she would never have to have. She kneels down and wipes tears from her face.

"You wanna know about your dad?"

Liam nods. Sarah nods along and puts her hands on his shoulders.

"Okay. Okay, you're right. You're old enough to know." Sarah takes another breath, "Your dad…"

A knock at the door interrupts them. Relief washes over Sarah's face. Sarah answers the door to a middle-aged woman in business casual with a clipboard and a badge on a lanyard.

"Go do your homework..." she says to Liam, shooing him away.

"Hello, Ms. Kenneth? I'm Donna Alderman, I'm with the County, Child Protective Services. May I come in?"

* * *

Sarah and Donna sit at the kitchenette while Liam works on a math worksheet on the living room couch.

"Are you able to provide medical documents to support your diagnosis?" Donna asks.

Sarah nods as she holds back tears.

"And you don't have any family or friends who can support you while you battle this?"

Sarah shrugs. "His dad is... He comes around when he can."

"What's the father's name?"

Sarah turns her gaze back at the couch to find Liam focused hard on his homework. She whispers, "Andrew Puente, but we call him Drew."

Over on the couch, Liam perks up.

"Can Mr. Puente make sure he gets to and from school, at least while you're in treatment?" Donna asks.

Sarah wants to say yes, and make this all go away, but she knows she can't make promises for Drew. "I'm trying my best."

Donna subtly shakes her head back and forth as her mouth tightens into an empathetic smile. "Listen. We're not the bad guys. We just want to make sure your child is being cared for. It's obvious you love your son and are providing for him. We all make mistakes, huh?"

Sarah musters a polite grin.

"Okay. Liam is a bit too young to make it to and from school on his own. He's eight, right?"

"Yes."

"Okay, so about this age we recommend children be home alone without adult supervision no longer than a few hours at a time, as long as they have some basic kitchen-safety training, have access to a cell phone, and know how to dial 9-1-1. If you're home and asleep, that doesn't count as him being alone. That's okay. Still counts as you being available as long as he has access to you. Does that sound okay?"

"Yes."

"Okay, so, I'm going to recommend that Liam register to take the school bus. That will get him to and from on the days you can't."

"Oh, no. We can't do that. We're out of district. The buses here don't go to his school."

Donna nods like she understands, but also has a solution. "That's okay. That's okay. Have you heard about the School and Health First program?"

"No. What's that?"

"Okay. That's a program that uses public transportation to get Liam to his school, no matter where it is. So, what he'll do is get on the bus every morning that stops right out here..." Donna points at the window, toward the street. "Doesn't matter what bus route or what time. Then that bus driver will let Liam ride along until she can call a public transport vehicle. It's like a minivan, to meet at the next stop and take Liam the rest of the way to his school."

"Oh? They have that?"

"Yes ma'am, it's for school children and elderly transport to the hospital, things like that. You'll have to apply for the program, and I can send you all that information."

Sarah nods, pleased, and a little relieved.

"Okay, good. Now that we got transportation out of the way. Can you schedule your treatments around Liam's school schedule?"

"Yes, I think so."

"Great. I'll write up my report, and as long as Liam isn't left alone at school, and doesn't walk by himself again, you shouldn't hear from us. How does that sound?"

Sarah smiles and nods.

"Alright, I do have to warn you though, that a second call for the same offense will cause to have to," Donna moves into a whisper, "remove the child from the home."

Sarah's mouth tightens, and her eyes fill with water.

"I *really* don't want to do that, though, and I think, if you follow our recommendation, we won't have to. I'll leave the rest to you then. Good luck to you both," Donna says, standing up and excusing herself. Sarah stands to walk her out and startles when she finds Liam standing right behind her.

"Momma?"

"Baby, go sit down. I'm gonna walk Ms. Donna out."

"Momma?" Liam says again.

Sarah's maternal antenna rises. She knows he's serious, but more important is getting the social worker out of their home. "One minute baby. Please."

Sarah follows Donna to the door, giving herself a moment to collect her thoughts and decide how she wants this conversation to go—it's happening whether she wants it to, or not. Sarah lets Donna out and shuts and bolts the door behind.

"Is Drew my… dad?" Liam says, his jaw clenching and his face twitching.

Sarah turns around to face her son. She grabs a throw blanket from the couch and drapes it around herself to cover her clammy, chemo skin.

"Baby, let's talk about this."

Liam's anxiety takes over as he shivers. "Drew's my dad!" He screams and cries. His fists tighten, and his teeth grind down on top of themselves. "You never… told me!"

Sarah collapses to her knees and pulls her son into her, keeping the throw as a barrier between their skin, and hugs him tight. "Baby, baby, baby. Calm down. Okay. It's okay. We're gonna talk about this."

Liam thrashes against his mother's embrace, ripping the throw blanket from Sarah's body.

"No! No! NO!" Liam screams.

Sarah reaches back with one arm—the blanket just out of reach. She cries, she begs. "It's okay, baby. It's okay. I got you. It's okay..." She finds the blanket, wraps it around Liam and fastens her arms around him.

Liam hits himself with his fists as Sarah pours all her strength into stopping him. He screams until all his aggression runs out and forces his release. He sobs with exhaustion. Sarah rocks him in her arms.

thirty-five

SARAH TUCKS LIAM INTO BED. He's calm, but sullen.

"Can I just sleep in your bed tonight, Mom?"

Sarah's pale face tries to hide her pain as she responds, "I'm sorry, baby, but the medicine is still in my body. It's gonna be a little bit before we can do that, okay?"

Liam nods, frowns, and looks away.

A ball tightens in Sarah's throat. She takes a deep breath. "What do you want to know about Drew? I'll answer any questions, but you have to promise me you won't get angry, okay?"

Liam turns back and nods agreement. "Why didn't Drew want to be my dad?"

Sarah fidgets with her fingernails as she searches for the right words. This is harder than she'd expected. "It's not that he didn't want to. Drew loves you very much. It's that Drew has some anger inside of him. When he was young, he got hurt, and he didn't have anyone to help him recover in the right way. That makes it hard for him to be his normal happy self sometimes. When he is not happy and is angry, he can't be around us because he doesn't want to hurt us. He goes away when he feels he is not safe and comes back when he feels better."

Liam's face contemplates. "Is that why I have anger inside me, too?"

Sarah rubs out her chest, the tightness becoming unbearable. "No, baby. The anger you have is normal. We all get angry sometimes. What's important is how you work with your anger. Like today, you got angry, and you tried to hurt someone, yes?"

Liam nods, but his shame pulls his face away.

"It's okay, baby. That was a mistake. Tomorrow you're going to apologize and we're gonna learn to be better. It's okay to feel angry, but it's never okay to hurt people. That's what makes you different from Drew."

"What happened when Drew was young? How did he get hurt?"

Sarah takes a pause and internally assures herself she'll choose the right way to answer the question she never thought she'd be the one responsible for. "Remember, I told you when momma was young, Grandma and Grandpa died in an accident?"

Liam nods.

"And remember I told you I was really, really sad?"

Liam nods.

"Well, when Drew was little, he never had a dad, and his mom got sick and passed away, just like Ms. Linda."

"Oh, no!" Liam gasps.

"Drew got so, so sad, and because he didn't have anyone to help him deal with his feelings, it turned into anger. His sadness and anger just didn't leave him. He became sad and angry with everything in the world. And he never learned to let it go."

Sarah sees the myriad of emotions clear on Liam's face. Sorrow, panic, and an eventual breakdown as he cries. "But... you're sick. Will that make him sad and angry again? Will it make me?"

"No! No, no, no. Baby, no." Sarah rubs Liam's head and wipes the tears off his face. "You and Drew are not the same, baby. I promise. You are a sweet, loving, innocent little boy and nothing bad is gonna happen to you or to me, okay?"

Liam sniffles his tears and wipes his eyes.

"Okay, baby." Sarah leans in to kiss Liam's forehead. She stays there and lets the kiss linger. "Good night, baby."

"Night," Liam says back as he rolls over.

Sarah tiptoes out of Liam's makeshift bedroom. She turns off the living room lamp. Her eyes pour tears as she walks into her bedroom.

Sarah collapses onto her bed, exhausted, both in her body and deep in her soul. But there's something else left to do before she can end her day. She pulls out her phone and scrolls through her messages. She types a message to Drew.

"CPS came by today. I don't know how I'm gonna do this alone, Drew. I need you."

* * *

Sarah is sound asleep in bed when an incessant and loud banging on the front door jolts her awake! The walls of Sarah's apartment rattle with an angry vibration. Sarah jumps, and rushes into the living room.

She clicks on the lamp and finds Liam standing, shivering, and focused on the door, shuddering BANG, BANG, BANG!

"It's okay, baby. It's probably just the police with the wrong apartment again." Sarah pulls on Liam's arm, distracting him from his frozen state of fear.

Liam sucks in quick breaths, and grabs onto his mother's waist.

"Go to my room. Go." Sarah pushes him away. Liam runs into the dark refuge of his mother's bedroom. He hides behind the door frame, and peaks back out.

BANG, BANG. BANG!

"Open the door, Sar!" Drew's voice shouts.

Sarah sighs in relief. An angry Drew she can handle. Liam's watchful eye relaxes too—it's just Drew, even in this state, is more welcome than any alternative could have been.

Sarah opens the door. Drew bursts into the apartment and swallows the space with his rage.

"CPS, Sar! CPS! You let CPS up in here?"

Sarah struggles to match his energy. "What is wrong with you, Drew? It's the middle of the night!"

"Wrong with me? With me! You gonna let CPS take my kid away? Huh? Whatchu think this is a game?"

Drew approaches Sarah, aggressive and intimidating, getting up into her personal space. Sarah steps back and trips on Liam's shoes in the middle of the floor. She stumbles, and falls back, looking up at Drew, who towers over her. Her eyes widen, and her face contorts into pure terror—he's never done this before, she's never felt afraid of him before, and she doesn't know what to do.

"Momma!" Liam screams, still hiding behind the doorframe. Fear keeps his feet glued to where he stands.

Nothing can stop Drew, not even the sight of his cowering son or bedridden lover gives him pause. He screams at her, unaware of his effect on the two terrified people shrinking beneath him. "You know what they did to us, Sar! You know! That's not gonna happen to my son!" He advances again, but this time, Liam finds the strength to un-stick his feet. He runs out of hiding and steps in front of his mother, acting as a shield from a father he's only just discovered. He squeezes his eyes shut, bracing himself with all his might and ready for anything, despite shaking with fear.

The spell breaks and Drew finally soaks in the sight of his child's will to protect his mother against the monster. His rage melts into fear, regret, and sadness.

"Oh god. Oh god, I'm so sorry. I'm sorry." He takes several small steps back, shakes his head, berating himself. "What are you doing? What are you doing!" Drew yells at himself and slaps his hands against his head, over and over. "Idiot, idiot! What are you doing?" The self-infliction progressively gets louder and more aggressive as Drew continues to abuse himself—hitting, pulling his hair, and banging his knuckles against the wall.

Liam opens his eyes and watches as Drew continues. He remains weary, still standing in a defensive stance over his mother, but allows his muscles to relax.

"I'm sorry, little man. I'm sorry, Sar." Drew blubbers. "I'm sorry, but I can't... I can't do this..." Drew turns away, too shamed to face them, and runs back out of the apartment.

Liam runs after and slams the door closed. He bolts it, and chain locks it. He takes a deep breath in. The sound of his mother crying on the floor brings him back to her.

"It's okay, momma. He's gone now. It's okay. I will not be angry like that, ever."

Sarah cries harder. "I know, baby. You're so good. I know."

"Why are you crying, momma? You don't have to cry."

"I'm sorry, baby. I just... He's gone now, and I don't know how I'm gonna do this without him." Sarah vents to her son, who's too young to understand. She realizes her misstep when she sees Liam's face fill with confusion.

"We don't need him. I'm gonna take care of you," Liam says.

Sarah nods, wipes away her tears, and forces a smile onto her face. "Thank you, baby. Thank you."

Sarah bootstraps herself up with a deep inhale and shakes it out of her muscles. It's time to mother up. She can sulk later when Liam's taken care of. She scoots Liam back off to bed and tucks him back in.

thirty-six

EMILY HOLDS her shoulders high and smiles brightly as she strides into The Daily Grind corporate headquarters, ready for the day with her lavender rice milk latte she picked up at the company-owned coffee house downstairs. The space is warm and inviting by design. An office block that's spared no expense in the color-matched decor and furniture on the top floor of a Westside skyscraper. The floor to ceiling windows on the back end boast a scenic view of the hills, where rich people frolic while shopping at expensive stores and dining with their equally wealthy friends. The receptionist greets her with enthusiasm.

"Emily! Welcome back. We missed you."

Emily wears her smile like she's performing in a play where the overemphasis of a character's actions become paramount to the plot and the audience's engagement. "Thanks, Carol. Happy to be back," she says as she continues her choreographed walk into her private office.

Inside, Emily slams the door closed. Alone where no one can see her, except the birds outside the floor-to-ceiling windows, she drops the fake smile and slumps into her chair. Sweat soaks through her caked-on foundation. Her heavy breaths turn into heaves. She puts a hand over her mouth, trying to hold the vomit that burns her throat at bay as it creeps up from her stomach. She searches the room for a trashcan, finds it under the desk, and collapses to her knees where she hurls her morning latte into the can.

A soft knock sounds on the door. Emily picks herself up, dusts herself off, and sits in the desk chair. She's dizzy, and her face is red, but she's got a job to do.

"Come in!" Emily says with a smile. She pats her face with the back of her hand and remembers to wipe away any evidence of what she's been through as Adrian walks in.

"Emily, oh my god, so happy to see you! You look fabulous," Adrian says, his own fake smile stretched across his face.

"Thank you, Adrian," she says, not looking at him, self-conscious of some kind of secret superpower that might allow him to know what she did in the trashcan, or smell what she left behind.

"So..." his voice is chipper and unassuming, with no sign of knowing. "Your mom wanted me to drop in and say hello, and make sure you got the materials on the new campaign. We're so happy to have you back and ready to work." Adrian directs his eyes down at his tablet, poking the screen with his stylus.

Emily doesn't respond. She knows she doesn't have to—he's running a script through his head. His comments are professional, not authentic.

"Okay!" Adrian says. With one last click on his screen, he looks up from his tablet. "All sent." His attention now on her, he notices the state of the room and finds her latte spilled on the floor. "Oh, can I get you another one of these?" He points to the purple mess soaking into the carpet.

Emily follows his gaze to where he points. "Oh!" She's mortified —hadn't even realized she'd made another mess. "Uh, no, thank you... I uh, sorry. How clumsy of me." Emily bends down to clean the mess, but as she does, another wave of nausea comes over her. She groans.

Adrian smiles a pitiful smile that reeks of the disgust he barely hides under his curated professionalism. "Oh, honey, don't. You're way too pretty for that. I'll have maintenance in here to clean this up." Adrian continues to smile derisively, but also brings a hand up to cover his nose as he rushes out of the room. Emily leans back in her chair, sinking into her embarrassment.

* * *

Emily forces herself through the day and busies herself with emails, phone calls, and meetings. Each pained smile earns her praise for "being so strong." She scoffs internally and imagines rolling her eyes at every mention of the words "strong", "brave", and "fighter." None of these things applies to her. She isn't strong; she's bending to her mother's will. Nor is she brave, allowing her cancer story to be exploited for the company's public favorability. A fighter she certainly is not, as cancer isn't a fight. It's her reality, and all she can do is cope.

By the end of the workday, Emily is beat. The energy it takes to finish the day is more than she had banked. The office quiets and darkens with the last of the workers leaving home to their families and separate lives. Helen's office, however, at the opposite end of the hall, remains lit.

Emily sits at her desk and stares at her computer screen. She exits out of emails and documents, clearing out her day. A quiet evening awaits her. Just before she's ready to pack up, she receives a notification on her computer screen. An email from Helen asks her to stop by on her way out.

"Ugh..." Emily huffs. She grabs her coat and bag, flicks off her office light, and heads out the door.

Emily approaches her mother's office, takes a deep breath in, and knocks.

"Come in." Helen's words welcome her, yet the tone of apathy has an opposite effect.

Emily enters the office, and to be sure no one else is listening, closes the door behind her. She sits in an adorned guest chair across from her mother, who works at an elaborate and oversized desk. Helen's eyes don't leave her computer screen as she continues to work, despite Emily's presence.

"How was your first day back?" Helen says, still looking into her computer screen.

"Just tired, I guess."

"Oh, come now. It's been a week! The treatment is only supposed to have you down for two, three days at most."

"Right, just a long day, then."

"It's not over yet. Don't you have the support group today?"

"I thought you didn't want me to see that woman anymore?"

"Well, don't bring home any strays, yes, but you're in a three-month treatment plan. We'll need photos and updates throughout. The marketing team designed the entire campaign around your protocol, Emily," Helen says, peering over the screen for only a second.

"Oh, yes. Of course... Have you talked to Kyle?"

"I'm handling it."

Emily nods. An inquisitive look crosses her face like she's got something else to say. "Um... You know, my doctor would prefer I work from home, considering I'm immunocompromised because of treatment. I was thinking I might take this time to work from home? Just as long as I'm in treatment, of course. It would be more restful, I think?"

"Work is not supposed to be restful, Emily. You're seated to become the CEO of this company. What would it do to moral if they all saw you kicking your Louboutins off to work from home? Absolutely not. We pay too much for this building to let it rot without any employees in it."

Emily half knew this would be the answer she'd get, and she's not surprised. Another fake smile masks her turmoil as she pretends all is well.

"Have a good evening, mother."

"See you tomorrow."

Emily rises from the guest chair, wobbles from a sudden light-headedness, and walks out.

thirty-seven

THE BREAST CANCER support group meeting hosts a large group. Emily watches newcomers, a mix of new patients and Emily's personal brand of Insta-girlies who must be following The Daily Grind's coffee for cancer campaign on their Instagram feeds. Even though Emily hasn't attended the group for long, she recognizes the difference between the two sets of women. The ones meant to be there come in with arms crossed, a subconscious comfort to their discomfort. The others, here for the spectacle, stick out with faces of health, wellness, and arrogance, and they congregate around the branded buffet service rather than mingle with the true patients and survivors.

Emily watches the Insta-girlies with a forlorn look. She doesn't want them to be here, but knows why they are. Their presence is a symptom of turning the intimate and private experience of breast cancer into a public campaign for her own personal fulfillment. Watching them drink free coffee and eat treats meant for anyone but them, she feels a sense of shame, like she's let the group down. Something that was meant for them only, she's taken away.

The meeting coordinator, Cheryl, hurries to add more chairs to the circle and welcomes in the newcomers. Emily sits in the same chair she always does, and her camera person tags close behind. Someone sits in the chair next to her, but it's not Sarah. Disappointment.

"Sorry... is this seat taken?" The woman asks Emily, draped in luxurious clothing, hair extensions, and too much makeup.

No way she has cancer. Emily thinks to herself while she forces the fake smile back onto her face. "Oh, no. Not at all. Please."

The woman smiles and sips her free coffee.

Cheryl approaches Emily. "Goodness! I guess word got out about the coffee goodies! Quite a group tonight."

"Oh good! I'm so glad The Daily Grind can support."

Click, flash. Emily smiles big for the camera.

"Oof!" Cheryl chuckles. "Remember to get my good side." She waves at the camera, into it now, Cheryl's reaction to the extra attention in stark contrast to Emily's feelings.

The seats fill as attendees trickle away from the coffee buffet station and into the circle of chairs and the crowd that's formed behind. A wide-eyed Cheryl begins the meeting.

"Well then. Welcome everyone. So nice to see more new faces today. And thank you again for our new sponsor, The Daily..."

A crack of the heavy entry doors opening interrupts the introduction. Late again, Sarah enters the room.

"Sorry, sorry..." Sarah excuses herself as she searches the room for an empty chair, but there is none.

A genuine smile creeps into Emily's face. She sits up a little taller and raises her hand to wave. She leans over to the woman sat next to her. "Excuse me, actually, she's here now. This is her seat. Do you mind?"

The woman frowns in shock, like she's never been so offended.

Emily holds a firm smile and stares at the women, unaffected by her show of disgust at the request. "Please. She has cancer."

With a huff, the woman stands up and leaves, but not before grabbing another free goodie bag on her way out the loud doors.

Satisfied, Emily smiles wide at Sarah and gestures for her to come sit. Sarah responds with a wave and makes her way toward the open chair.

"Sarah, come on in," Cheryl says and acknowledges her. "We're just getting started."

"Okay, does anyone have any good news updates to start off the evening?" Cheryl asks the crowd.

* * *

A mob of her adorning Instagram fans rush Emily after the meeting ends. Sarah, who's sat quietly next to her throughout the meeting, slinks away without a word. Emily's fans take up her time with fake thank you's and requests for photos. She accepts their appreciation with grace and the camera catches it all.

The patrons empty the room and scuttle out of their seats. Some proceed to the coffee station to pick at the last bits of what's leftover, while others rush out. Emily says her goodbyes as the mob slowly dissipates. Her eyes dart through the room in pursuit of something, someone. When she doesn't find them, a subtle note of disappointment courses through her. She shakes it off, gathers her purse, and leaves.

Outside, in the hall, Sarah leans against the wall, waiting.

"Oh! Hi!" Emily says, perking up.

"Hey," Sarah responds with a warm smile. "Sorry, I didn't wanna interrupt you."

"Were you waiting for me?" Emily blushes.

"Uh... yeah, I uh... wanted to thank you for saving me a seat. And... to give you something." Sarah reaches in her crossbody bag and digs around—it's big. She pulls out an item wrapped in a plastic grocery bag. "I hope you like how they turned out." She unwraps the plastic to reveal two pink coffee mugs, etched with the message *WHO SAYS COFFEE CAN'T CURE CANCER?* across the face.

Emily gasps! "Oh, my god!" she laughs. "I love it! Are these...?"

Sarah nods, her smile brightens to match Emily's, but holds a weakness within it that Emily can't pinpoint. "Yeah, I finished them this week and wanted to make sure you got yours."

"One's for me?" Emily asks, struck with warmth and glee as the gesture pierces an emotional muscle she didn't know she had.

"Um, yeah, of course. You made one. It's yours." Sarah laughs and holds out the mugs. "Here, I brought both so you could pick, but this one came out a little better." Sarah presents the better-looking mug. "You should take this one."

Emily accepts it with a reverence like she's never received something so thoughtful, like a million dollars couldn't compare. She wants to speak, but can't. The gesture of friendship more powerful than her words could ever describe. Her lips curl into a frown, she squints, trying to control the tears that threaten to fall.

Sarah notices Emily's emotions and backtracks. "Sorry, is this okay? I didn't mean to..."

Emily wipes away an escaped tear and forces her frown into the smile it's hiding. "No, no. Gosh, sorry. This is so sweet. Um... I guess I... just didn't realize how much I need a friend right now. Thank you. So much."

Sarah reaches over to rub Emily's shoulder.

"Hey, are you hungry? I could kill for a cheeseburger right now," Sarah says.

Emily laughs out loud—part at Sarah's joke and part appreciation for the distraction from her feelings. She stares at the coffee cup. Her mother's words swirl in her head. *Don't bring home any strays.*

"You know what..." Emily says. "Yeah. Yeah, I'd love a cheeseburger."

thirty-eight

EMILY AND SARAH sit across from each other at a booth in a diner with menus in front of their faces.

"This is like the first time I'm actually hungry since chemo," Sarah says.

"I know. I've had like zero appetite all week. How's the week been for you?"

Sarah puts her menu down. Emily mimics the action.

"It's been, uh, not fun," Sarah says. "We had a little issue with Liam getting to school."

"Oh, no! What happened?"

"You girls ready to order?" A server in a simple T-shirt uniform and pony-tailed hair approaches with a notepad.

"Oh! Uh..." Sarah goes back to her menu. "Yeah, I'm gonna have the number two. No tomatoes."

"French fries or Cole slaw?"

"Fries. Please."

"Gotcha," the server says, jotting down the order. "And for you?"

Emily studies her menu again. "Uh, same please. Tomatoes are too acidic for me right now."

"Exactly," Sarah says.

"Got it. No tomatoes. Drinks?"

"Do you have Pepsi?" Sarah asks.

"Coke." the server says as she shakes her head.

"Okay, that's fine."

"Two?"

Emily nods.

"Comin' up." The server holds a smile as she walks away.

"Wait... what happened with Liam?" Emily asks, back to the conversation.

"I had a little trouble getting him to school and picking him up." Sarah's words catch in her throat as she stifles her emotions. "They, uh, they called CPS on us."

"Oh, my god! Really? Are you in trouble? Is Drew helping you?"

Sarah avoids her gaze, looking around for the server and tapping her fingers on the tabletop, but Emily persists.

"Sarah, is Drew helping you?"

Sarah covers her face with her hands. "No. I'm doing this alone." Her muffled voice sounds wet with tears.

"What? What does that even mean? That's impossible. You've got treatment every week for the next three months, at least. Have you shared your treatment calendar with him?" Emily's tone gradually turns frantic. "Can he at least commit to driving Liam to school? How else are you supposed to get better if you don't have his support? Is there anyone else who can? You said you..."

Sarah raises her hands in surrender. "It's okay. This isn't your problem, and we have a recommendation for—"

Emily interjects. "Sarah, I don't mean to be intrusive, but there's just no way you're going to get through this without help."

"Uh... I don't know. I think that, as time goes on, my body will adjust to treatment and I'll still be able to do all the things. I can still rest, as long as Liam gets to and from. He can make chicken nuggets. We'll be okay."

Emily laughs out loud, but not intending to be hurtful. "Sarah, no. Your treatment comes first and you need to have a committed support team. I'm going to take care of this for you. We'll do it together."

"Oh, no. I'm fine. I promise."

"No. Nope. Nope. Nope." Emily crosses her arms and shakes her head. "I can't accept that. We'll continue doing our treatments together, and I'll make sure a car is at your apartment every morning to take Liam to school and pick him up. You're not fighting me on this."

"But..."

Emily holds Sarah's hand and Sarah melts into the gesture of affection.

"Thank you, Emily. You don't know how much this means to me and Liam."

"Oh my god, of course. It's nothing, really." Emily feels good about doing something good. It's a feeling no amount of charity work or public appearances has ever afforded her. It's different, and she likes it.

"Ugh!" Sarah shivers involuntarily. "I hate talking about myself. What about you? Kyle back home yet?"

Emily shrugs, her turn to avoid Sarah's scrutiny. "No. But I'm sure he's just taking time to process..."

"Right, right..." Sarah says, boring her well-meaning gaze into Emily.

"Cokes?" the server says as she approaches with two red plastic cups full of soda. She places them in front of the women and pulls two wrapped straws from her waist apron.

"Thank you," Emily and Sarah say, but Sarah continues to stare at Emily while Emily tries to look anywhere else.

Emily's façade cracks as she rips open her straw, places it in her cup, and sips. "Other than that, it's been really nice to get back to work, back to the office. Everyone's been really supportive, and my mom is happy to have me back, so..."

Sarah stares daggers at Emily. "Uh-huh, sure. Emily, I know we haven't been friends for more than two seconds, and, I probably should just shut up, but... when you're alone, like I've always been, you learn to make it out here you have to lean on other people. You have to let them in and let them help."

Emily waves her off. "Sure, but. I have all the help I could ever need."

"Yeah, I think the problem is, you don't see how alone you really are."

Emily sits up, a little shocked, and mostly offended. "That's not true!"

"You're lying to yourself. All this *help*, but still, no one who cares..."

"Excuse you!" Emily stands up, but rethinks when she sees Sarah's concern, and sits back down.

"Yeah, I mean, sorry, but you're sitting here giving me the greeting card version of your cancer experience. Kyle will be back soon. Your mom's happy you're back, blah, blah, bullshit. You literally could die of cancer and you're talking about how good it is to be back at work?" Sarah doesn't mince her words, yet she reeks of warmth that Emily wants to strangle at the moment.

"Sarah!" she shouts, too frazzled to put together a full sentence.

"It's okay to be vulnerable sometimes. No one's gonna judge you for having feelings."

"Well..." Emily waits for the words to come. She crosses her arms over her chest in self-defense. "You... just... don't understand what it's like to be me! I have rules and expectations and..."

"Okay, okay, Miss Director of Marketing..."

"Chief Marketing Officer," Emily corrects.

"Whatever. Sure. You're right. I don't understand. I don't know a lot of things you do, Emily. But what I know is that money's not gonna get you through this, and if you *don't* get through this, you can't take any of it with you, anyway."

"Well, that's a bold statement coming from the girl who would rather ignore the reality of her own baby daddy drama than have a real father for her son!"

The women standoff in a tense staring contest.

"Alrighty!" The server approaches the table with two identical plates of cheeseburgers with fries. "Here we go, girls." She sets the plates on the table. "Enjoy."

thirty-nine

SARAH AND EMILY act like old high school friends who grow up and pretend not to notice one another when they pass each other by chance in public. At the support group, Sarah sits opposite Emily, and they complete the next set of treatments separately. What was becoming an unlikely friendship is thwarted over Cokes and cheeseburgers.

"Where's Miss Emily today? Thought you two we're sticking together through this?" Nurse Jackie asks Sarah as she sets her up in an infusion chair for another round of chemo.

"Oh, we're not friends, or anything," Sarah says. "We just know of one another from group." The look on Sarah's face shows a furrowed brow and telling eyes that reveal a hidden pain.

Sarah slinks into the group late, and no seats are open. Emily sees her come in, but doesn't act to make room for her like she did before. Instead, she keeps herself busy snapping photos and chatting with her Insta-fam while she pretends not to notice Sarah sitting alone in the back of a crowd.

"Okay! Let's get started, everyone!" Cheryl says to her group attendees. "Sarah, you have a new round of treatment coming up soon, right?"

All eyes turn to Sarah.

"Yup," Sarah says, averting her gaze away from the attention.

"Wow!" Cheryl responds, trying to keep the interview going. "That means you've completed your first round? Another week off and then round two?"

The watchful eyes of the audience burn into her. Sarah ignores her nerves and nods.

"Okay then..." Cheryl says. "That means you too, Emily! You're also coming to the end of your first round, right?"

"That's right!" Emily says, cheerful. "First round down, I can't believe it's almost been one mo—" Emily stops herself from finishing the sentence. Her eyes shift to Sarah like she's remembered something about her. "Month... It's been one month. One... billing cycle."

The rest of the room clocks a look at Emily—it's the look a puppy gives you when they don't understand a command, their head turns sideways and they stare into your eyes, deeply wanting to know the words coming out of your mouth. The one person who understands is the only face in the room, avoiding Emily by fidgeting with her fingernails and chewing on her bottom lip, Sarah.

Emily takes in a deep breath, feeling compelled to say something. "Right, Sarah? It's been a month?" Her voice shakes. She knows she's being confrontational, and Sarah never responds well to that. But one billing cycle means the grace period Doctor Evan gave her is up and Sarah needs to have her medical card to continue treatment.

Sarah clears her throat and finds her confidence. "Not quite," she says out loud. "Three weeks of treatment and one week off. Next week will be one month. I still have a week."

The other women are even more confused, unable to discern they were only a medium for Sarah and Emily's conversation.

"One week for what, Sarah?" Cheryl asks.

Sarah shakes her head and gestures for Cheryl to move on, but Emily continues to look at her, despite her disappointment at Sarah's unwillingness to talk about it.

Cheryl looks at Emily for clarification. "Something we should know about?" she asks.

Emily smiles, remembering where she is and who's watching. "No. Nothing."

* * *

Sarah rushes through the morning routine with Liam. But they're already late.

"Come on, come on. Let's go baby. Socks and shoes, socks and shoes!"

Sarah shuffles through a stack of mail, desperate for something important hiding among the junk. Her face contorts in defeat when she accepts it's not there.

"Ugh, come on!" she whispers to herself as she tosses the stack of mail onto the kitchenette table.

"What's wrong, momma?"

"Nothing. Nothing's wrong, baby." Sarah rubs her brow with frustration. There was indeed something wrong. She's been attending the group, just like Doctor Evan told her to, but one month has passed and her new insurance card has not arrived. She was keeping up her end of the deal, and until today, so was he. Today marks not only the end of his grace period but also the beginning of a fresh round of treatment. She needs her insurance to continue receiving her prescribed chemotherapies. But that little green plastic Medi-Cal card did not arrive, and she didn't know what would happen at her appointment today. Would they turn her away? Could this all be over? Her thoughts reel and try to suck her into them. But she's got no time. She's too busy getting Liam ready for school to stop now.

Liam runs through the apartment, a yogurt tube hanging from his mouth as he hops on one foot while putting on his socks. He loses balance and gets distracted by his backpack, stuffing it with a binder and loose papers. Sarah claps her hands, encouraging him to go faster. Liam finds his shoes, and sits down to finish putting on his socks, before placing them on his feet.

"Laces!" Liam shouts as he completes the task.

"Okay, momma's gonna take you to school, then I gotta go to my doctor's appointment. Momma's gonna be really tired afterward and you're taking the bus home. Remember? You get on the bus and tell them you're with the Schools and Health First program."

"Okay, Mom, I already know this..." Liam says with an annoyed groan.

She finishes tying up his laces. "Okay, okay, let's go!"

Sarah opens her apartment door and startles as a small scream escapes her mouth.

A tall man in a black suit stands right in front of her.

"Oh, my god. You scared me," Sarah says.

"Excuse me, miss."

Sarah relaxes when she realizes he's not a threat. "Uh, hi. Can I help you?"

"Here to take Mr. Liam to school and you to your appointment."

Sarah jerks back. "Wait, who sent you?"

"Ms. Emily Cassius sent me, Miss Kenneth."

"Are you serious?"

"Yes. Ms. Cassius has arranged all transportation for the next two months with an option to extend, should your treatment call for it."

Sarah can't believe it. She rolls her eyes with annoyance. "I told her not to."

"She thought you might say something like that, so she asked me to give you this note." He hands a folded note to Sarah.

Sarah studies his face with slight-eyes and snatches the note from his hand.

This is me, reaching out to help. And this is you letting yourself be vulnerable because no one's judging you for having feelings.

Sarah chuckles. "Doesn't even make sense..." she mumbles to herself. "Whatever. Okay!" she addresses the driver. "Take us to school, I guess."

Liam does a little jig, pointing to the shiny black SUV in the parking lot. "Is that our ride?"

"Yes, Mr. Liam. Please follow me."

forty

THE DRIVER HOLDS OPEN the door to the Breast Health Center for Sarah. She carries herself like someone made her princess for a day. She spots Emily in the lobby, scrolling on her phone as she waits. Her shoulders tighten as nerves take over. Emily lets out a deep breath and approaches.

"Hi," Emily says first.

"Hi."

Both attempt an apology but stumble on their words as they cut each other off. The nervous laughter that proceeds is enough to lighten the mood.

"Me first..." Sarah says.

Emily nods.

"I'm sorry for what I said. I was insensitive and kinda mean."

"No, you were only sharing your experience and trying to help me open up. And you were right. I try to pretend that everything is roses, but it's not real, no matter how hard I pretend it to be. And I know I don't have to pretend with you."

"Good. I hope you don't anymore. It's not your money that makes you cool, ya know? It's definitely the cancer," Sarah says, nodding vigorously, to emphasize the point.

The women laugh out loud.

"That's gonna take some getting used to, though," Emily says, regarding Sarah's blunt and unforgiving honesty.

"Really appreciate the escort. You didn't have to do that," Sarah says.

"Eh, it's nothing. I know I've been ignoring you at group lately. I'm sorry. I wanted to apologize."

"I guess Director of Marketing pulls in more scratch than I imagined."

Emily laughs. "I uh, yes. Well, it's Chief Marketing Officer, but my mother owns the company."

Sarah's eyes display their shock. "Oh, so... oh..." As the initial surprise weans, Sarah's body twitches with discomfort. She sinks inside herself as her gaze shifts down.

Emily notices and tries to backtrack. "But it's whatever. I just have a little more money that average, I guess."

"Ya think?" Sarah scoffs.

"Come on. Let's check in."

"Oh, yeah... uh..." Sarah rubs the back of her neck to calm her stressed nerves.

Emily looks back. "Something wrong? Did you get your card? Your Medi-Cal came through, right?"

"Uh..." Sarah doesn't answer the question, but drags her feet over to the reception desk.

"Welcome in, ladies. How can I help you?" The receptionist greets them warmly, as Emily follows close behind and hovers.

"Hi. Sarah Kenneth." Her smile tightens and her pulse races. She's nervous as she watches the receptionist click into the computer.

"Oh. We're going to need your Medi-Cal card today. Can you provide that to us?"

"Uh, so... that's the thing. I..."

"Here!" Emily says, poking herself forward and presenting an AmEx black card. "Please charge this. And keep it on file."

"What? No! Absolutely not. I can't. That's insane!" Sarah spirals, unable to accept to the gesture of kindness and responding only to the feeling of overwhelm.

"Sarah. Please. Just let me do it this time." Emily is adamant, not a crack visible.

"It's too much," Sarah says in protest.

Emily knows no amount of money could be a burden to her. Paying for cancer treatment might as well be buying a friend a cup of coffee. But she also understands Sarah doesn't understand what that's like. They come from different worlds and no amount of explaining could make a difference.

Emily must think fast to convince Sarah to be okay with this, and decides a bit of Sarah's own brash honesty might do the trick. "Well, you have no other choice, so this is happening," she says and forces the black card toward the receptionist, urging her to accept it.

The receptionist looks from Emily's victorious smile to Sarah's wide but accepting eyes and receives the metal black card without.

"Okay, we have a back charge of one billing cycle. The total is twelve-thousand, four-hundred, and seventeen dollars and eighty-three cents. Plus, today's treatment starts a new cycle, and we'll need a first payment of four-thousand, three-hundred and seventy-five dollars and thirty-two cents. Are you comfortable with that?"

"Oh, my god…" Sarah holds her stomach like she's going to be sick.

"Yes, that's fine. Thank you."

The receptionist swipes the card and completes the transaction. "Do you need a receipt?"

Emily waves her hand and shakes her head.

"Okay, you ladies are all set. Have a seat."

Sarah's still overwhelmed and at a loss for words at the generosity. Emily smiles like she's got warm-fuzzies. This whole *helping others* thing is settling in as something fun for her.

Emily recognizes Nurse Jackie at the door to the treatment room, takes in her warm smile and shies away, embarrassed, like being caught doing a good deed has shame attached to it. A lifetime of living for herself, and now, using her privilege to help someone else, she feels insecure in her act of goodness when it's caught by an outside observer.

"This way, ladies." Nurse Jackie says as she invites them back.

* * *

Sarah and Emily sit side by side in their infusion chairs. They take a deep breath, knowing what to expect this time, but still not looking forward to any of it. Nurse Jackie finishes setting up and administers the drip bags of medication.

"Alright then. Holler if you need me."

"Thanks," Emily offers a polite but forced smile.

Sarah doesn't react. She's lost deep in her thoughts. Emily notices, but waits for Nurse Jackie to leave before she speaks.

"Hey, you okay?"

Sarah snaps out of her head. "Huh? Yeah. Sorry, uh... Say something to distract me."

"Uhh, okay." Emily is grateful for the opportunity to distract herself as well. "What's Liam's favorite TV show right now? Does he like Blippi? Or is that just a little kid thing?"

"Hey, did you say your family *owns The Daily Grind*? Like the whole thing or just one store?" Sarah skirts the question to respond with her own line of questioning.

Emily shakes her head with mild embarrassment. "The whole thing. It's no big deal, it's..."

"Ugh! I can't believe I gave you a stupid coffee cup!" Sarah says, slapping her palm no her forehead.

"What? No! I love my coffee cup!" Emily's look turns to shock and dismay, like she's a little girl and someone's just stolen her ice cream cone mid-lick.

"It's okay. You don't have to be nice about it. It was a stupid gift."

"Hey," sincerity floods Emily's voice. "No, it wasn't. I told you. No one's ever given me such a thoughtful gift, and I meant it. I loved the gift, and I'm so grateful."

Sarah shakes off her own embarrassment. "So, uh... you don't have money, you have *monn-aaaayyyy?*"

Emily chuckles. "Yes. More than we know what to do with. But you were right. It's not important. Not like laying in a bed of it is gonna make it any easier when I die."

"Eh, no, but that would make pretty cool photos for The Gram."

The women laugh.

"You know..." Emily says. She pauses before she continues, like she has to think it through first.

"It's okay. You can say it."

Emily hesitates, but the longing in her eyes gives her up. "My whole life, the only value I ever held was how well I could protect the money."

Sarah smiles a nod of encouragement at Emily.

"It was always *'do this because we need their allegiance.'* Or, *'marry him because he's from the right family,'* *'be friends with her because she's low risk...'* No one ever asked me what I wanted. No one wanted to know how I felt, what was important to me. It's never been about anything other than 'protecting the money.'"

Sarah listens with intention. Her face shows compassion and empathy, as Emily explains.

"And for what? Why?" The fire inside Emily grows until her cheeks flush and her eyes narrow. Her voice pitches into anger and the pace of her words quickens. "So that when I die of breast cancer, my legacy will be a bank account full of zeros? I don't have anything real! No one! My best friend won't answer my calls. My husband's god knows where doing god knows what... And my mom? My only remaining family because she hated my dad and just used him for his money until he died and now any extended family wants nothing to do with us! Or, I don't know. Knowing her, she probably pushed them all away so she wouldn't have to share any of it." Emily's out of breath and all worked up.

Sarah reaches over her hand and waits for Emily to notice. Emily sucks in her breath, trying to catch up with herself before she sees the hand. She reaches over and grabs onto it as if Sarah's hand is a lifeline and the both of them are thrashing through a turbulent ocean.

"I'm sorry you've been so alone." Sarah squeezes Emily's hand tight and smiles.

Emily feels the gesture in her heart as her internal sea calms.

* * *

Emily and Sarah try their best to maintain composure despite the exhaustion and queasy bellies, but it's too hard.

"I'm sorry, can I just…" Sarah says as she leans into Emily and rests her head in Emily's lap. Emily smiles, even as she struggles through her own pain. The women groan when their car moves through the streets and try to brace themselves as they tolerate the bumpy ride.

"Is Drew able to help with dinner for you and Liam tonight?" Emily asks, curious, but also prying slightly.

Sarah lifts her head at a slight angle and lets out a deep sigh. "I'm gonna tell you something, but I don't want you to freak out, okay?"

Emily straightens herself up, while Sarah hides her face in Emily's lap.

"There was an incident. Drew got kinda mad about the whole CPS thing. He came barging into our apartment, screaming and acting insane. I fell down, Liam got scared, and Drew basically left with his tail tucked up pretty tight."

"What? Did he hit you? Did you call the cops? You have to press charges!"

"No, no, no. It wasn't like that. Drew is… complicated. He knows he's got issues, and he keeps himself at a distance because of them."

"Sarah! That's no excuse to hit you!"

"Okay, hold on, hold on. He didn't hit me. He kinda just... accidentally knocked into me, and I tripped."

"Uh, huh? Who's making excuses now?"

"Okay, yeah. I know. But this has been a lot for him. I told you what happened to his mom when he was a kid. This is all very triggering. He's afraid for Liam. That's all."

Emily wants to call out the excuses again, but refrains for Sarah's sake, understanding what's done is done and all she can do is ask what Sarah will do now. "Well, are you at least gonna do something, so he doesn't come back?"

"He won't. He doesn't want to hurt us. He just doesn't know how to help. He'll be gone for a long time now. Not my first rodeo with him."

"So, he's done this before?"

Sarah shrugs and shakes her head. "Never like this, but *this* is a lot. For anyone. Especially him."

The driver stops in the parking lot of Sarah's apartment building. He gets out and opens the passenger door for Sarah, who unwillingly peels herself up from the comfort of Emily's lap. Sarah pulls Emily in for a hug and they melt into each other's embrace.

"Thank you so much for everything," Sarah says.

"Course. Get some rest. Liam has a key to get in, right?"

"Yeah, he does. Thanks for that too, but, uh, outside all this," she gestures to the car, the driver. "Stop paying for stuff, please? It's weird now." Sarah shivers, feigning exaggerated disgust.

"Oh, get over it." Emily's breath releases a half-hearted chuckle.

"Okay, okay. Jeez!" Sarah uses what little energy she has to raise her hands in surrender, but makes it only halfway, her arms too heavy to finish. "Text me later," she says as she moves to close the door behind her. The driver intervenes, holds up his hands in a gesture of *I got it*. Sarah smiles at him and relents. "Yeah, I still gotta get used to this princess stuff."

"It's kinda cool. Perks of being friends with me."

forty-one

KYLE STANDS in front of a fancy bathroom mirror. He buttons the top button of his dress shirt when his cell phone rings.

"Ugh..." he groans. "What now?"

A toilet flushes behind him and Tiffany comes out wearing a silk nighty. She wraps her arms around his waist and squeezes him in a playful hug.

"Aren't you gonna wash your hands?" Kyle says, ignoring her cuddle.

Tiffany's mouth drops open and she snatches her arms away from him.

Kyle is oblivious to her surprise at his remark. He grabs his phone and walks away to answer the call.

"Hello, Ms. Helen."

"You get it out of your system yet?" Helen says with a growl.

"Ms. Helen, what are you implying? No..."

"Save it, boy! I've given you and your father an entire month to consider my offer. If your car hasn't left that bimbo's driveway in the next twenty minutes, consider my generosity revoked!"

Kyle hurries to put on a tie, suit jacket, dress shoes, and rushes out of the bedroom.

Before she can finish washing her hands, Tiffany hears the front door slam. She shakes her head as the realization of their brief escapade ending washes over her. Not surprised, she continues to primp, as she expected Helen's call to come much sooner. The mirror holds her gaze for a brief second as her eyes reflect her loneliness back at her, before a smile creeps back in. She's got something cooking, an idea. She wipes her hands, and skips into her bedroom, where she stares at her phone, picking at her cuticles. 1, 2, 3, 4, 5... she counts and then picks up her phone, opens her messages, and scrolls to the text chain with Emily.

"Hey, Emily! Can't believe I missed this. I miss you! Let's meet up? Are you free?"

* * *

Emily vomits into a bedpan on the side of her bed.

Dana comes to her aid. "Oh, miss Emily," she says as she brushes Emily's hair from her face. "Anything I can get for you?"

"No, Dana. Thank you."

Dana picks up the full bedpan and excuses herself from the room. Emily lays back on her bed, her breaths labored.

A text message pings on her phone. She ignores it, still recuperating from the last bout of nausea and dizziness. Her phone pings the two-minute notification reminder.

"Urrrggghhhhh," Emily groans, still without the energy to engage with her phone.

Emily hobbles into her bathroom. She washes her face at the sink as she sways side to side, all her strength gathered to keep her knees from buckling beneath her. She wipes the fresh water from her face and stares at her face in the mirror. This time, it's worse, illustrated by eyes more deeply sunk into her sockets and skin paler in comparison. Her face is gaunter than she remembers from last time, the queasiness in her stomach and the weight of her tiny body harder to bear than her last round of treatment. She doesn't understand why it feels worse this time.

She looks back out of the bathroom door toward her bedroom and thinks she can make it. It's not that far, but only after she takes another moment to build some strength. She leans against the bathroom counter in rest, and gathers herself for the trip back to bed.

A single step forward starts the journey. The second, continues it. As her feet pull her weight forward, her heart races, and her face pours sweat. She groans out as her stomach turns and her vision blurs. She can do this, she tells herself. But each step seems to pull the bed further away as her field of vision distorts. Is she going backward now? No. She can't be. But is she? Dizziness confuses her. A few more steps and her thighs touch the side of her bed. She collapses onto it with heavy breaths, but the pain coursing through her veins is now so intense, she cries out. Frustration at her weakness, anger at her diagnosis, and denial of how her life has crumbled around her throughout the process, all pour out of her eyes and puddle on her comforter.

Once it's all out and she has nothing left to cry, she wills her heart rate to slow with several calming breaths. She takes the rest of her strength to pull herself back into a somewhat comfortable position in bed. Her vision blurs and goes black again at the subtle movement. When it returns, faster this time, the first thing she sees is her phone, and remembers she has a message waiting. Tiffany's name shows on the screen and the sight of it peps her up. She almost can't believe it. A half-smile creeps onto her sweaty face as she reads and types out a message to respond.

"Hey, Tiffany! Yeah, now's not great. But I should be feeling better this weekend?" Emily waits and watches the screen. The response ellipses appear.

"Great! Bottomless mimosa brunch it is! See you Saturday!"

Emily looks at her screen in uncertainty and whispers, "Mimosas?" The thought makes her stomach turn and her cheeks puff. "Ugh. Whatever."

"Sounds great. See you then." Send.

Emily drops her phone and sinks back into bed, whimpering to herself in her own little pity-party.

* * *

The early morning sun lights Emily's bedroom as her automatic shades pull up on cue. A soft alarm of classical music plays, gently stirring Emily awake. Her eyes flutter open. She lays still in the light-filled room as if she's taking a moment to gauge how she's feeling. After a full night's rest, she decides she feels well enough to pull herself up. With slow movements, she sets herself up against fluffy pillows as Dana enters the room.

"Tea this morning, Ms. Emily. Better than coffee for your belly aches."

"Thank you, Dana."

Dana nods and excuses herself.

Emily reaches over to the cold side of the bed and grabs her laptop. As she attempts to sip tea against a nausea that keeps her guessing whether she'll be able to, she opens her laptop and types into the search bar. A search page offers her a list of links for *Breast Cancer*. She clicks the top result. It brings her to the homepage of *The Breast Cancer Awareness Foundation*. She clicks and sips and finds a page for *facts and statistics.* Click.

The bulleted list presents itself as facts, but offers little more than terror.

- About 1 in 8 women in the United States develop invasive breast cancer during their lifetime.
- The risk of developing breast cancer by age 30 is less than 0.49%.
- The 5-year relative survival rate for women with non-metastatic breast cancer is 91%

- The 5-year relative survival rate for women with metastatic breast cancer is 22%
- Only 2%-5% of research funding raised for breast cancer is dedicated to the study of metastasis.
- Every year 200,000 Americans are diagnosed with breast cancer, 6–10% of these diagnoses are metastatic.

The bottom of the list hosts a large pink button begging, DONATE NOW.

"Oh, my god… 0.49%…" Emily covers her mouth as quiet tears stream down her face. Her thoughts spiral as she considers how a disease like breast cancer, just a few months ago, wasn't something that'd ever crossed her mind, but now, she was part of the 0.49% of people for whom it would become the forefront of every thought. How, at twenty-five years old, in the prime of planning her future and building a life with her new husband, everything has changed, and she now lives in a place where nothing is certain anymore. There is no guarantee, and money can't buy back her health.

* * *

Emily stands over her bathroom counter. She runs the tap to splash cool water on her face. She looks in the mirror, but doesn't recognize herself. Down in the sink, strands of fallen hair cover the white marble. A light gasp of shock escapes her as she notices.

She touches her head with soft fingers. Several more strands of hair fall away. But she can't muster the energy to even weep at the loss. Instead, she turns on the sink to wash it away. The hair gathers in a clump at the drain and reminds her of a hamster she had as a pet once. There's so much of it. She picks it up in her hand, and holds it softly in her palm with a sullen look of loss, the same way she held her hamster as she put it in an old shoebox the day it died.

forty-two

SARAH FIGHTS against exhaustion as she pedals her turntable. The balcony, once full of bright colors and crafted pieces of her soul, is now almost bare in comparison. The clutter of art supplies remains, but the artifacts have gone to new homes. Replenishment and new creations have become difficult as her illness persists. Still, this is her solace, her obsession, and her livelihood, the fruit of which has hit a season of lull, but she goes on, because she must.

Her hands hold tight to the clay on the round as it forms into a tall vase and takes its shape. But it's like her body is giving up on her. The muscles of her hands cannot follow the commands of her neurons. She can't squeeze it tight enough. The clay is too loose—weak, like her.

Sweat beads on her strained brow. Her shoulders shake. She can't. Her hands drop, the clay folds and deflates into a puddle of soft ceramic walls fallen over on themselves. She stops the pedal. The table follows. She sinks in defeat and brings hands wet with clay to cover her face full of tears.

A knock on the apartment door distracts her. She wipes her hands across her eyes, leaving a trail on her cheek. She reaches for the damp rag on the table next to the box of clay and drags it across her face to clean herself, but because her strength is gone, more streaks of clay paint her skin. Next, she pulls the rag across her hands and fingers, only smearing the gray—good enough.

* * *

"He—" Emily walks in. "Oh... are you okay?" she says, surprised and concerned seeing Sarah's inflamed eyes, and cheeks stained with gray.
"It's just... so... hard!" Sarah breaks into tears.
Emily pulls her close and embraces her. The women hold one another, Emily enduring Sarah's weight.
"Hey. I brought dinner!" Emily says, sensing that Sarah's cries have subsided and she's shifted her bodyweight back onto her own feet. The women separate and Sarah gestures for Emily to come inside. Emily complies and holds up a brown paper bag of takeout.
"Dinner?" Liam says as he pokes his head out from behind the tapestries of his *bedroom*.

* * *

Liam sits at the TV and eats from his cardboard takeout box. Sarah and Emily sit at the kitchenette, their own takeout boxes in front of them, mostly untouched. Instead, they poke at the food, push it around on their plates, and sigh. Hunger is a sensation that's missed them both.
"How's the week been this time?" Emily asks.
Sarah shrugs. "The car has been super helpful, thank you."
"Have you been resting?" Emily asks.
Sarah's head moves up and down only once in a depressed nod.
Emily responds with a subtle and understanding smile. "That's great."
"Are you feeling better?" Sarah asks.
Emily's shoulders rise only halfway, both offering movement

JENNIFER LUCIC

that only just gets the point across. "Enough to get out of the house. Back at work again." Emily's head points down, almost shamed. "But also, I have to go to brunch tomorrow. So, that should be fun."

Sarah huffs at Emily with crossed arms and a piercing stare.

"What? I can go to brunch."

"With who?" Sarah asks, her tone Emily absorbs as judgment.

"Whatever, Sarah..." Emily says, reading between the lines. "Just because I acknowledge my friendships are somewhat... manufactured, doesn't mean I can't still enjoy them."

"I mean, do what you want, but are you really enjoying them or are you obligated to them cause mommy told you so?

"Can we talk about something else?" Emily waves her off.

"Just sayin... we both get limited time here. You really wanna spend it being fake?"

"No!" Emily says with a snap, not thinking.

Sarah looks at her with a satisfied smile, knowing she's made her point.

Emily takes in a breath to compose herself and tries again. "No, I don't. But I also don't know what that means yet."

"Okay, well, that's something..." she says as she twirls one of her dreadlocks in her fingers; it breaks off from her scalp, and FALLS IN HER PALM! Sarah's shock radiates through her face.

Emily covers her mouth as her eyes try to escape their sockets.

The women stare at each other, both wait for the other to speak. Sarah goes first when she lets out a full and deep belly laugh. But the fright in her eyes and the frowned corners of her mouth give away any pretense of joy. It's a laugh of pain. One that comes from the pit of the stomach and the darkest places of despair. The *if I don't laugh, I'll cry* kind of laugh. The laugh that, instead of hiding anxiety and pain, brings it to the surface in a desperate show of despondency.

Emily's heart breaks for Sarah, for both of them. She raises her hand to her own head, pulls on her hair, and a clump falls out into her palm. The women together howl with pain masquerading as laughter.

* * *

The two women stand in front of the small bathroom mirror in Sarah's apartment.

"You ready?" Sarah says.

Emily hesitates, but nods. "Uh, you first."

The buzz of an electric hair clipper startles Emily. Sarah holds the vibrating machine. She raises it to the top of her head. Emily grits her teeth and squints as Sarah makes contact, and drags the clippers over her scalp, detaching dreadlocks and leaving a lawnmower trail as she goes.

Emily shrieks and continues until all of Sarah's hair is gone!

"Ooohhhhh yeahhhhh, baby!" Sarah says, twirling the clippers in the air.

Emily cries and laughs, her rollercoaster of emotions unsure of where to settle.

One last stripe down her head, Sarah passes the clippers over to Emily. "Let's go! Get it!"

"Ahhhh! No, I can't, I can't!" Emily takes a deep breath. "Okay, give it to me," Emily says as she rips the clippers from Sarah's grasp.

"Oh, okay! Here we go!"

Emily squeaks her voice as she commits the act. The clippers drag across her head, and hair falls.

Sarah cheers, skipping around as much as her body allows, while Emily yelps.

* * *

Sarah and Emily sit in the moonlight on Sarah's balcony. Their bright and bald scalps reflect a shine.

"We did it," Emily says as her hands feel her bare scalp, discovering a part of her body she's never known.

"Yeah. We did." Sarah smiles with warmth and places her hand on Emily's bald head. The women chuckle together until silence takes over. Sarah leans her head into Emily and Emily leans into Sarah until they allow their scalps to connect. Here they stay and revere one another's touch.

The moment passes as a subtle chortle pulls them back away.

"So, uh, I know you have brunch plans tomorrow, but if you change your mind, I'm going to the market. I got a few new pieces to sell. You should come."

"Hmmm, I've never been the one behind the booth before."

"It's fun. Me and Liam, my little pottery wrapper."

"Thanks for the invite. I'll let you know if I finish up early."

Polite smiles exchange between the two of them. Emily isn't going, and she knows it.

forty-three

A RESTAURANT PERCHED on the beach with an ocean sand patio overlooks the Malibu coast. Inside, tuxedoed servers offer gastronomy themed cocktails that trail a line of smoke from the glass, or bubble like a cauldron with small plates of trendy food items to designer-clad and accessorized patrons.

Emily struts in through the front door. She sports red-soled high heels, designer garb, and a brightly patterned silk scarf wrapped around her head. Her dress is a suit of confidence that makes her feel like herself again. She holds a smile across pink painted lips and finds comfort in the familiarity of her surroundings.

Emily raises her hand in a wave. At the bar, Tiffany sits pretty in a vivid red tube dress. She sips a crystal glass mimosa, and waves back.

"Tiffany! Hi! How are you?" Emily says as she approaches.

"Yay! Hi! Oh, I've missed you so much!"

The two friends offer one another a half hug. The gesture is unmatched to the enthusiasm in their voice as they play pretend with one another.

"Ugh, I love that scarf! I wish I could pull that off!"

"Oh, you know, chemo hair." Emily chuckles.

"Oh, my god, yes. Sit, sit, sit! Tell me all about that?"

Emily sits at the bar next to Tiffany. Without a formal order, the bartender serves her a mimosa.

"Thank you," Emily acknowledges the service. "Um, yeah, it's been going well. I have a scan next week, hopefully all good news. Treatment's been rough, but no worse than a hangover!" Emily laughs, used to being fake and knowing Tiffany won't pry, anyway.

"Oh, yay! I'm so glad to hear it's been easy for you. There're just all these stories of these poor women who just *suffer* and it's like, ugh, gross."

Emily's head snaps back with surprise at the comment. The plastered fake smile on her face cracks.

"Um, well, uh…" Emily can't find the words. "I mean, it's not… easy per se…"

"Oh, come on, girl. I've seen you on some of your worst morning afters. Can't be much worse than Maldives two summers ago. Do you even remember the cabana boys?" Tiffany laughs her off and changes the subject. "Oh, how's Kyle, by the way? He back home yet?"

"Uh… I never told you he left." Emily's face flushes under her makeup and her eyes narrow.

"Oh, honey. You're turning red. Are you having a hot flash? I heard that was a side effect of the chemo," Tiffany says as she fans Emily's face with a napkin.

Emily swats Tiffany's hand back, making her gasp in an exaggerated show of offense.

"Why did you really call me here today, Tiffany? We haven't spoken in months, but you seem to already know everything about my diagnosis, my treatment, and MY HUSBAND!"

"You're my friend, Emily. I've been keeping track of your awareness campaign on Insta. Of course, I know what you've been up to."

"Kyle was not part of the campaign. How'd you know he hasn't been home?"

Tiffany stumbles over her words, scoffs, and tries to cover up.

"What are you talking about? Of course he was. It's all everyone's talking about."

Emily and Tiffany's conversation degrades into a stare off. Emily stiffens, glaring at Tiffany who cowers, retreating into herself, unable to face the confrontation she's stepped too far into by mistake. Inside, Emily panics through spiraled thoughts, but outside she's protected by years of extensive social training.

Why is she so interested in Kyle? It's all she ever talks about any time I see her. Does she know something? Was my mother right? Is Tiffany... no.

Emily notices Tiffany's phone on the bar. In one swift movement, she swipes it. It's in her hand and her possession. She holds it up high, a victory. All those years of *social training* quickly disintegrating under a threat Emily perceives as more important than maintaining her composure.

"Emily!" Tiffany growls with gritted teeth. "You're being ridiculous!" She attempts to recapture her phone, but can't create a scene at the risk of public embarrassment.

"Let's see, your passcode still as basic as you? 2468?"

"Emily!" Tiffany's voice grumbles a little deeper, and tries to stretch forward a little further.

Emily moves out of Tiffany's grasp, keeping her prize close. She types in the code. "Wow. Really!" Emily says, not surprised as the phone unlocks.

Emily laughs as she scrolls through the messages, but not for long, because Tiffany lunges and tackles her. Emily and Tiffany both crash to the floor. The two fight for the phone rolling around in a heap of expensive textiles and body parts. Tiffany's tube dress slips below her breast, exposing her, as she reaches for and rips Emily's scarf from her head. Patrons and workers both gawk and gasp at the spectacle. Emily won't give up her pursuit, still scrolling through the messages while trying to keep Tiffany from snatching the phone as they roll around on the bar floor.

"WHAT!" Emily screams out loud.

Tiffany stops the attack, scooting her body back and waiting with bated breath for Emily to respond further.

"You're sleeping with my husband!"

Emily melts into a full tantrum. She screams, cries, and throws Tiffany's phone. Tiffany slinks her body away and up from the floor. She grabs her phone from where it lands. Defeated, she makes a quick exit, leaving Emily to deal with herself, by herself.

forty-four

EMILY RACES her G-Wagon down a windy canyon road bawling her eyes out as her car swerves in and out of traffic, her vision compromised. Rage guides her pained honks, screams, and thrashes against the steering wheel.

"Out of my way! Get out!" Emily shouts out the window as she cuts off another driver, forcing them into the shoulder.

The stereo interrupts her with a phone call. She bangs the accept call button on the in-dash monitor.

"Mom, Mom, Mom! Tiffany's STOLEN my husband!" Emily screams and wails.

"Oh dear god, did Kyle tell you?" Helen says.

"What? Did you know about this?" Her own shock silences her.

"Of course I did, Emily. And don't blame her. This is Kyle's doing, but he's just a man. You can't expect anything of the lesser sex."

"How could you keep this from me?"

"Emily, control yourself. I've made sure to end the affair and get him back home. I told you, you needed to fix this quick. I even gave you the opportunity to do it on your own. But you didn't. You left it to mommy, like a good girl. Now, everything is taken care of and he'll be home this evening."

"What? No! No! I don't want him home. He's not allowed in my home."

"What you want in this scenario is irrelevant. Kyle will be home this evening, and so will you."

"NO! I'm not going home! I'm going to Sarah. She's the only person who cares about me!"

"You'll do no such thing! I forbid you from any further interactions with that woman. You don't belong to her class, Emily. I can't spin this campaign any further than I already have."

Emily deflates. She sniffles through her words, "My life isn't a publicity stunt, Mom. I just want a friend…"

Helen gives an annoyed sigh. "Oh, Christ, Emily. There are more important things in this world than your feelings. The sooner you realize that, the easier this becomes."

Emily takes a moment to collect her thoughts. She breathes out a deep breath. "Right… the money. Always protect the money."

"Yes, Emily. The money. The money that's afforded you every comfort and luxury your little heart could ever desire. I've toiled my life away, building this empire for you, for us. When you were little, it was just the two of us, against the world. Do you remember that? And all I've ever asked in return is you respect my sacrifice. Is that too much to ask, dear daughter?"

Emily nods in silence. "But what if I don't want it anymore? This… *empire?*"

"THAT HAS NEVER BEEN AND NEVER WILL BE AN OPTION!"

Emily shakes with fear as her mother's words attack her.

"This conversation is over, Emily. You'll be home this evening, ready for dinner at six pm sharp. I've arranged for Dana to prepare a meal for the three of us, where we'll get this settled and behind us."

Emily finds her courage to speak. "Sarah invited me to the farmer's market. I'm going."

"You are not!" Helen says in a low growl, losing her patience.

"Yes, I am."

"Emily!" Helen warns.

"To say goodbye! If this is what you want, mother, I'll do whatever you want... but I have one condition. Sarah and her son will continue to have my financial support, even if from a distance."

"You're talking about driving her child to school?"

"Yes, and... whatever else she might need through treatment. I won't compromise on this."

"Oh, Emily, fine! We'll add it in as part of the campaign, I suppose. You'll say goodbye at the farmer's market, and group meetings remain cordial but at a distance, or the support stops. Do we have a deal?"

"We do. Bye, Mom," Emily says with calm clarity.

*　*　*

Emily parks her G-Wagon in a crowded parking lot. As good of a place to cry as any, and lets the welling up inside her flow out. This is it, the moment the walls of her Insta-worthy life crumble beneath her. She's lost her husband, her best friend, her mother considers her a public affairs fiasco, and money tied to the family business keeps her beholden to expectation that's become an invisible strangulation device. She wants freedom, but what would that even look like? Could she buy a van and live #vanlife on the open road? Could she jet-set off to Paris and pretend to be French? Oh, that's right, there's that other thing, that cute little pink ribbon thing—cancer. In this life she doesn't want anymore, anyway, all she can do is obey, because it's all she knows how to do.

After a long cry, Emily goes numb. Having purged it all, she has nothing left to squeeze out of herself. She prepares herself for what she knows must happen next. She'll go home and speak to Kyle, just like mother said. They'll make up, at least publicly, and she'll continue with her treatments, the campaign, work, the support group, all while keeping a safe distance from the new, and only genuine friend she's ever had.

She settles into a new reality—her life is a lie, a sacrifice, because that's what it means to have one like hers. Emily steps out of her head and studies her surroundings. The parking lot bustles. A sign advertises the *Saturday Morning Farmer's Market*. She takes in a deep breath and braces for what comes next.

forty-five

EMILY WALKS through the farmer's market, her silk scarf re-wrapped around her head. Her eyes search the booths for any sign of Sarah's. She almost misses them, her gaze sweeping over an almost bare table with only a handful of painted ceramic pieces. Emily watches as Sarah seems to finish a sale. Liam wraps the piece with gentle hands. Emily watches the interaction between Sarah and her customer. The two talk like old friends.

"I hope Jack enjoys his new bowl!" Sarah says to the customer as she hands him his wrapped purchase.

Liam notices her first.

"Momma! Momma! It's Emily!"

Sarah looks up and sees her. "Hey! You made it."

"Hi." Emily approaches the booth. "Uh, do you know him? Who's Jack?"

"Oh, no. Just a customer. Jack's his dog, a Jack Russell. He was purchasing a new dog bowl for him. One of my favs, actually. I'm glad it found a home."

"But he's just a customer. Why were you talking about his dog?"

"Just to talk."

"So, like a marketing strategy?"

Sarah shakes her head. "Not all human interactions are transactional. Even when they are. He didn't come to buy anything. But we were connecting, so he bought the dog bowl because now he has a little memento to remind him of the human experience he had *that one day at the market*. Life's about collecting little moments. Not strategy."

Emily thinks on the comment as she absorbs the words, a perspective she's never considered. "So, you like talking to strangers?"

Sarah chuckles. "The more we reach out, the less strange the world becomes."

"Hmmm..." Emily says.

Sarah changes the subject. "How was the mimosa brunch?"

Emily's eyes well at the memory, and her chin quivers slightly.

"What happened?" Sarah says as concern washes over her face.

Emily's eyes dart over to Liam. He's too close.

Sarah recognizes the signal. "Baby boy, can you go get us some popcorn from Julie?" Sarah says as she hands Liam a five-dollar bill.

"Yes!" Liam says and jets off.

Sarah refocuses on Emily..

"He's sleeping with her," Emily whispers.

"WHAT!" Sarah shouts, louder than she wanted to. "Your husband and *best friend?*"

Emily nods with a teary smile.

"Oh, no way! Are you gonna fight her? Can I?"

Emily laughs out loud. "Well, actually..."

"What? You fought her? At brunch!" An exuberant energy laces Sarah's voice like she's watching a live sporting event and getting riled up with the rest of the crowd.

"Oh my god, guuurl! I don't even know this chick and I wish I could have seen that!"

"Her boob popped out of her dress!"

"Stop! Ha! What a floozie!"

The women can't help themselves. The laughter grows stronger and they attract attention. They don't care; they collect the moment.

But Emily's smile vanishes when she remembers why she's there—this is supposed to be goodbye.

"Um, wow," Emily says as she prepares herself. "Listen, I actually wanted to talk to you about something."

"What's up?"

"Things are getting crazy again at work, and I've really gotta get on it with the fall product lineup. I've enjoyed spending time with you, but unfortunately, I'll be fairly busy coming up."

"Oh…" Sarah says, disappointed and confused.

"You'll still have a car every morning and afternoon for Liam, and The Daily Grind is so moved by your story, we want to offer you anything else you might need. We will still help with your treatments, elective procedures, reconstruction surgery, even groceries, and rent. We want to make sure you're taken care of, so you don't have to do the markets while you're healing."

"What? What are you talking about? Are you trying to buy my silence or something?" Sarah's confusion turns to anger. "Is this about Kyle? Are you gonna go make up with your shit-bag husband, and you want me to keep my mouth shut?"

"No! No, no. Not at all. Say whatever you want. I don't care. Kyle deserves what's coming to him. I just want to help. You've been so kind to…"

"Emily," Sarah says, cutting Emily off. "I've been on my own since I was a kid. You think because you're some rich-chick you can come along and patronize me into eternal servitude for your handouts?"

"Servitude? What are you…"

"I'm not gonna grovel at your feet because you buy my groceries or pay for my boob job when they have to cut this thing out of me."

"Sarah, please, that's not…"

"Just say it, Emily. Own it! You don't wanna be my friend! You never did!"

"That's not true!"

"No, you know what? I'm good. I've always been good, and I don't need you throwing money at me to stay good." Sarah has an anxious urge to leave, get out, run away. She picks up her wares and packs them into their boxes—tearing down the display.

Emily's eyes tear. "Let me help you, please." Emily reaches out for a plate.

"You've done enough!" Sarah says and yanks the plate out of Emily's hand. Emily doesn't let go while Sarah's fingers fumble. Emily finally processes, and let's go, but Sarah's hand is no longer there to receive, and the plate crashes to the asphalt beneath them, shattering into small pieces.

Emily gasps. "Oh, no! I'm so sorry!" she says as she bends down and scrambles to pick up the pieces.

Sarah bends down next to her. "Just stop, Emily. Go. I don't need your help." She says, refusing to look back at Emily.

Emily gulps at the tightness in her throat. There's nothing left to say.

Liam comes back with a giant plastic bag of kettle corn.

"Momma! Julie gave me the big bag!"

Both women stare back at one another. One angry, one sad, and both afraid. Liam's eyes go back and forth as he watches them both huddled on the ground around broken pieces of ceramic.

"Oh..." Liam whispers as he steps behind the booth and sits on the floor with his popcorn bag.

"I'm sorry, Sarah," Emily whimpers, standing up. "I am... so sorry."

Sarah crosses her arms over her chest and watches Emily turn and walk away.

forty-six

EMILY'S adorned dining room holds candles and celebratory balloons. An expensive floral centerpiece rests in the middle of the ornate table. Kyle stands at the table's head, color-coordinated to match the decor, and holds three-dozen long-stemmed red roses. Next to him is Helen, also coordinated with the decor, holds a bottle of Vevue champagne.

Kyle's bored expression doesn't fool Helen.

"Straighten out that face or I will!" Helen commands.

Kyle snaps to attention and forces a smile.

"You've made this hard enough for me already. We can't afford any mistakes tonight."

"Yes, Ms. Helen. Thank you for the opportunity…"

Helen rolls her eyes with contempt. Kyle doesn't bother finishing his sentence.

The front door jiggles and Kyle and Helen stiffen, ready to put on the show. They greet Emily as she enters with warm smiles she knows aren't real. Nothing in this life is.

"Darling!" Helen says as she walks toward her and presents her with the bottle.

"Sweetheart!" Kyle follows with the same smile, like they've all just walked into a cocktail party.

Kyle hands her the roses. Emily accepts the champagne, out of obligation and without feeling grateful, only weighed down by the gestures.

"Uh... It's not six yet. I thought I had time to..."

"Of course, of course, dear," Helen says.

Dana walks in from nowhere, takes the roses and champagne from Emily's hands with a smile.

"Dana will put these in water for you," Helen says. "Go freshen up and we'll see you in the dining room for champagne." Helen smiles widely, the same way she smiles at her shareholders.

* * *

Emily, Helen, and Kyle sit at the dining room table and eat in quiet. The polite scratches of fork and knife on the china are the only background noise. Emily bites into her filet minion and sips champagne. She keeps her eyes averted from Kyle's gaze.

The air conditioner kicks on, so loud in the silence.

"Wow, we should probably get that looked at, huh, babe?" Kyle says with a nervous chuckle.

Emily shrugs but doesn't look up from her plate. "Yeah, I guess."

"This filet is magnificent, Ms. Helen. My compliments to the menu planner."

"Thank you, Kyle," Helen says, "but it wasn't me. Adrian truly spoils me when I ask for an occasion on a whim. We're so lucky to be able to afford such modern luxuries as assistants and private chefs. Wouldn't you agree, Emily?"

Emily rolls her eyes.

"Emily," Helen commands her daughter's attention.

Emily looks up from her plate, past Kyle, and straight at her mother. "Yes, mother?"

"Your husband has been so gracious to join us tonight. Isn't that nice?"

"Gracious?" Emily laughs. "You're kidding, right?"

Helen crosses her arms, annoyed, but is unwilling to shout over the unnatural laughter. Kyle slumps his shoulders and hangs his head in shame.

"Make her stop...." Kyle grumbles, his face flushed red in response to Emily's cackling.

"Emily," Helen says to calm Emily, but it doesn't work.

"Stop." Kyle raises his voice to be heard.

"Gracious?" Emily can't stop herself. "For listening to daddy and coming home like a good little boy?" Emily sways, running her hands over the scarf covering her head.

"Stop it!" Kyle stands, his face red like the lobster shell that rests on his plate. "Stop it! Stop laughing at me!" Kyle screams and brings his fist down hard on the table. The dishes shudder, and Helen and Emily jump in their chairs. Emily covers her mouth.

Kyle stays silent, chest heaving, until he collects himself. He wipes his mouth with his silk napkin. "I'll settle into the guest room for now. Thank you for dinner, Ms. Helen. Goodnight, sweetheart," Kyle says before he trots out of the room.

Emily stifles a laugh, but can't hold back a small snicker.

"Emily!" Helen corrects her in a harsh whisper.

"What? I think that went well," Emily says with unadulterated sarcasm.

"Enough. Tonight was supposed to be about reconciliation, not humiliating him because he's a man."

Emily scoffs. "Why do you always talk about *men* like they can't help themselves? Like we owe them some kind of pass because what's between their legs makes them monsters?"

"Emily, it's not their... that makes them monsters. It's the world they've built for themselves and the mere crumbs they've set aside for us. This is their world and if you want a bigger piece of it, make them feel like they have control."

"He's the one who cheated on me! I'm not reconciling anything. That wasn't part of the deal."

"It absolutely was! You think you can pull off a sham marriage for the rest of your life?"

Emily shrugs like a disrespectful teenager. "Can't be that hard. You did it."

Helen stands. "Your father was a wonderful man!"

"Oh, please. You only put up with one another because he gave you money for the coffee shop."

"Exactly! That's life, Emily! Relationships are transactional. When are you going to grow up to realize that?"

Emily is silenced. Her head swirls with the conversation she had with Sarah at the farmer's market. *Human interactions aren't all transactional.* It was a perspective she felt her mother could benefit from, but would never allow herself to hear.

Helen rubs her temples, trying to destress. "Oh, Emily... I'm leaving. Tonight was a disaster, but at least he's home. If you can stomach it, go in there and be a wife. He'll forgive you, if you at least give him that."

Emily doesn't respond in words, but shakes her head. Her lips and nose curl and she squints, disgusted at the idea of having to earn Kyle's forgiveness.

"See you at the office," Helen says, and leaves. The walk from the dining room to the front door interspersed with her heels clicking on the floor.

forty-seven

EMILY SITS in her office chair behind her desk. Her body is smaller now against the tall chair back, her silk scarf seems to take up more of her head, and her eyes have sunk into their sockets. Months of chemo and elective cancer therapies have ravaged her, despite the supplements, tonics, and mental exercises she'd invested in that promised relief, an easier recovery, or fewer symptoms. None of it worked in hiding what cancer did to her, evidenced by a drastic weight loss, lack of energy, and a brain fog that took over most of her days now. Emily spent the last two months of her treatment plan opting for complementary therapies because it was an excuse to get out of the house, ignore her husband, or keep herself distracted from her aggressive and lonely treatment schedule without Sarah.

Sarah had stopped coming to the support group. Emily hadn't seen her since the day at the farmer's market. She knew through the grapevine that Sarah's treatments were continuing, which meant Sarah was still being supported by The Daily Grind and Helen was keeping up her side of their deal. As long as Sarah was being taken care of, Emily would keep up hers, and wouldn't reach out. The last two months were long, quiet, and difficult. But today was going to be a good day, because it was the day her doctor would call her to tell her how her most recent scans went. Today she would find out if this would be the end of her cancer journey, and she hoped against her anxiety, it would be.

Emily taps her knee as anxious energy takes over her body. The office phone rings. "Yes?" she answers.

"I have Doctor Stevens on line one."

"Put him through, please. Thank you."

The line clicks over.

"Hello, Doctor Stevens?" Emily announces herself.

"Well, Emily! We have good news for you today," Doctor Stevens says.

"You do?"

"This is always the best part of my job. It seems our treatment plan was a success! Your cancer is undetectable. Congratulations, Emily. Your cancer is in remission."

Emily's mouth opens. She can't believe it. "Oh, my god! I'm cancer free!"

The doctor offers a polite laugh. "Well, we don't call it that anymore. You'll still need to come in for regular checkups, and to prevent a recurrence, we will need to continue a treatment plan, but you shouldn't experience chemo symptoms in the same way you have been. This will be a lighter treatment to ward off any future cancer. But, today, you get to celebrate."

"Thank you, Doctor Stevens! Thank you so much!" Emily laughs out loud and slams the receiver down, too excited to care about manners. She shakes her head and dances in her chair. A celebration for only her.

* * *

Sarah works alone on her patio. The rhythmic turn of her clay-caked turntable beneath her gray stained hands offers a meditative ambiance. A distraction from the yellowing of her skin, her sinking cheekbones, and the sickness of her soul highlighted by the glow of the afternoon sun.

Her phone rings. She stops her foot pedal, wipes clay from her hands, and answers.

"Hello?"

"Hi, Ms. Kenneth. This is the reception from the Breast Health Center."

"Hi, yes. My scans? Did they come back?" Sarah manages a weak smile for no one but herself. Hope of a positive result bubbles inside her.

"Uh, yes, but unfortunately, I'm not allowed to discuss results. I'm calling because the doctor would like to get you in right away for a new treatment plan and will discuss the results with you at the same time. Can you come in this afternoon?"

Sarah lets out a defeated sigh. It's the same phone call she's had before, and she knows where this road leads. "Like today? That bad, huh?" Sarah titters.

"The sooner the better, Ms. Kenneth."

"Um, okay, well, what time?"

"The doctor has set time aside for you now. We'll see you shortly."

"Okay, thanks."

Sarah clicks off the line. She covers her eyes and lets out a frustrated growl, which turns into a scream.

forty-eight

THE WEEKLY BREAST cancer support group meets again in its usual place. The chairs form a circle, and women of various ages and stages of disease fill the seats and help themselves to the day's offerings from The Daily Grind's donated coffee buffet table. Cheryl smiles as she greets her attendees.

"Hello, Anna, how are you?" Cheryl says to Anna, who holds a plate of coffee cake. "Got your goodies? Did you try the new tea they brought today?"

"New tea? Oh no, I didn't see that. Where?"

Cheryl guides Anna back to the table, a wide and excited smile on her face.

Emily waves hellos and politely nods as she shuffles to her seat. She's greeted back with wide smiles and big waves—the women of the group have grown to appreciate the coffee reprieve as a welcome, albeit short, relief from their diagnosis. She sees Sarah, already there, and, huh? Sarah's here? Emily wonders why Sarah's there, when she hasn't attended the group in months. The thought leaves her as she's overcome by a happiness at seeing her face again. It's been a long time, and she looks different. Tired, ill, and beaten down. So does Emily, although it's different for her as she nurses the hope of her remission. Sarah's shoulders stay weighted down, and hopeless.

The women notice each other and offer an awkward smile. It's been enough time to let anger subside, but not enough time to repair the relationship—not that it's allowed. Emily understands her instructions and the stakes. She tells herself this is what's best for both of them.

Today is a special day at group. It's the day Emily announces her treatment is over, her cancer in remission, and the Breast Cancer support campaign offered by The Daily Grind is coming to a close. This will be Emily's last support group meeting and she's secretly happy Sarah is here to see it and hear the announcement. She wonders if Sarah will feel proud of her, happy for her, or anything at all. The photographer, sent to commemorate the occasion and document Emily's announcement to the group, follows her in.

Emily takes her seat, and Cheryl begins the meeting.

"Okay, let's get started, everyone. Thank you all for being here, as always. Who'd like to share today?" Cheryl says.

Emily is a ball of nerves. Her hand shoots up like an anxious teacher's pet begging to answer the question posed to class.

"Emily, please. How'd your scans go this week?"

Excitement pours out of Emily as she speaks. The click and flash of her entourage acts as her soundtrack.

"Hi! Sorry. I'm so excited! Yes. My scans came back, and…. I'm in remission! Ahhhh!"

The room erupts in applause, all the strength these women have, forced into celebration of her news.

Click, flash, click, flash.

Emily looks across the room and watches Sarah's face. As the world around her celebrates, Sarah's face remains dim, unchanged, and unaffected, except for a micro-curl of her lips into a smile with a subtleness rivaled only by the Mona Lisa. Was she smiling? Or wasn't she? Emily racks her brain, desperate to read Sarah's expression, but can't.

"Congratulations. Emily. That's wonderful news," Cheryl exclaims. "What's the first thing you're going to do to celebrate?"

"Um, gosh... I hadn't thought about that. I'm sure my husband has something special planned for me back at home. We'll see!" Emily says as she holds onto the public perception she's here to defend.

Her audience offers polite nods and smiles.

"Um, so, as you can probably guess, because of this, today will be my last meeting."

Hushed whispers peek through the silence as the women gossip among each other.

"Now, ladies. Hold on, let's give Emily a change to explain," Cheryl gestures for everyone to pay attention.

The reaction surprises Emily. "Oh, I uh... I mean I'm done. This was only ever supposed to be a three-month program. It's over now."

Cheryl quiets the reignited whispering again with her arms.

"Emily, remission is an exciting time. We're all so happy for you. But, it's still recommended you attend group when you're able. It's easy to forget what a cancer diagnosis means in the long term once you disconnect from the support group."

"Oh, well, of course I'll still send goodies. The Daily Grind fully intends to keep supporting the group." Emily looks out over the circle of filled chairs, absorbs their shock, offense, and shaking heads.

"While we appreciate the donations, our concern is you, Emily. Not the free coffee," Cheryl corrects Emily's misstep.

"Sorry. I didn't mean to..." Emily shakes off her embarrassment, reinstalls her smile, and moves on. "Well, anyway. Thank you all for the support. It's been wonderful getting to know all of you. I'm so happy to be cancer free! Uhhh... in remission. Sorry, remission."

"Well, best of luck to you, Emily. We hope to see you again regularly, regardless. Anyone else like to share?" Cheryl searches the room. "Sarah, you had scans this week too, yes? How'd they go?"

Sarah half smiles and wipes a single tear off her cheek.

"Congratulations, Emily. I'm so happy for you," Sarah says first.

Emily mouths a thank you with a smile, only because the lump in her throat stops her from being able to speak. She's moved by Sarah's words, simple, but profound, even if only to her.

"Uh..." Sarah goes on. "Hi. Thanks. Yeah, scans... So, I guess the original plan was that after the first round of chemo, the past three months, the tumor was supposed to shrink, then do the surgery. But, instead, the tumor broke off into little pieces and spread into the lymph nodes. So, it's metasick? Metasta...?"

"It's metastasized!" Emily gasps.

"That's it," Sarah says.

"Emily, we try not to interrupt," Cheryl says.

"What do you mean? How is that possible?" Emily panics.

"Emily, please give space for..."

"You've been at every single treatment. You did everything you were supposed to do!" Emily says, her voice rising in anger. "I just... I don't understand. You were supposed to get better. We were both getting better..."

Sarah stands from her chair and rushes to Emily's side. She pulls Emily out of her seat and in for a hug. Emily calms from her anxious outburst, breaking into soft sobs. The women hold each other up as they cry into each other's shoulders.

* * *

Emily and Sarah sit together in the hallway outside the support group. The other women shuffle out and wave goodbye. The two remain silent until Cheryl closes up the meeting room and shuts the door behind her.

"You girls need anything before I head out?" Cheryl asks.

"No, thank you. We're fine," Sarah says.

Cheryl nods a goodbye and leaves them.

"I've been reading about metastatic breast cancer. It's absolutely horrible." Emily says.

"Yeah, my doctor didn't seem too optimistic. But I did an MRI today."

"But if it's just the lymph nodes, that's only stage three. Can't they just hurry and take the whole breast?"

Sarah shakes her head. "I was already stage three, grade three poorly-differentiated, because of the size of the tumor. It's stage four now. The MRI will show if there's more. Or, not *if*, but *where*."

"You were already stage 3! Why didn't you tell me?"

"I don't know! Because I'm twenty-seven years old. None of this even makes sense! How was I supposed to know to take this seriously? I still eat chicken nuggets and EasyMac with my kid!"

"Ugh, Sarah. I never would have had you drinking champagne with me if I knew you were stage three!"

Sarah waves her off. "Wouldn't have mattered."

"Maybe it would have. You don't know."

"Yeah, well, neither do you. All we know is what's in front of us, and champagne in front of me equals, yes."

The women force a smile, despite the tension.

"Oh, my doctor told me about a trial I might be eligible for. Some new drug that uses the body's own immune system to kill off the cancer cells? I don't know."

"Oh! That's great! The Daily Grind is gonna cover the cost too, as promised."

Sarah shrugs. "Well, first I have to quality. Depends on the MRI and what else we're dealing with. He said something about cancerous fluid in the lungs? If there's that, then the trial is a no-go."

"Oh, okay. Well, how's your breathing been lately? Can you take a deep breath? Take a deep breath with me."

Emily sucks in a hard breath. Sarah follows. The women sit together, deep-breathing as if the diagnostic test they just made up holds any scientific water.

"Well?" Emily says. "How does it feel?"

Sarah takes one last deep breath. "Yeah, I mean. I can do it. Is this normal?" She deep-breathes again.

"Yeah. I think so, yeah!"

Emily and Sarah both smile at the prospect of what this could mean—naivety offering hope in an otherwise helpless moment.

"Have you told Liam?" Emily asks.

"I don't know how." Her eyes well and her voice weakens. "He's... he's just a baby... and I'm all he's got."

Emily leans into Sarah for another hug. "I'm gonna help you figure this out, okay?"

Sarah collects herself and pulls back. She wipes her eyes and nose. "I don't need your pity just cause my scans didn't go as well as yours did."

Emily sighs with deep regret. "Sarah, it's not like that. I'm thrilled you came to group tonight because seeing you helped me realize how bad I messed up. You were my friend and I let my mom get to me. I'm sorry. I never should have listened to her. I..." Emily wants to say her next words, but it's hard. Being vulnerable was never a skill set she learned, because it wasn't ever supposed to be a necessary part of the life she led. "I miss you! Okay? There I said it. I miss being your friend."

"Oh my god, you're such a weirdo!" Sarah laughs out loud and playfully smacks her on the shoulder.

Emily laughs. The women embrace. All forgiven.

"Ms. Cassius." A deep voice interrupts the moment.

A black suit stands at the open exit door. "It's time to get you home. Your husband and mother have called for you."

"I'll come when I'm ready." Emily barks at her driver. Her face softens again, and she addresses Sarah. "I'll text you later. Do you have a way home?"

"Yeah, I'm good. I drove. Good luck!" Sarah says as she also picks herself up from their cuddle puddle.

forty-nine

EMILY ENTERS HER HOME, exhausted and emotional, yet lifted.

"Surprise!" Helen says, startling Emily.

Emily takes a breath and reexamines her surroundings. Helen and Kyle stand in the living room with a bottle of champagne and roses. Emily rolls her eyes at the familiar scene.

"Ugh, champagne and roses again? What'd you do this time, Kyle?"

"Emily, manners," Helen interjects. "We are celebrating your being cancer free. We knew you would pull through, darling, and we're so happy to finally put this all behind us."

Kyle clears his throat, smiles, and steps forward. "Yes. Congratulations, sweetheart." He presents her with the roses.

Emily pushes past him and ignores the gesture. Kyle swallows the rejection. He follows her into the dining room. Beautifully aesthetic settings, once again, decorate the space.

"Oh, lookie-here. Another romantic dinner. How repetitive and mundane." Emily snickers.

"Emily, please. We're trying to celebrate you," Helen snaps at Emily.

"I don't need another manufactured celebration, Mom. What do you both want, really? Let's just get to it, okay?"

Helen takes a moment to gauge her daughter's sincerity. "Fine. Sit."

Emily rolls her eyes and sits across from Helen at the candle-lit table. Kyle sits next to her. Emily retreats, creating a distance between the two of them. She sips at a glass of champagne for comfort.

"First and foremost, our sincerest congratulations. We are truly happy to be done with this. The campaign went wonderfully. Our latest poll reveals not only that the shareholders would trust you as the company leader, but they also sympathize with your diagnosis. And now, because you're cured, we expect them to only grow in their support of you, knowing you are no longer sick. We've achieved our objective. Well done," Helen says.

Emily listens, her arms crossed. "Great. Whatever," she says as she dismisses the accolades. This isn't about Emily being cancer free, it's about the shareholders, the company, about always protecting the money—the same old tune.

"Now," Helen says, "I've spoken with your doctor, and we've discussed your fertility. A pregnancy isn't advisable yet, but..."

"A pregnancy?" Emily almost chokes on her saliva. "You're joking!"

"What's there to joke about, Emily? The question of your fertility was what started this whole mess to begin with. Now this has been dealt with, and we can get back to planning your future."

"I am *not* getting pregnant!" Emily scoffs and points. "By him? Absolutely not!"

"We had already figured you might feel that way, which is why we've come up with a solution," Helen says.

Emily shakes her head, already in disagreement about whatever it is they've connived together.

"Go ahead, Kyle."

"Thank you, Ms. Helen. Yes. We're so glad you're better, sweetheart. Truly. We can get back to what we were, and I think moving forward with our family can be healing for us, and what we've both been through."

"What we've been through? Yeah, okay."

"Yes, Emily. We. Your diagnosis was hard on me, too. It forced me into the arms of another woman! Do you actually believe I wanted to do that to you, to us? I had no choice!"

"My god. They really are as stupid as you paint them to be, Mom," Emily says.

"Pitiful creatures. I've always said so," Helen says.

"I'm right HERE!" Kyle yells.

"Alright, alright. Enough of that," Helen commands control of the room. "Kyle, continue."

Kyle shakes it off. "Anyway, what your mother and I had discussed was an egg donor and surrogate."

"Oh, wonderful, Kyle, yes..." Emily's voice is thick with sarcasm. "And did you have someone in mind already?"

"Yes, actually..." Kyle clears his throat. "Tiffany has offered to..."

"There it is! Yup!" Emily loses it. "Little Ms. Back-stabber wants to weasel her way back in there, huh? Well... she can have you, because I am DONE!"

"Emily. Control yourself," Helen commands, to no avail.

"Why do I have to have kids with him? Why do I have to be married? This is all so ridiculous!"

"I'm just trying to think of solutions!" Kyle screams.

"BECAUSE YOU NEED AN HEIR!" Helen shouts.

"A what?" Emily says in complete shock. "Is this the dark ages? Are we worried about protecting a kingdom or something?"

"Yes! Yes, Emily. We are protecting the empire we have built, and you will protect the sacrifice I made to do so."

"Sacrifice? Right, because you had to sleep with a rich, disgusting old man to get ahead in life and you've never forgiven yourself for it!"

Helen's hand raises above her head, and before Emily can even process it, the hand comes crashing into her face. The shock mixed with the pain of the slap is visceral. Kyle's mouth falls open.

Helen points a finger in Emily's face.

"The Daily Grind is merging with the coffee table book industry in a way that's never been done before! Every other coffee shop that thinks they can compete with us won't be able to! We're cornering the market of intellectual coffee drinkers and this is how we grow our market share. A baby brings a wholesome message to the new marketing campaign. This is the plan, and you will comply."

The room falls silent as Emily soaks in the new information.

"I... I..." Emily stammers as she re-finds her voice and processes her shock. "I want a divorce. I want my own life! I'm done living yours, mother! I want out!"

"Emily!" Helen shouts.

The three of them yell over each other until a thunder of voices clouds the room.

"You want out?" A final roar from Helen regains attention.

Emily's eyes squint, and her neck recoils as she braces for another hit.

"Fine!" Helen says. "But if you'll not be married anymore, you'll not live in my house."

"This is *my house!*" Emily says.

"That I bought as a wedding present! I own the trust! The Daily Grind, me! You will follow this plan, you *WILL BE* a mother, or you *WILL BE OUT!*"

Helen finishes her champagne in one giant gulp, and slams the glass on the table. Without another word, she stomps out. The front door slams behind her.

Kyle studies Emily and waits for a response. "It's what's expected of us, Emily..."

"Expected of us?" Emily scoffs. "There's more to life than following *their rules*, Kyle!" Her clarity is stronger than ever, her face turns toward Kyle, for the first time, with pity. "You and I never had a chance. Don't you see that? They stuck us together when we were kids, and it was *expected of us* to fall in line. You don't love me. You don't want a family with me. And neither do I. What mommy and daddy want doesn't have to be what we settle for. Don't... don't you want more?" Emily's eyes fill with water.

Kyle's eyes narrow and his face becomes pensive as he contemplates her question, but he can't face the truth. Emily cries, because she knows he can't, and this is truly goodbye.

fifty

EMILY TRAPS herself in her bedroom. The salt of dried tears streak her face and make organic lines down her cheeks. She's unsure what to do with herself, and restless. The choice is simple, go to bed, wake up tomorrow, go to work, and pretend like nothing happened as she moves forward with her mother's demands, or, pack her things and leave her home, her life, and every comfort and luxury attached to it. The choice is simple, yet not clear. She paces her room and mulls in her thoughts when her phone chimes with a notification. A smile bends the lines of her dried tears.

"Hey! We gotta celebrate you! Officially in remission!"

Another message comes through—a picture of a sickly Sarah pouring sparkling wine into her pink cancer mug.

Emily responds with a text. "You're not supposed to be drinking!"

"I'm not. I'm not. This one's for you. Bring your cup so we can cheer. Promise I won't have any. But you deserve a sip."

Emily feels reassured, then excited. She rushes out of her bedroom and into the kitchen. Dana is doing the dishes and cleaning up the evening's dinner.

"Hi, Dana. Have you seen my pink coffee cup?"

"Yes, Ms. Emily." Dana stops her work to help Emily find the cup. She opens a cabinet and retrieves the mug.

"Thank you! Thank you!" Emily takes the mug and runs out. The front door slams as she leaves.

* * *

Emily knocks on Sarah's apartment door.

"Come in!" Sarah answers from behind the door. Emily opens the door and is met with...

"SURPRISE!" Liam and Sarah shout as they blow party horns and set off poppers! The space is decorated with breath-filled balloons scattering the floor, streamers taped to the walls, confetti everywhere, and party hats.

"Congratulations, Aunt Emily!" Liam exclaims as he brings a party hat over to Emily. He squeezes her body in a warm hug.

"Aww, thanks, buddy." The gesture brings Emily to tears, but she remembers Sarah is ill, and this is too much. "Sarah, what is all this? You should be resting."

"Would you relax. I'm gonna rest, later. Right now, we party!" Sarah fist pumps the air and joins in on the hug.

"But you're ill..."

"Nope, nope, nope. None of that. You're free! Cancer ain't got you no more. You ready to do this?"

"Do what?" Emily says, confused.

"Did you never look inside your cup?"

"What?"

"Look!" Sarah says, imploring Emily to comply as she points at the inside of the cup.

Emily looks, and can't believe she never noticed it before. On the inside bottom of the cup, in white letters that contrast the pink hue, a message reads: *I get to smash this cup when I'm cancer free.*

Emily gasps. "Oh, my god!"

"Let's go girl."

* * *

Emily, Sarah, and Liam stand outside the apartment door on the concrete sidewalk. Emily holds her empty coffee mug in her hands.

"Smash! Smash! Smash!" Sarah encourages.

Liam joins in, "Smash, smash, smash…"

The chant grows louder as Emily gets ready. She lifts the cup over her head, she shrieks…

"Smash, SMASH, SMASH!" Their feet stomp out a rhythm as they clap, getting louder still. "SMASH! SMASH! SMASH!"

Emily brings her arm down hard, releases the cup, and watches as it crashes against the concrete and explodes into broken bits. Ceramic pieces scatter on the ground, near and far.

The three jump up and down in celebration! They scream, they hug, they cry—a victory dance all their own.

fifty-one

EMILY AND SARAH CUDDLE on the couch and share a cup of hot tea out of Sarah's still intact pink coffee mug. Liam's snores are audible despite the tapestry. The women giggle as they whisper.

"I can't with those little noises. So cute!" Emily says.

"I know. It's even more adorable when he gets to talking in his sleep."

They giggle, but this time, it is not out of enthusiasm, as the mood turns somber.

"Hey? You okay?" Sarah asks.

"I'm so glad you called me over tonight. I needed a minute."

"What's up?"

Emily shakes her head as tension builds in her head. "Ugh! My mom, Kyle. She's not thrilled with me right now, so I don't know what's gonna happen as far as the support we've been providing."

"Huh? What are you talking about?"

"The payments for your treatments... the chauffer?" Emily says with a puzzled brow.

"Yeah, I mean..." Sarah doesn't quite know how to respond. "We appreciated that, that one time a few months back. But we haven't spoken in so long. Liam and I both qualify for the public bus program. Schools and Health First. It takes him to school and me to treatment. Pretty cool program actually..."

"Wait... WHAT?" Emily fumes with anger, not meaning to cut Sarah off.

"Sorry. Why haven't you been using my driver? And how are you paying for treatments?"

"Uhhhh... there hasn't been a driver. And I didn't know you were still offering. After the farmer's market, that was the last I heard from you. I stopped going to group because my insurance kicked in, and that's how I've been paying for it. Good ol' fashion, social welfare." Sarah laughs.

Emily realizes her mother has tricked her and the deal they made was a sham. Her mother had never intended to follow through, because it wasn't necessary to get Emily to follow through. "Wow," she says out loud and laughs at herself. "I'm such an idiot."

"Why is that funny?"

"She's so fake. SO FAKE!" Emily laughs harder. "I can't believe she actually lied to me about something so big! It's like she knew all along. She didn't have to keep up her end of the deal. She just had to make me believe she would. And I fell for it! I fell for all of it!" Emily's emotions are a rollercoaster as she twists and turns in her own thoughts, trying to make sense of her life under the rule of her mother.

Sarah watches Emily spiral. She offers a soft hand on her back, a gift of comfort through physical touch.

Emily's shame takes over. "Oh, god. And I just left you! And all for what? Ugh. I can't believe this." Emily sinks into the couch and into Sarah's touch.

"Who are we talking about now?"

"My mom! She wants me to get back to everything like none of this ever happened. Like I never got cancer, like Kyle never had an affair, like I never met you. And like she never made promises she never intended to keep... I just... I don't know if I can live like this. It's all fake." Emily laughs through her tears. "And you know the funny thing? Now she's telling me if I don't follow her plan, I'm out! Can you believe that? I don't want this life anymore. But what else am I supposed to do?"

"Eh, that's an easy one."

"What do you mean?"

"You just said you don't want this life. SO... why would it matter if she kicked you out of it? She's doing you a favor."

Emily laughs again, this time with a frantic energy. Her emotional outpouring has her manic one moment, depressed the next, and pulling her in every other opposite direction throughout. "Sarah, you don't understand." Her voice and nose raise in contempt.

"I don't. Okay. But I know a thing or two about having everything ripped away, starting from nothing, and building out the life *I chose for myself.*"

The statement sinks into Emily, and she's humbled again. "I'm sorry, I didn't mean..."

Sarah shrugs. "All good, us peasants don't know anything, anyway."

"Oh, god. I'm so sorry, Sarah."

Sarah holds up a hand and gestures for Emily to stop with her pleas. The mood is tense. "You know what I think, Emily. I think you're scared. You're scared to take what you want. Yeah, it might be hard. Nothing worth having isn't. That's life. You fight for what you want, for what you love."

Her naivety, the cost of such a privileged life, shames Emily.

"Like the cancer? Do you consider yourself fighting... against your disease?"

Sarah muses for a moment as she considers the question. "No. I'm not fighting cancer. I'm fighting for my life, for my son. The things I love. Cancer happens to be the thing standing in the way of all that. Maybe your mom or your designer bag lifestyle is what's standing in the way of yours?"

Emily soaks in a new revelation. Fighting for what we love is not the same as fighting against what we fear, because love is the absence of fear.

"I'm gonna crash, feel free to crash on the couch." Sarah stands to leave. "Congrats, again. Happy for you."

"Thanks," Emily whispers, lost in thought.

fifty-two

SARAH CLOSES her bedroom door behind her. She collapses onto her bed, but moans in agony as her chest hits the soft surface. She rolls over, her hands holding her left breast in pain. A few deep breaths help her brace through the pain as she waits for it to subside.

A little composed, she reaches for her phone, opens a new text chain, and types a message to Drew.

"You done yet?" Send.

* * *

In a small, but dirtier and dingier apartment, Drew paces the living room with his phone in his hand. He types out messages to Sarah, shaking his head, "Na, na, na..." He deletes it, and tries again...

"Yo, I miss you..." Delete, he sucks his teeth and shakes his head.

"Can I see my son?" Pfft, no, delete.

"Can we talk?" Ugh... delete.

Drew falls onto his couch, defeated and lost. His phone pings with a message from Sarah. His fingers stumble on the screen as he rushes to open the text.

"You done yet?" From Sarah. Drew smiles. He types a response.

* * *

Sarah holds her phone close to her face as she stares at the message chain to Drew.

"Sup, shawty! Knew you couldn't stay gone for long!"

Sarah scoffs, rolls her eyes, and dials Drew on the phone. The line trills.

"What up, what up!" Drew's overconfident voice answers the call.

"I couldn't stay gone? Me? You're lucky I'm even calling you right now!"

Drew restrains himself to a calm chuckle. "I know, I know. I'm just playin' with you. Come on, girl."

"You better quit playin' cause this ain't a game."

"I know. I gotchu. I's just excited to hear from you. I'm sorry. I miss you and little man."

"Mmm-hmm. Whatever." The tone shifts into playful as Sarah lets her guard down a bit.

"How are you? Can I come through? Come on?"

Sarah chuckles. "Listen, I called you because…" Sarah chokes on her words. "I got something going on tomorrow, and, in case I don't wake up, I need you to know that…."

"Whoa, whoa, whoa… what are you talking about?"

Sarah sniffles through her response. "Um, they're taking me into surgery tomorrow…" Her voice pitches as her throat closes. She coughs to open it again. "I'm scared." She dissolves into soft cries.

Drew breathes out a captured breath. "Yo." His voice is sullen and soft. "You got this, ma. I know you can do this." He forces a smile she can't see, to keep himself from crying with her. "Ain't nuthin ever come up for us we couldn't handle. Cancer ain't no thang we haven't seen before. It's gonna be different this time. I promise you. It has to be." The reassurance is for him as much as it is for her.

"I'm so afraid to die," Sarah says as she gently weeps. She curls into a ball and hugs her knees with one arm while she holds her phone to her ear with the other.

Drew clears his throat, coughs, and beats on his chest. His eyes are red and wet. His chest heaves, just once, but he sucks it back in and up. "You are not gonna die. Okay!" He deepens his voice, a defense mechanism, like how a person caught in the woods with a bear tries to make themselves bigger and scarier than the bear. "It's gonna be different this time. Okay?"

Sarah doesn't answer, but just continues to cry.

"Sar, please." Drew says, unable to stave off his fear much longer. "Please don't cry, Sar." He sniffles up his emotions and wipes the wetness from his eyes. "Ima be right with you tomorrow. Okay? What time you gotta be there?"

"After Liam's school."

"I'll be there. Okay, Sar. Ima be there." He takes a deep breath in. "And Sar…"

"Yeah?"

"I'm sorry, okay? I'm sorry for everything. I'm sorry for being such a screwup. I shoulda been there before. For you and Liam when we lost Ms. Linda. For you when you CPS came. You were scared, and I messed everything up. I scared you and our son. And… I don't know why I'm like this. But I don't wanna be." Drew breaks down into muted sobs. He holds his breath to stop them, but some escape anyway.

Sarah wipes her tears and lets out a deep breath. "I'll see you tomorrow. I love you." Sarah clicks off the line and cuddles herself to sleep.

fifty-three

THE MORNING SUN shines a beam of light through the sliding glass window of Sarah's apartment onto Emily's face, asleep on the couch. She stirs and rolls over as the light touches her.

"Morning!" Liam's voice startles her, too close to her head. Emily jumps up, and there he is, two inches from where she slept.

"Oh! Hi, Liam. Morning."

"Hi," Liam says. He stands still with eyes locked onto her.

Emily squirms and adjusts herself on the couch to sit up. Liam watches her.

"Uhhh, how's school been, buddy?"

"I don't know... school's lame."

"How come? What's going on?"

Liam sits himself on the couch next to Emily. He crosses his arms and keeps his gaze toward the ground.

"Kid thinks he can mess with me."

"Someone's bullying you?" Emily stiffens up with silent rage.

"Yeah..."

"Does your mom know about this?"

"We're working on it." Sarah's head pokes out from the kitchen. A steaming cup of coffee in her hands. She gestures to Liam, pointing her neck and eyes toward the bathroom, telling him there's something else he should be doing right now.

"Ugh!" Liam groans and throws his head back—deeply inconvenienced.

Sarah saunters in from the kitchen.

"Coffee?" Sarah says. She passes the cup to Emily.

"Thanks." Emily accepts with grace.

Sarah sits next to Emily on the couch.

"Nothing for you? Can I get you a cup?" Emily says.

Sarah shakes her head. "Can't. I got surgery after I drop Liam at school."

"Surgery?" Emily shakes the shock out of her expression. "You didn't mention that last night! How are you…"

"I got it. We're good. Drew's coming to the hospital."

"Drew? You're talking again?"

Sarah shrugs. "Since last night, yeah…"

"Um. Okay… Wait. Didn't the last time you saw him… didn't he… attack you? Am I understanding this right? Did he even apologize? How can you just reconcile and forget like that never happened?"

"How could you let your husband move back in with you after he had an affair with your best friend?"

"Hey! That's not fair."

"Emily, I don't have to understand your choices any more than you have to understand mine. Drew and I are family, just like you and your mom are family. And I hope someday you and your mom reconcile, because she's what you get in this world. Drew's what I get. That's all you have to understand."

Emily sighs, "My God, can you, like, stop being profound for two seconds!"

Sarah chuckles. "Cancer's brought it outta me."

The women chortle.

"Is there anything I can help…"

"Nope." Sarah cuts her off.

"Stay as long as you want. Just lock the door when you leave."

Sarah gets up off the couch. She grabs her coat and puts on shoes. Liam comes out from the bedroom, ready for school. Sarah helps him with his backpack and shoes.

"Bye, Aunt Emily!" Liam says, his cheery attitude oblivious to the tension in the room.

Sarah smiles and waves goodbye as the door shuts behind them. Emily sits in quiet reflection on the couch as she sips her warm coffee. The art, the colors, the clutter… Every choice in this space belongs to Sarah, from the furniture to the shoes left in the middle of the entryway. From who she allows to enter, to who she keeps out. It's all hers. This life belongs to her. It's a thought she's had before, but one she can never get used to, because it's such a stark contrast to her own, now more than ever, as she continues to hold on to the lie of what her mother wants her life to be.

Emily thinks hard about her own home, relationships, and life. How none of it belongs to her, how she came close enough to losing all of it, and it wouldn't have mattered, anyway. Cancer could have taken her breath away, and there would have been nothing left because never was there a remnant of her in her own life, anywhere.

She soaks in her thoughts until she concludes and her choice no longer haunts her. She wants her own slice of life, no matter how small or uncomfortable it might be to grow. In that moment, she decides she'd rather give up all her luxuries if only she could make one choice for herself. She wants something to belong to her.

Settled in her thoughts, she takes another sip of her coffee. Her phone rings. It's Mom. She answers.

"Hi, Mom."

"Emily, please tell me you've thought about what I said and have come to your senses. I truly don't have the time to go through the hassle of all this anymore."

"I have thought about it."

"Oh, thank god. Good, then I need you to…"

"And I've decided I don't need anything from you anymore."

"Excuse me?"

"Sell the house. I'm gonna buy my own. Right after I file for divorce."

"Is that so? And where exactly will you get the money to buy a new house? Or hire an attorney? Or, anything, really?"

"Um, from my job, thanks."

"What job? The one I gave you? Hmmm.... Seems like that would be something you still need from me, so we'll have to eliminate that, too. Along with your health insurance. And since you won't be working for The Daily Grind anymore, no need to continue the campaign to help your little cancer friend."

"Oh, you mean the help you said you were giving her to trick me into staying with your little hand-picked-puppet-husband when really she's had no help from us in over TWO MONTHS!"

Helen holds her tongue.

"Oh, didn't think I'd find out about that, did you? Well! I did! You lied to me! You've always lied to me!"

"Enough of this! You want to see what it's like to live on your own? Fine! Go find out what the real world is like with *those people!*"

"Those people? We both got the same disease and they'll put us in the same ground!"

"So be it!"

"Fine!" Emily clicks off the phone with an aggression unmet by the silent tap of the end call button.

"Arrrgghhh!" Emily says, getting in the last word.

* * *

The tires on Emily's G-Wagon rip into her driveway. She stops just short of the fancy front entrance but takes out a planter filled with expensive and well-maintained florals. Emily storms out of the driver's side, her feet land in destroyed earth and broken flowers. She doesn't stop to notice but continues to tear into the front porch, each stomp of her foot louder than the last.

At the front door, she struggles against the key pad as her hands shake with fury. Her fingers miss the correct code. She can't manage it.

"Oh, come on!" Emily says with a growl through gritted teeth.

Her hands tremble as she types in the lock code one more time. Emily rips through her house, collecting her personal effects and things, pulling out the matching sets of her suitcases—Louis Vuitton, Chanel, Gucci. She tosses the Birkin bags from her closet into a pile on the floor. Designer shoes, pants suits, dresses, and jewelry follow. Emily's rage keeps her going as she gathers her most expensive things and stuffs them into suitcases.

Back in the living room, Emily pulls on her luggage, now full and heavier than she'd expected. Her body's still weak, and she's never had to carry her own before. It's not as easy as she's seen it done, but she doesn't relent. Her brow sweats as she heaves and tugs against the baggage, even with four wheels on their bottoms.

She makes it back out to the driveway. One by one, each piece of luggage finds its way to the back of her G-Wagon. But the task still isn't over. Emily takes a breath. She can do this. With her back, she hoists each piece into the trunk while she strains against herself, but she prevails. She takes a step back and smiles as she admires her achievement. Uneven and forced-into-place pieces of her luxury life stuff the capacity of the back of her car.

Emily slams the trunk of her G-Wagon, pleased with herself. She walks with calm confidence back to the front door and takes one last peek inside. The first choice she'd made on her own is to toss, turn, and leave her home in disarray, and it's marvelous. She sucks in a deep breath of air and contemplates what she's about to do. Anxiety washes over her. Is this the right choice?

Emily shakes away the doubt and resolves to follow through with what she's already done. She slams the door, presses the lock button on the keypad, and marches away with her nose up and her shoulders stiff.

fifty-four

EMILY SITS in a cold hospital waiting room. She scrolls on her phone, bites her nails, eats cheese cracker snacks from the vending machine—anything to pass the time. A nurse in scrubs enters the room. Emily perks up and listens to hear her name.

"For Sarah Kenneth," the nurse calls out.

Emily jumps to attention. "Yes, hi. Me."

But she's not the only one.

"Yo. Who are you?" Drew says, barking at Emily.

She sees him for the first time. Tattooed and intimidating. Drew towers over Emily. They both approach the nurse's call.

"Uh, I... I'm Emily. I'm a friend."

"Oh, okay, okay. The rich white chick... So, check it. I'm here. She don't need you. Go home," Drew says, his tone demanding Emily's compliance.

Emily cowers, and her expression begs the nurse for help.

"Hold on, sir, what's your name?" the nurse asks.

"Drew. Puente."

"Uh-huh. And you, miss?"

"Emily Cassius."

"Got it. I have both of you on the list here. You're both entitled to be here."

Drew's face sours, but he relents. A slight gesture of his hands shows the nurse his surrender.

"Okay, well, the surgery went well. Sarah is back in recovery and ready for visitors. You're both free to go in."

"Thank you, ma'am," Drew says.

"Thanks," Emily says, less confident than her counterpart.

Drew takes a step back and motions with his hands for Emily to go ahead, mocking a gentleman's impression. "After you."

Emily walks ahead.

* * *

Emily calculates if she should be the first to go in, or if she should allow Drew. Who would Sarah want to see first? She steps aside, allowing Drew to take charge. He doesn't hesitate and pushes past her. Emily stays back at the door and observes as Drew greets Sarah.

Sarah rests with her eyes closed in a hospital bed. She's wrapped in white bandages around her chest and covered in blankets at the waist. I.V. drips and machines surround her. A heart rate monitor beeps. The fluorescent overhead light brightens the yellow of her skin and casts shadows that flaunt depth in the concave curves of her face. The sight is shocking. Emily holds her hand over her mouth as her eyes take in the visual. For Drew it's different. He looks at Sarah, with soft eyes and a forlorn face, like he doesn't like what he sees, but it's something he's seen before.

"Sup, Sar," Drew says with a quiet voice as he approaches the bed.

He picks up her hand, an I.V. line taped to the skin. He brings her hand up only slightly, and lowers his head, meeting in the middle. His gentle lips kiss the top of her hand, making sure not to disturb the I.V. Sarah smiles and her eyes flutter open.

"Sup," Sarah says in a whisper back to Drew.

Her face squelches in pain—it's too difficult to breathe.

Drew's face knots into concern. He takes a knee and closes the distance between the two of them.

"Yo. Yo, yo. You're good. I'm right here. I'm here," Drew says, his words a knot in the back of his throat as he tries to damn the overflow of his pain.

Sarah closes her eyes and smiles. Drew sniffles back the water that fills his eyes. He drops his head and hides. He shudders as silent tears force their release despite his greatest efforts to keep them contained.

Emily scoots further inside the room but stays a respectful distance back.

Drew hears Emily's movement and stands up, wiping his eyes with his sleeves. He steps aside to allow Emily space to say hello. Emily mouths a *thank you* as she takes his spot at Sarah's bedside.

"Hey," Emily whispers with a sad smile.

Sarah's eyes open halfway. She smiles. "Thank you," Sarah whispers, clenching her jaw in pain.

It hurts Emily to see Sarah hurting, and when she looks at Drew, she recognizes the ache in him as well, and something changes. They have something in common, their love for the woman in the bed before them.

Sarah's eyes close again, and she drifts back to sleep. Drew gives Emily a once over with his eyes. He takes time to consider his thoughts, but it's clear he's thinking about her by the intensity of his eyes as he studies her. It's almost unnerving for Emily as she waits for some kind of reaction, a word, an explosion, anything.

Drew lets out a soft sigh, breaking his stare. At ease, he addresses her with a respect that wasn't there before.

"Yo, sorry about before."

"No, not at all. I'm a stranger, and I'm sure you've heard things about me."

Drew scoffs a laugh. "I got my own record. We're good."

Emily nods. The two understand each other.

"I gotta get little man from school and bring him back here. You got her here for a bit?"

"Yeah, yeah. I'll stay with her. Thanks."

"Cool, cool. Be right back."

Emily sits in the guest chair and watches Sarah sleep. Silent tears roll down her cheeks as her thoughts turn melancholic. Why is it Sarah there in the bed, and not her? Why did circumstance finally bring her a true friend, only to have to watch her slowly fade away? Why is life so cruel and so unfair?

fifty-five

DREW PULLS his vintage Honda with rusted plates and sunburnt paint into the lot of Liam's elementary school, and waits in the car line. He turns off the key. The car settles into silence. Drew's knee bounces with anxiety. He takes in deep breaths. This will be the first time he's seen Liam since his breakdown, and he's apprehensive of how Liam might react.

He doesn't have much time to prepare as the bell rings and children pour out onto the front lawn. Drew scans the crowd for Liam and finds him first. A soft smile comes to his face. Drew has missed his little buddy.

But Liam is too distracted to notice anything but except his bully, who taunts him from several yards away behind a fence. Liam huffs, but keeps walking, until he can't take it anymore.

"I hate you! I HATE YOU!" Liam screams.

Drew watches on tenterhooks, not sure if he should intervene, but tense, waiting to see how this plays out.

Liam rushes at the bully, on the attack.

"No!" Drew says out loud as he jolts into action and hops out of the car.

Liam bangs into the fence and growls. "I hate you! I hate you!" He shakes and thrashes against the fence, letting out all his anger and accidentally cutting his face against a broken link.

The kid takes a few steps back, but only laughs, knowing he's protected by a chain link.

Out of nowhere, Ms. Lucy swoops in and grabs Liam's backpack, pulls him back and away. She plucks Liam away from the conflict and leads him back toward the car pick up lane. Liam is fuming as a stripe of blood gathers on his face from the cut. He hides his anger and faces down as he's pulled further away. In the background, his bully laughs, points, and absorbs no consequences.

Drew rushes to greet Liam and Ms. Lucy in a state of fear. He shouts to announce his approach. "Liam!"

The sound of Drew's voice pulls Liam's head up. His face of anger switches to confusion, until he sees where the voice is coming from, and is shocked to a freeze, like a deer threatened by a sound from the woods. Drew waves and tries to crack through the tension.

"Yo! Little Man!" Drew gulps. As he approaches, he sees the blood on Liam's face. He shakes his head and reaches out a hand to cup Liam's chin.

Liam pulls away, not ready for the touch. Drew's face falls to shame because he knows exactly why.

"Ma'am," Drew says to Ms. Lucy. "Do you have a..." Drew points to Liam's face.

Ms. Lucy looks to where Drew points and gasps. "Oh, my!" She searches her fanny pack, pulls out an individually wrapped First-Aid wipe, and hands it to Drew.

Drew accepts and taps it in his hand while he searches his head for words. "Thank you." he says to Ms. Lucy. "I got it from here."

Ms. Lucy understands, but can't leave. "I'll have to write up an incident report, especially with this injury..."

"Today's a big day. We gotta get back to the hospital. Can we take care of that tomorrow?" Drew asks.

Ms. Lucy ruminates and smiles understanding. "Course." she says and walks away.

Liam lets out a breath and crosses his arms, expressing his unhappiness toward Drew.

"You alright, little man?" Drew says and holds out his hand for the secret handshake.

Liam doesn't respond, and just makes his way to the car.

"Wait, wait, stop." Drew holds Liam back by his arm, and takes a knee, now eye level with Liam. "Ay man. I get it. But there's some things I wanna say to you. Can we go talk?" Drew rips open the packaging of the First-Aid wipe and gently applies it to Liam's wound.

Liam winces at the burn while he contemplates his answer. Drew finishes cleaning the blood to reveal a minor scratch. Resolved, Liam nods.

"My man... ice cream?"

Liam offers another nod, this time with a smile.

***

Liam sits on an outdoor mesh metal table with a cup of chocolate ice cream and a messy plastic spoon, the scratch on his face dried and beginning to scab. Drew sits across.

"Good stuff?" Drew asks Liam.

Liam nods as he eats.

"Listen. I owe you an apology. I know it's been a minute since I came around, and I know I scared you and your mom real bad the last time."

Liam watches Drew as he speaks, not reacting to the words. His only focus is the sweet taste of chocolate in his mouth.

"I was wrong. A real man never comes up on a woman like that. But you tryin' to protect your mom like that. That was real man stuff. Proud of you."

Liam licks his spoon. "If you're my dad, how come I have to call you Drew? How come you never played catch with me? How come you don't come home every night for dinner with us?" Liam shovels bites of ice cream into his mouth between breaths. "All my friends at school say their dads do all those things. But you never do. How come?"

Drew doesn't know how to answer the question. "Uh..." Drew lets out a pressured breath. "Little man... I've made a lot of mistakes. I have a lot of anger inside from stuff that's got nuthin to do with you. You understand?"

Liam shrugs as he gets closer to the bottom of his ice cream cup.

"What happened with that bully today? It's that same kind of anger. You gotta stop that, man."

"Ugh! But it wasn't my fault! He was messin' with me!"

"I know. Trust me, I know. But you gotta take responsibility for yourself. That's what men do. That's what I'm tryin' to do." Drew takes a breath. "I know. I got a lot more to apologize for. And not just to you."

Liam scrapes the bottom of his paper cup with his spoon. He takes his last bite. "Can we go see my mom now?"

Drew chuckles. "Yeah. Let's go."

fifty-six

SARAH STIRS FROM HER SLEEP. With eyes still closed, she lets out a whisper. "Did he leave?"

Emily's eyes open with surprise. "Uh, yes... Sarah?"

Sarah squints open her eyes and smiles.

"Oh, I didn't know you were awake," Emily says as she relaxes and straightens up.

"Oh god, quit fussin'," Sarah laughs, but the pain stops her. "Oh, don't make me laugh."

Emily chuckles. Even in this state, Sarah is still playful. "Sorry."

Sarah tries to sit herself up in bed, but it's too difficult. The pain is too intense.

"Hold on, let me help you." Emily reaches for the bed controls and presses the buttons until the bed adjusts and helps Sarah into a more upright position.

"I have to tell you something," Sarah says softly. She uses as little air as she has to, to get the words out as every inhale stings her chest.

"Yeah?" Emily says as she braces herself.

"You can't tell Drew... It's too much for him... right now," she says, pausing to breathe between each word.

"Okay..."

"My MRI."

Emily is still hoping for the best, but the way Sarah's face turns down to evade Emily's eyes tells her good news might be the most unlikely scenario. "Okay, and?"

Sarah's chin quivers as she searches for the words.

Emily's breath catches and is on the verge of hyperventilating. Her only saving grace is Sarah; she needs to be stronger for her. But she can't help the lump in her throat and the tears that show up to betray her. She reaches over to hold Sarah's hand.

"Uh..." Sarah says. "It's not just the lymph nodes..."

Emily stares at Sarah blankly, not wanting to hear the words.

"It's in my chest cavity... with that fluid around my lungs... in my brain... and some spots on my bones."

Emily shakes her head, pressing Sarah's hand.

"But the trial?" Emily whispers.

Sarah shakes her head. "No trial."

Sarah's words break into fragments and circle in Emily's head. No trial. Chest cavity. Brain. Fluid. Lungs. Bones. Emily had done enough research by now to know what all these words together meant. Sarah, the only real friend she'd ever know, is officially terminal, and someday, too soon, would be no more.

Emily and Sarah fall into a hug, the only available comfort, and sob in Sarah's hospital bed.

"Momma!" Liam's voice interrupts them. Liam rushes into the room and up to Sarah's bedside. Emily moves aside. Drew comes in, not far behind.

"Hey, baby!" Sarah musters a smile for him. "How was school?"

Liam climbs up on the bed to sit next to her. "Are you better now? Is the cancer gone?"

Sarah smiles through the pain. Emily turns away, unable to face it.

"No, baby... The cancer's not gone."

One second, Drew is full of calm confidence as he walks into the hospital room with his little boy. The next his expression contorts into horror as four little words, *the cancer's not gone,* trigger his fall into sadness. "Wait... what?" His eyes dart side to side like he can't make sense of this information. "Whatchu mean, Sar?"

Emily reaches out to Drew from behind. She touches his shoulder and squeezes. Drew turns back toward the touch. He sees Emily's face full of pain and settles into submission. Sarah refocuses on Liam.

"Baby. This surgery helped momma feel better, but..." Her smile holds strong, but her eyes give her away. "The doctor found some new cancer in different places."

Drew sobs, "No..."

Emily pulls him into a half hug.

"So, momma is gonna still need some help... but I'm feeling okay today... and that's good, right?" Sarah holds her smile tight as she watches Liam's face for his response.

Liam's, still too young to understand nuance and only able to take words at face value, accepts Sarah's response. "Yeah... I guess..."

Sarah pushes through her own pain to rub Liam's shoulders—his comfort more important than hers. "This is gonna be a longer journey. And I need you to be strong. Can you stay strong for momma?"

Liam hesitates, "But how much longer?" his voice quivers.

"Well, probably quite a bit longer. And I'm gonna need a little more help. But I've already talked to Aunt Emily and Drew. I think they're both gonna be around a bit more to help. We're all gonna get through this together, okay?"

Liam's face smiles with hope as he believes the words his mother offers. "Okay, momma. I can be strong for you. I can help too."

"Thanks, baby. I need your help now more than ever."

Liam collapses onto her and hugs her with all his might.

Sarah grunts with discomfort but hugs him back, anyway. Drew tries to intervene and moves to pull Liam off her, but Sarah holds up a hand to stop him—*It's okay.*

fifty-seven

DREW WHEELS SARAH into her apartment. She's still bandaged from surgery, but the soft expression on her face says she's happy to be home. Emily and Liam follow close behind.

"Aight, I gotcha, I gotcha," Drew says as he parks Sarah's wheelchair by the couch. "You ready?"

Sarah nods.

"Let's do it!" Drew says with fervor. He lifts Sarah out of her wheelchair slowly and places her on the couch. "You good?" he asks, his face still close to hers, and holding onto her, like he can't let go until she confirms it's okay.

"Yeah. Good," she says as she waves him off of her.

"Can I get you anything?" Emily says, kneeling to Sarah's level.

"I can help! I can get it!" Liam shouts, eager to include himself.

Sarah scoffs and with a playful tone, flaps her arms and hands at them. "All of you better stop. Chill. I'm home. I don't need anything."

Drew nods. Emily understands. Despite the circumstances, there's an unspoken urge to get back to normal, as much as possible.

"Uh... you want me to get dinner?" Drew says with hands on his hips and a face searching for a task to complete.

"Oh my god, you're too much... fine. Go," Sarah says as she relaxes into her position on the couch.

Drew claps, excited to feel useful. "Alright! Let's go, little man! You and me!" The boys hurry off to the kitchen, ready to tackle their chore.

Emily stands there, fidgeting with her fingers as she too searches the space for something to do.

"Sit!" Sarah says. "You're freaking me out."

Emily complies and chuckles lightly. "Sorry."

"Lotta suitcases in the back of your car... I noticed," Sarah says.

"Oh, yeah... uh... I left."

"Good for you." Sarah nods. "Kyle or your mom?"

"Both of them. I'm done. I have no money, no credit, no place to go, and no clue how I'm gonna figure this out, but... I'm not going back."

"Roomies official?"

"Oh, you don't have to do that. You don't have enough space here and you're gonna need room for medical stuff, and..."

"Hey, hey," Sarah cuts through her ramble.

"Sorry."

"It's okay. We both need help right now."

"But you have Drew now. I'd just be in the way."

"Drew can't throw clay! And we still need to pay these bills. I'm putting you to work, girl."

Emily smiles, humbled, yet again. "I mean, I do have quite a few Birkins to sell..."

"To who? The Beverly Hills Housewives?"

The women laugh at themselves.

"We're gonna be alright. Just gotta stay positive. It'll work itself out. And now I get to show you how *my half* lives." Sarah nods with enthusiasm, a gesture of faith.

A smile stretches across Emily's face. "Can't wait!"

fifty-eight

THE DOOR of Sarah's bedroom cracks open and Emily walks in, traversing through piles of clothes, plastic garbage bags, and more clutter than typical. The space inside is dark; tin-foiled windows block the morning light.

"Morning! I brought you coffee," Emily says as she approaches the bed. "Can I please take down this foil? It's so dark in here. You need sunshine." Emily doesn't wait for an answer, instead she sets down the coffee cup and tears an opening in the foil. A ray of bright light illuminates the space.

Sarah expresses lament with sound as she groans. "Noooooo!"

"Oh, come on. You're not gonna melt..." Emily tears away another piece.

Sarah pulls the covers over her head and lets out another painful groan.

The sound of Sarah hurting pulls Emily's attention away from the window. Concern paints her voice. "Are you okay?"

Sarah whimpers.

"Oh, shoot! It probably hurts because it's been twenty-four hours. We have to change your bandage. Come on." Emily takes great care as she pulls the covers back down and off Sarah.

Sarah squint as they struggle to adjust to the room illuminated by sunlight.

"Go away...." Sarah says with a moan.

Emily hands the steaming cup of coffee to Sarah. "Here. Sip," she says with a gentle smile.

Sarah accepts the offer grudgingly, angry she has to do this, angry at the pain, angry at the light, but knowing there is no other way.

"Why are you so happy?" Sarah grumbles.

"Uh, I don't know. Happy thoughts. We gotta stay positive. We're gonna get through this, right?"

Sarah sips her coffee with a suspicious stare. "Yeah, one way or another. I guess we're all getting through this..." Sarah's tone reveals a secret message, not talking about getting through this, but about getting to the end.

"Ugh. Sarah. Don't say that. We have to stay positive." Emily says as she gathers bandages, ointment, and medical tape off Sarah's dresser.

"What's the point? It doesn't matter, anyway. I'm dead, even if you don't want to believe it."

Emily stops her nursing routine. She sits next to Sarah, sensing Sarah needs her to just be. "You're not dead yet. Now, you wanna sit around feeling sorry for yourself, or you wanna watch cartoons with your son later?" Emily says, moving the conversation out of the darkness and into an opportunity to look forward.

"Cartoons," Sarah suggests, a brief twinkle in her eye.

Emily, pleased with herself, picks up the bandages and ointment again. "Alright. Here we go. Let's get this done."

Sarah complies and does her best to scoot herself up in bed, her face contorting in pain. Emily helps and pulls her up further. In the correct position, Emily gets to work. She unfastens a compression garment wrapped around Sarah's torso. With a pair of medical scissors, she cuts through the old bandage and opens it up. Emily works to clean and re-bandage the wound. The room is silent, and the energy is dark.

"Cool battle scar, huh?" Sarah says, taking it upon herself to lighten the mood.

Emily chortles.

"It's like a bear attack! Took my whole nip!"

The women find their laughter.

"Oh my god, stop!"

"What? This is nuthin. You should see the bear!" Sarah jokes, but pain invades her smile.

Emily sees her pain and shakes her head. "Okay, okay. Calm down."

Emily tosses her hands up. The goal is complete. "Okay! Done! You can have some pain medicine now. You wanna take a chill pill and relax for a bit, or you want me to help you out of bed and to the couch?"

"Eh... Where's Liam?"

"Already at school."

"Okay, I'll stay here. Gimme the chill pill."

Emily jolts to action. She finds a perception pill bottle on the dresser, retrieves one pill, and brings it back to Sarah in bed. Sarah tosses the pill in her mouth. Emily holds up a water cup with a straw.

"Okay. I'm gonna get on the computer for a minute. I'll come back and check on you soon."

Sarah rolls over back into bed.

* * *

Emily closes Sarah's bedroom door behind her with a soft click of the latch across the lock plate. She sits down at the kitchenette table with her laptop, in business mode. Strewn in the kitchen behind her on the counters, floors, and over the stove are her Birkins, shoes, matching sets, and jewelry. Each piece neatly categorized into an overwhelming mess of luxury. Emily opens the internet browser to an online consignment shop website. A top page banner highlights "Sell your LUX!"

"Okay! I've been making money my whole life; how hard can this be?"

Emily dives deep into her task of photographing, uploading, and listing her sellable items. Confidence pours out of her fingertips as she pecks at the keyboard.

fifty-nine

EMILY AND SARAH sit together in the circle at their support group. They're tired, out of luck, and same on hope. The room is emptier, colder, and more fluorescent. Emily isn't being trailed by a photographer. The donated goodies table doesn't exist, not even a traditional coffee warmer filled with hot water or instant coffee powder. No more The Daily Grind paraphernalia to entice the attendees or paint Emily as the martyr.

The women clap as one of them finishes sharing a story. Emily and Sarah move through the motions as they follow along, but their eyes have a glaze and their expression is stoic. Both of them are distracted, but for different reasons.

"Sarah?" Cheryl interrupts the women as they gaze off into nothing.

"Hmm? Yeah." Sarah responds. Emily snaps back to attention.

"I said, we're all so pleased to see you back here so soon after surgery. How did it go?"

"Oh, the mastectomy was a success. While they were in there, they did a thor-o... A thorasetic?"

"Thoracentesis," Emily says.

"Emily, it's important we let Sarah share her experience without interrupting."

"Yeah. That," Sarah says, back to the story. "And as soon as I recover, they have me slated for radio-stereo... uh..."

"Stereotactic radiosurgery for brain metastases."

"Emily, I've asked you not to interrupt..." Cheryl says in a harsh tone as she loses control of her annoyance and crosses her arms.

"Hahaha!" Emily laughs out loud, cuts Cheryl off, and crumbles into an emotional rant. "Right! Don't interrupt. Like how cancer totally interrupted my whole life and destroyed my marriage?"

"Emily, please..." Cheryl tries, but fails.

"Like how I finally find a friend right before we find out she's dying and, ya know, *dying* is gonna interrupt the rest of her life. Oh, and how her eight-year-old son will be left without a mother for the rest of *his* life. And how I don't have the slightest clue how to help with any of it, or where I even belong in this reality I've somehow stumbled into. But hey! Anyone wanna buy a Birkin? We got Birkins coming out of our ears and need the money for, ya know, this stupid life where everything's too expensive in comparison to the money that's available and it doesn't even make sense how people live like this. But yeah. You're right, Cheryl. Let's not interrupt because cancer's done enough of that already."

The room is stunned to silence. Sarah reaches over and grabs Emily's hand in hers. A soft smile comes to her face, and Emily realizes what she's done.

"Oh, my god. I'm so sorry," Emily breaks down into tears and her cheeks flush with embarrassment.

"It's okay," Sarah says as she squeezes Emily's hand. "You're okay."

sixty

SARAH AND EMILY settle into a new life supporting one another. Sarah teaches Emily more about pottery, and how to survive in a world they're out-priced in. Emily practices on the turntable until she's good enough to sell pieces at the market. This, with Drew's help where he can, and Emily's occasional sale of her fancy items online, sustains them. They struggle, but as Sarah predicted, they make it.

Emily's hair grows back in curly this time, which amuses her. It feels like a change to match the change in her life. Sarah continues with various treatments, staving off the inevitable and buying them more time. The procedures are sometimes brutal, but Sarah has youth on her side, her twenty-seven-year-old body able to take the punishment and bounce back in recovery. Over the weeks and months, Sarah cycles through various phases of health and demise. For some periods of time, the bags under her eyes are dark, her skin is pale, and her body is weak. Others, her face seems vibrant, her hair grows an inch, and her demeanor offers the illusion of health.

On this day of her twenty-eighth birthday, Sarah boasts a radiance as she stands tall and proud. Her hair's fallen out again, and the port under the skin of her chest is puffy and newly traumatized, but today's a day that she won't let her disease take from her.

Sarah sits at her kitchenette, a birthday party hat on her bare head. Liam blows on a party kazoo, a matching hat on his head. Drew, also with a party hat, chews on a slice of pizza, sat next to Sarah at the table. Emily carries in a small birthday cake with two candles lit on top in the shape of the number two and the number eight. A number weighted with a silent knowledge—there won't be many more.

"Happy birthday to…" Emily sings, and the rest follow.

"… you. Happy birthday to you…"

Emily places the cake in front of a jubilant Sarah.

"Happy birthday, dear Sarah. Happy birthday to you!"

Sarah blows out her candles. The room breaks into applause with shouts and yays.

"And many more! On channel four!" Liam sings out with glee.

"What?" Liam says as the smiles fade, the energy dampens, and the applause quiets.

Emily clears her throat. "I, uh… I'll get plates!" and rushes to busy herself.

Sarah smiles at her son. "Nothing, baby. It's okay. Ready for cake?"

"Yes!" Liam makes a fist and pulls it down like he's scored a touchdown.

Emily slices the cake on the kitchen counter and serves out the pieces on paper party plates. Her phone pings a notification. She pauses, the cake cutting to lick frosting off her fingers and open her phone screen. Text message from Mom with the number 35 in parentheses—she's been ignoring Mom for quite a while.

"Ugh…" Emily mumbles to herself. "Go away…" She presses the lockscreen and shoves the phone back in her pocket. "Okay! Who wants cake!" she announces as she gathers the party plates and brings them to the table.

* * *

Emily and Sarah rest in their apartment. The couch hosts their bodies bundled under blankets and the moonlight that creeps in through the sliding glass door.

"It's colder in here than usual, right?" Emily says.

"Gas bill."

"What?"

"I couldn't pay the gas bill. Drew's supposed to come through with some change, though. We'll get it back in a couple days."

"Oh..."

"It happens."

"My Birkins haven't exactly been flying off the shelf. But we got market in a couple days, that'll be good."

"Rent's due, too."

Emily sighs. "Forget this. Should I just call her? She'll make some kind of deal with me."

"I think you should call your mom. But not transactionally. Like it or not, she's what you get, and all you'll have left after I'm gone."

"Do you think it's time to talk about that? What you want that to look like? Your wishes?" The mood turns dour as Emily contemplates the finality of what this really means.

"Yeah. I think so."

They're not ready, but they both know they're running out of time.

The women sit in a moment of silence.

"So... you start. I don't know..." Emily says.

"Oh my god, no. You please. I don't know what to say!" Sarah's voice pitches into an almost playful tone.

"What am I supposed to say?" Emily's voice matches.

"I don't know. I don't know. Just ask me questions and I'll answer," Sarah says, almost excited to make it a game.

"Uh. Okay, okay. Hold on." Emily thinks. They know this is serious, despite both wishing it didn't have to be. "Um... burial or cremation?"

"Uh. Whatever's cheapest."

"Okay... your stuff? Who gets your arts supplies, your pieces?"

Sarah smiles wide. "You do."

The gesture moves Emily, and she feels a tense pang in her chest, the beginning of tears, but holds them back. "Oh. Thank you." She takes a moment to think about her next words. "And, um... Liam?"

The smile drops off Sarah's face. She takes a deep breath in and holds Emily's gaze. "Liam. We both know Drew loves Liam. But I also know Drew. He's been who he is as long as I've known him. He's a bomb without a warning tick."

"Yeah..."

"Things are okay now, but there will be another time when they won't be, and I can't take the chance of that happening when I'm not around."

Emily nods.

Sarah lets out a deep breath. The words that come tangle themselves in her tears. "I would love it if you would take custody of Liam."

The request knocks the air out of Emily's chest. She takes a deep breath in, and slow exhale out. "Uhhh."

"It's a lot to ask. I know." Sarah shakes her head like she wants to take it back, only she doesn't. "Liam loves you and I know you'd make a great mom."

Emily sits in her thoughts. "Uh... sorry." Emily shakes her head like she's shaking out any doubts and dismissing herself for even having them. "Yeah. Yes. Of course. Of course I'll take Liam."

"Oh my god, thank you!" Sarah says as she lunges into Emily and grabs her in a warm hug. "Thank you! Thank you!"

"Course."

sixty-one

EMILY SIPS MORNING coffee in the kitchen while she scrolls her online listings of Birkin bags, designer shoes, clothes, and jewelry. She lets out a gruff when she sees her shop portal shows no new sales.

"Course." Emily mummers to herself. "Why doesn't anybody want this stuff?"

She clicks open a new tab and types in the search bar. *Why won't people buy what I'm selling.* An AI generated response page pops up on the screen. She reads the text aloud to herself.

"There are many reasons why people won't buy what you're selling, including..." Emily browses through the bulleted list. "No need. No trust. Lack of awareness..." Ugh! Emily gives up, frustrated and bored. "I'm a Chief Marketing Officer! What am I doing wrong?"

Emily slams her laptop closed. She steps over to the kitchen sink. Plate by plate, and cup by cup, she stress-cleans, letting out her frustration as she scrubs. Until she comes across Sarah's pink cancer cup. Coffee-stained and sitting off to the side by itself. A calmness rushes over her as she holds the cup in her hand. Then, an idea comes to her.

"Lack of awareness..." she says out loud.

Emily rushes back to her computer, opens it up, and types into the search bar, *Metastatic breast cancer awareness.* A page populates with facts and statistics about metastatic breast cancer.

- Metastatic breast cancer awareness day is October 13
- MBC occurs when breast cancer spreads to other areas of the body, usually the lungs or liver.
- There is no cure for MBC.
- Research on metastasis is challenging for many reasons, however, the biggest obstacle is lack of funding.

Emily's phone pings. Another text from mom. "Ugh! What do you want?" She huffs as she opens the text chain and is met with walls of text from her mother. The messages beg her to speak, to please answer her, to come back. Offers of money, cars, homes, promotions, new husbands, anything material that could ever be acquired waiting for Emily to say the word, and it's hers. All she has to do is call her mother.

Emily bites her fingernails as she reads through the temptation. A knock at the door distracts her. She answers the front door to find… no one there. A single sheet of paper taped outside the door catches her eye. The bold title on the paper reads, 'Eviction notice. 30-days to pay or quit.'

"Oh, no!" Emily rips the paper from the door, slams it closed, and stomps back inside.

Back at the kitchen table, Emily picks up her phone and types a response to Mom.

"I'm ready to talk."

sixty-two

EMILY STRUTS into The Daily Grind's office headquarters with her shoulders back and her head high. The receptionist offers a kind greeting, but the surprise on her face shows this visit is unexpected.

"Emily! Gosh! Hello. So happy to have you back."

"I'm not back. I'm here to speak to her."

"Uh... yes. Of course. Hold on." The receptionist dials her phone with nervous fingers. "Hello, Ms. Helen. Um. Emily is here to see you?"

There's a long, silent pause as the receptionist waits for a response.

"Yes, of course. Thank you." The receptionist looks up. "She'll see you."

"Thank you."

"Great to have you back!" the receptionist shouts as Emily walks away and out of earshot.

Emily approaches Helen's office. The door is closed, and the blinds drawn. She knocks.

"Come in," Helen's voice calls from inside.

Emily opens the door and sails gingerly into the space, confident and ready.

"Hello, mother."

Helen stands tall, glares at Emily, but doesn't respond. Emily waits, unsure of how to proceed. In the grip of Helen's stare, Emily's confidence seeps away.

"Close the door," Helen says.

Emily complies. The door clicks shut. The sound of the strike plate meeting the latch bolt triggers Helen into a full breakdown, muted only by her will to not embarrass herself. She sobs, sniffles, and lets go of years of pent-up emotions. Tears stream down her face. Snot dribbles from her nose. Her throat constricts, as she cannot contain her misery.

Emily stands in disbelief. She's seen nothing like this before. "Mom?"

Helen collapses into her desk chair. She pulls tissues from a box to help herself.

"Oh, Emily." She moans.

"What is going on?" Emily says with an incredulous snort.

Helen dabs her eyes, her nose, and takes in a deep breath. This sight of her mother's breakdown is too much. Emily can't take it. Her heart fills with compassion she never knew could exist for her mother.

"It's okay, Mom!" Emily says as she approaches the broken woman. She reaches out a hand and touches it to Helen's shoulder. The moment is awkward, but Emily pushes past it.

The touch takes Helen by surprise as she lets out a small gasp. Her sobs quiet, and her breaths normalize.

"Well, then!" Helen clears her throat and straightens up.

Emily startles. The moment's over, it's back to business. Emily makes her way back around the desk and sits in a guest chair. Helen straightens her clothing and sits tall in her place of power.

"Thank you for coming, Emily," Helen says. "I... uh... things have not been the same since you left." Her face changes from intermittent strength to gratitude and softness as she speaks. "As soon as the campaign ended, it got out on social media that The Daily Grind had stopped supporting the meetings. We've been canceled, sales are down, and last month's shareholder summit was pitiful... I... took you for granted, Emily. You do more here than I let you believe."

Emily slumps in her seat. "Oh, so this was just about the company... Okay, I get it." Emily steeps in disappointment—stupid of her for thinking her mother might have missed her.

Helen sighs. "No, Emily. That's not all."

"I..." Helen struggles in her seat, uncomfortable. "When I met your father, I was entranced by him. He was charming, funny, he held a presence in the room. I was young, your age. And yes, he was 20-years older than me, but in the beginning, he wasn't just some old rich guy. I didn't even know about the money, until it was too late, and we were married... When you were a baby, he cheated on me, with the secretary." Helen scoffs at herself. "I know, I'm a cliche.

Anyway, he made no effort to hide his affair, and it was clear he wouldn't let me leave easily. I had nowhere to go and an infant to think about, so I stayed, without a fight, and the walls of my heart hardened around you and me. I blocked everything else out. Yes, I put up with him for the sake of money. Yes, he let me start the coffee shop and I poured all my energy into it. From him, I learned business, how to build, and how to protect what I'd grown. Control and power were key. At some point, you became part of that, and I stopped letting you live your own life. I wanted safety and security for you. I wanted you to have everything, because all we had was each other. I wanted more for you than to feel alone in this world, like I did. Since you've been gone, I've realized I went about all of it the wrong way. Money is not the most important thing in this world. You are."

Emily sits up a little taller in her seat. She takes it all in. "I appreciate you saying that," Emily says, still processing.

"If you come back, you can have the house back. You don't have to stay married to Kyle. I'll even help with hurrying along the divorce. Whatever you want." Helen's voice begs, desperate for reconciliation.

"I appreciate that too, but that's not what brought me here today. I have a proposition for you."

Helen leans in with full attention.

"These last several months with Sarah and her son have been hard, but I've been grateful for them because I've discovered that helping others makes the struggle worth it."

"But what do you want, Emily?"

"I want you to listen to me."

Helen sits back, white-flagged as she throws up her arms in surrender.

"Two-hundred and ninety-seven thousand women will be diagnosed with breast cancer this year. One in three women will be diagnosed within their lifetime. Between 20-30% of all early-stage breast cancer will become metastatic, and only 2-5% of all research dollars are funded to the study of metastasis."

"Emily, I fail to understand…"

"I want to start The Daily Grind's non-profit arm to benefit the study of metastatic breast cancer, and make treatment more affordable."

"Emily, if this is about helping your friend and her child, fine. I won't fight you on that anymore. You can have whatever money you want to support them, no need to start a whole organization just to…"

"This isn't about the money. It's too late for Sarah. But together we can help the other two-hundred and ninety-seven thousand women, and their families, who suffer through this disease."

Helen sits with her thoughts. "How?"

Emily rifles through her bag, pulls out Sarah's pink cancer mug, and places it on the desk in front of them. "We'll sell limited edition pink coffee mugs, the proceeds of which will go toward the cause. I'll be back here every day, working to build the campaign and the agency as an extension. I'll move back home, and Sarah and Liam will move into the guest rooms. And we'll require 100% support for any medical equipment and transportation necessary for both Sarah and Liam."

"Anything else?"

"Yes." Emily catches her breath. "I've agreed to take on full custody of Liam at the time of Sarah's death. I'll require your support and legal representation with the adoption process."

Helen sizes Emily up and searches for a point of negotiation. Emily sits tall. Her determination lets Helen know there is none.

"You're back to work full-time starting Monday and you'll do an interview with Business Insider about the divorce, and use that as a pivot into the new non-profit venture. Do we have a deal?"

Emily celebrates in her seat, stomps her feet, and shakes her fists, as covertly as possible. She did it. "Thank you, Mom! Thank you!"

Emily stands and rushes Helen for a hug. Helen's shoulders tense with surprise, but then, release into the embrace—the first time, in a long time.

sixty-three

EMILY WEARS a huge smile as she marches in through the double doors of the Breast Health Center. She approaches the reception with a child-like excitement.

"Hi! Just here to sit with Sarah. Can I go back?"

"Yes, Miss Emily. Go ahead." The receptionist waves her back.

Like she owns the place, Emily marches through the halls to the infusion room. Nurse Jackie greets her first.

"Well, hey there. Thought we were gonna miss you today."

"Oh, come on, Nurse Jackie, you know me better than that!" The women chuckle together. Nurse Jackie goes back to her task and tends to Sarah seated in an infusion chair.

"Took you long enough," Sarah says.

"Sorry! I know. My mom talked forever. But I have news!" Emily says as she sits in an adjacent guest chair.

"Me too."

"Huh? Oh, you first, then!"

"You want the good or bad first?"

Emily's face shows surprise. "Is this about the eviction notice? I saw it this morning, but don't worry about that, we're gonna be..."

"No." Sarah cuts her off. "Not that. I know you saw it. You left it on the table."

"Oh... well, then... what? What's wrong?"

"Good or bad?" Sarah says, now annoyed.

"Oh. Sorry. Good!"

"I reached out to that social worker, Donna? From forever ago. She said she might be able to help me find a pro bono attorney to help with legal stuff for Liam's adoption. A trust, or whatever she called it..."

"Oh! Okay, but also don't worry about that. I talked to..."

"And the bad..." Sarah cuts her off again. "Is I told Drew. I don't think he took it too well."

"Oh, no! What'd he do?"

"I don't know. It was over the phone. He kinda just made a weird screaming sound and hung up."

"Oh!"

"It's probably all he needed to set off. I don't think we'll hear from him for a while. Typical."

"Well, why do you think he's so upset? He doesn't even want Liam? Or he can't, I mean."

"No, it's way more self-serving than that. Liam getting adopted means I'm dead, and he's lost another one. It's about him and his inability to cope with this. It's not about you or even about Liam." Sarah's face twists into discomfort as she dry heaves. She points toward a countertop. Nurse Jackie brings her a kidney dish. Without a second to spare, Sarah vomits into the dish.

Emily rubs Sarah's back.

Sarah takes a few heavy breaths, spits, and wipes her mouth. "Ugh... What happened with your mom?"

"Oh... relax. We'll talk about it later."

"Think you can take care of market this weekend?" Sarah catches her breath. "I have a feeling I'm not gonna be up for it."

Emily smiles. "Don't worry about it."

* * *

Emily thanks Nurse Jackie as the two of them help Sarah out of the infusion chair and into a wheelchair.

"Thanks again. See you next week."

"Alright, girls. Take care." Nurse Jackie smiles as Emily wheels Sarah out of the center.

Emily drives while Sarah rests in the front seat. The ride home is quiet. When they pull up to their apartment, Emily notices it first. The apartment door is ajar.

"What the..." Emily says.

"What?" Sarah says, wrestled awake as the vehicle stops.

Emily throws the car in park and jumps out of the driver's seat. She jogs up to the door, but maintains a safe distance. Sarah, now alert, musters her strength to get herself out of the car and hobbles out behind Emily.

"Hello?" Emily shouts. "Hello?" she says a little louder.

"What happened?" Sarah pushes past Emily and into the apartment.

It's destroyed. Everything. Liam's tapestries are torn from the walls. His dresser flipped. The couch cushions show their stuffing, opened with a knife and shredded. The floor holds a now broken TV, knocked off its rickety entertainment center. The tables and chairs rest across the room and upside down—thrown haphazardly and likely in anger. Sarah's bed is wet. Her art, her photos, her memories, ripped from their resting places and stomped on the ground.

"No!" Sarah cries.

This sight makes Emily's mouth drop open.

Sarah keels over but holds herself up by bracing her hands on her knees. She fights against her condition and hurries to the back. Pieces of the shattered sliding glass door scatter across the floor. Then she sees it—her balcony respite destroyed. A sight that rips the breath out of her chest. Her pottery turned to broken shards. Her art supplies scattered and wasted. The turntable hammered into bits. Nothing spared.

Sarah can't breathe. She tries, but her throat is closed and won't let in air. She hyperventilates and falls to the ground.

"Sarah!" Emily screams and runs to her side. On the ground with her, Emily gathers Sarah in her arms and pulls her up into a hug.

"He smashed... my cup! Noooo! He smashed it!" Sarah cries.

In the darkness, Emily remembers a glimmer of light. "No. He didn't!" Emily's face lights up in a sparkle.

"What?" Sarah takes a breath, curious.

Emily searches through her bag and finds Sarah's pink cancer mug. She presents it to Sarah with gentle hands.

Sarah sniffles, tears roll down her face and over her smile. She takes the cup and spends a moment with it in her hands. Her gaze shifts outward again and her eyes rummage through the rubble for answers. With none to be found, she relents again to tears.

sixty-four

SARAH SITS atop her knees as she mines through the broken pieces of her life now scattered on the floor of her apartment. Emily assists and rummages through her own pile of rubble in an adjacent corner. Every shard of a memory brings Sarah to tears, while it fills Emily with rage.

"You just tell me what I'm allowed to do to this jerk, Sarah. Say the words, and it's done."

Sarah shakes her head as she whimpers. "I just want…" the sound of broken glass as her hand moves through the destruction. "My memories." She pulls out a paper photo of her and baby Liam in the hospital on the day he was born. "Ow!" she shouts. Blood drips down her hand.

"What?" Emily rushes over to see.

"The glass must have…" Sarah says, bleeding profusely now.

Emily gasps! "You're on blood thinners!" She runs into the kitchen, artifacts crunch beneath her steps. She rummages through the open drawers and cabinets. The break-in leaves a single dishrag undisturbed, still folded in its drawer. She grabs it, and hurries back to Sarah, who waits helplessly and weeping on the living room floor.

Emily grasps Sarah's hand with the rag and presses hard to stop the blood. The visible deflation of Sarah's spirit incites Emily's heart to ache with empathy.

"Distract me. Please?" Sarah says.

"Um... okay... I..." Emily flounders.

"What did your mom say? Talk about that," Sarah says, desperately, gritting her teeth.

"Oh! Yes! I went to see my mom. She's agreed to my terms, and we're going to start a non-profit arm of The Daily Grind to benefit metastasis and provide more affordable treatments to people who need it."

Sarah's breaths soften, and the words calm her. "That's great. I'm really happy for you." Sarah tries, but her attention goes back to the mess they're enveloped in.

"No..." Emily says, pulling Sarah's focus back to her. "It's not for me. This is for both of us. And Liam. Part of the terms was you and Liam moving in with me where I can take care of you, and we won't need that pro bono attorney. Everything is taken care of."

"Oh." Sarah soaks it in. "OH!" and laughs out loud. "You mean..."

Emily nods hard as a cheese-ball smile widens her face.

"Oh, my god! Oh, my god!" Sarah says, her continuing tears now confused with relief.

"We're gonna be leaving now, okay? Right now. I'll have someone come clean all this up."

"Um..." Sarah pauses. "I need you to understand something."

"Yeah. Anything, what?"

"Drew doesn't know what he's doing. He's been hurt, and he never learned how to cope."

"Ugh! Sarah! Come on! Look at this place! He doesn't deserve..."

"But," Sarah cuts Emily off, shy smiles, and begs for mercy. "This has to be it. My son's safety comes first. What's left of me, and *you* are Liam's only family now."

Emily nods she understands. "Come on. Let's go."

Emily helps Sarah off the floor. Sarah grabs her stomach and clenches her face as she lifts herself up. Emily pulls Sarah's arm up and around her shoulders, and the two move toward the front door.

sixty-five

EMILY PULLS into the driveway of the home she used to share with Kyle and parks next to another fancy car. Several other professional trucks and vans fill the rest of the driveway. The planter she left broken is back together, with new foliage, like nothing ever happened. Sarah sleeps in the front seat.

"Why is my mom's car here?" Emily says to herself, waking Sarah from her nap.

"Your mom?" Sarah says, rubbing her eyes.

"Uh... it's okay. Hold on. You stay here. Let me go see what's going on." Emily jumps out of her car and approaches the front door with apprehension.

"Hello? Mom?" Emily says as she pokes her head in the doorway.

Inside is a bustling team of uniformed service professionals as they work to prepare the home. There are chefs in the kitchen, cleaners walk around with brooms and spray bottles, a scrubbed nurse readies medical equipment in one of the guest rooms, an interior designer places children's furniture and play sets in the other, and a moving company removes any trace of a husband.

Emily walks in, astonished at what she sees before her.

JENNIFER LUCIC

"I apologize, we're not quite ready yet," Helen's voice pops up and surprises Emily.

"Oh!" Emily turns around. "Mom, this is… amazing!" Emily rushes to her mother and hugs her.

Helen smiles. "Will this suffice, then?"

Emily belly-laughs. "Yes! Yes, this is perfect." Emily takes another look around, her face full of wonder, like a child on Christmas morning. "Um. Do you want to meet her?"

Helen clears her throat, stands up a little straighter. "Is she here?"

"Yeah. She's in the car. You want to?"

* * *

Sarah stays still in Emily's car and watches the front door as it cracks open. She sucks in her breath. Emily walks out with Helen. A smile on her face tells Sarah to relax.

Emily and Helen approach the car, and Emily opens the passenger side door, merriment exuding from her. Sarah smiles, nervous, but calm.

"Sarah, this is my mom, Helen. Mom, Sarah," Emily says as she steps aside so the two can meet.

"Sarah, hello. So nice to meet you," Helen smiles and holds out her right hand.

"Uh…" Sarah looks at the hand, not sure what to do with it. "Hi… Nice to meet you, too," Sarah says as she extends her hand.

Helen gives a firm business handshake.

"I hope you'll be comfortable here. Apologies for not being ready sooner. I wasn't sure exactly when the two of you would arrive home."

Sarah smiles again.

"Come on, we'll show you around," Emily says, excited for Sarah to see everything going on inside.

* * *

Emily brings Sarah inside in a wheelchair. Helen trails close behind and introduces each part of the house as they walk through.

"I hope you're hungry. I've had our private chef and his team working hard to build a welcome home dinner for us," Helen says.

Sarah holds her hand over her mouth to stop herself from crying.

Helen leads them down a hall to the guest rooms, Liam's first. An interior designer works to place toys and furniture to ready the space.

"This will be Liam's room. We weren't sure what toys and things he might like, so we took a few guesses. I hope that's alright?"

Sarah can't stop herself any longer and bursts into happy tears. "This is… Thank you." She manages a few words and collects herself. "He's never had his own room before."

"This way, please." Helen guides them to the next room, Sarah's. Inside, Nurse Jackie is readying the bed. A fully functional infusion chair and the required medical equipment sit off to the side.

"Hey, girls! Thanks for havin' me!" Nurse Jackie says when she sees them.

Sarah and Emily turn to Helen and search for understanding.

"I took the liberty of hiring your nurse to come on as a private medical concierge. You'll be able to receive your treatments here, from the comfort of your own home. You will still have to go to the hospital for any surgeries or emergency procedures, but all regularly scheduled infusions and doctor visits can happen right here."

"Mom, this is…" her mother's generosity floors Emily.

"Too much… It's too much. I can't…" Sarah says with a weak voice.

"Please, Sarah." Helen lays a warm hand on Sarah's shoulder. "This was all pre-arranged for Emily before plans changed. No sense in wasting the registration fees."

Nurse Jackie finishes straightening the bed. She approaches

Sarah with the warm smile Sarah and Emily have come to find comfort in. "You ready?"

Sarah nods. Nurse Jackie lifts her from her wheelchair and helps her hobble over and into the bed.

"Thank you, Nurse Jackie," Emily says, grateful.

"Oh, you got it. We're gonna let Miss Sarah get some rest now. I got it from here," Nurse Jackie says as she shoos away the bystanders.

sixty-six

OVER THE NEXT SEVERAL MONTHS, life ebbs and flows for the happy trio in their new life and home. Emily goes back to work, builds out the pink coffee cup campaign—*who says coffee can't cure cancer*—and finalizes her divorce. Sarah pursues treatment, becomes ever weaker as her cancer grows, and Liam attends a new school, free of bullies. Drew remains at a distance, or at least that's what they assume, as they blocked him from their phones, social media, and email accounts, and he doesn't know where Emily lives.

As Sarah gets sicker, Emily tries her best to keep spirits up. Between new toys and expensive electronics for Liam, and a new clay and artists setup in the backyard for her and Sarah, Emily relies on what her money can buy as she seeks temporary relief from the pain of their reality. While no amount of stuff will ever be enough to fill the holes burrowing in their hearts at the impending loss they will soon face, that doesn't stop Emily from trying.

With each passing treatment or emergency hospital stay, the holes inside them grow deeper and wider as the imminence of Sarah's final moment draws nearer. Never-the-less, the new-formed family finds reasons and moments to be grateful, and share joy.

Sarah and Liam cheer as Emily strikes the final signature on her divorce papers.

Emily invites Helen over for dinner, who brings a gift for Liam. The warm meal compliments the joy the group shares at the table as they talk about Liam's new private school, his new friends, and plans for the future. The world is now open to him with the gift of opportunity.

Emily and Sarah laugh over messages as Kyle slides into Emily's DMs and begs for another chance. Sarah pokes fun at how pathetic he presents in pictures he sent that showcase him posing with a stoic scowl on the bow of a yacht—his desperate plea for sympathy. Emily cackles at a reflection she sees on a mirrored surface, the same photo, none other than Tiffany behind the camera.

Sarah, thinner and more yellowed in her skin, sits in meditation behind her clay turntable in the backyard. Her foot pedals, her hand shapes the clay. Emily enters, suited in business casual home from work, pulls up a stool and joins her at the adjacent turntable. Stacks of pink coffee mugs rests on the counter behind them.

Nurse Jackie tends to Sarah in her infusion chair, comfortable in her own room and surrounded by photos of memories she, Emily, Liam, and Helen have made over the past several months. A trip to a tropical paradise, dinners at fancy restaurants, a performance at Liam's new school, soccer games, an award ceremony, and Liam's birthday party surrounded by friends and presents.

The pink coffee cup campaign does better than Helen or Emily imagined. The Daily Grind surges in popularity again as social media videos of pink *Who Says Coffee Can't Cure Cancer* coffee cups go viral. Emily and Helen hire a manufacturer to make and distribute the cups to meet the new demand.

At the breast cancer support group, new members and supporters fill the seats and standing room as The Daily Grind hosts a birthday party for Sarah. Twenty-nine candles fill a multi-tiered cake. A weak wheelchair bound Sarah, wearing a silk scarf on her head, blows hard on her candles to the cheers of the audience.

Back at home, Nurse Jackie tucks Sarah into bed. Before the covers are even pulled over her shoulders, Sarah is fast asleep. Nurse Jackie smiles down at her, as if to say goodbye with silence.

Nurse Jackie hands a file over to a new nurse, Nurse Hernandez. Her face is sullen like this time is goodbye. Nurse Hernandez accepts the file with a solemn glance, a passing of the torch.

Nurse Jackie approaches Emily, who waits at the door, and reaches out to touch her shoulder, and Emily pulls her into a deep hug.

"Thank you for all you've done for us, Nurse Jackie. It's meant so much."

"Oh, you're sweet. You be strong, alright? Nurse Hernandez is a great hospice nurse. He'll take good care of her."

Emily nods and wipes away a tear as Nurse Jackie shows herself out. Nurse Hernandez tends to the machines around Sarah that burr and beep. Emily stands at the door and watches Sarah sleep.

sixty-seven

EMILY PREPARES a breakfast of scrambled eggs and bacon with a blueberry muffin. She assembles the items on two plates with a delicate touch.

"Liam! Breakfast!" she shouts from the kitchen.

Liam heeds the call and shuffles in, holding his backpack, ready for the day. He perches himself on the breakfast table in front of one of the steaming plates of food. Emily sits beside him, the second plate of food in front of her.

"You say good morning to your mom yet?"

Liam shakes his head with a morose nod. "Still sleeping."

Emily puts down her fork to rub Liam's back. "You know, now that Mom's on hospice, she'll be sleeping a lot more. Do you remember what we talked about, about what hospice means?"

Liam nods again and pushes bits of eggs around on his plate.

"You wanna talk about it?"

Liam lets out a sigh. "What happens next? After mom dies?"

"You stay right here with me, buddy. And we heal together." Emily squeezes Liam in a hug as she speaks.

"But what if you don't want me?"

"Why would you think such a thing?"

Liam shrugs. "Drew didn't want me."

Emily swallows the pain in her chest while she thinks about how to respond. Nervous chuckles get her through. "Well, first of all, nobody could ever NOT want you. Captain of your soccer team? Coolest V.R. setup of anyone in school? Come on!"

Liam offers a polite chuckle.

"Second, Drew is... Well, I don't know him all that well, but I think you're old enough to know."

Liam perks his shoulders and turns his head up. "What?"

"You remember how Drew used to come and go? How'd he'd spend time with you and mom but then and disappear?"

"Yeah. But he always came back before."

"He did. Because your mom let him. But she finally got to a place where she couldn't anymore because that might mean, the next time, he could hurt you. Your mom sent him away, and I plan to continue that, to protect you."

"But he's my dad! You can't do that! You can't keep him from me!" Liam screams and runs away from Emily.

"Liam! Wait!"

But it's too late, he's gone. The front door slams. Emily runs after him, swings the door back open, and finds Liam as he makes his way into a hired car, ready to take him to school. Emily sighs in relief.

"We'll talk about this when you get home," Emily says as she shuts the door.

Emily saunters back into the kitchen and grabs a protein milk from the fridge. She takes it with her to the closed entry of Sarah's bedroom. She knocks.

"Hello?" Emily says as she cracks open the door and peeks into the room.

Sarah stirs in her hospice bed. I.V. lines, tapes, and tubes crowd the space on the bedding. Monitors and medical machines surround the bed like idle visitors. Her eyes open and she smacks her dry lips.

"Hey! How'd you sleep?"

Sarah reaches up a hand to her throat and touches it.

"Thirsty? Here." Emily opens up the protein milk and places a plastic straw into the opening. She moves it toward Sarah's mouth and she labors through a sip. Emily watches the milk travel upward through the translucent straw, only long enough for it to touch Sarah's tongue, and she spits it back out. Sarah shakes her head in disgust and pushes the bottle away. Her eyes flutter close again.

"Okay, sorry. You want water instead?"

With eyes still closed, Sarah shakes her head.

Emily sits at Sarah's bedside, at a loss for what else to do, but not ready to leave.

"Liam's off to school."

Sarah doesn't respond.

"He's not too happy with me today… I told him about Drew, and *our* decision to keep him safe and away." Emily scoffs. "He did not like that."

Still no response as Sarah sleeps.

Emily takes Sarah's hand in hers. She kisses it as tears roll down her face. "I want you to know I'm gonna take care of him. I promise. He'll always have me, okay? He'll grow up with every stupid toy a kid could ever ask for, but I promise to make sure he learns, too. What you taught me… about life, about living for yourself and making your own way. About how it's okay to stand up for yourself but also to ask for help. How to be thankful for every moment we get, even when it seems like everything else's taken away. Your friendship saved me, Sarah. I'm sorry I couldn't save you back."

Emily rests her head on the bed as she wails. Alone with her friend, she allows herself to feel how close they are to the end.

sixty-eight

EMILY WAITS on the living room couch with a glass of wine, tears flowing down her eyes. The front door of the home opens and Liam walks in with his head down, as though he knows he's in trouble. He closes the door and stands there, not comfortable enough to move.

"It's okay, buddy. Come here," Emily says.

Liam tiptoes over to the couch. His head stays down and avoids eye contact as he sits next to Emily.

"How was school?" Emily panics and stalls as best she can.

Liam shrugs.

"You're not in trouble, buddy. I'm sorry I upset you this morning."

Liam looks up at Emily with puppy eyes.

"I, uh, I lived my whole life following orders that other people set for me. It was good of you to stand up for yourself and demand to be heard. I'll never punish you for that you. Okay?"

Liam nods.

"However, running out like that, we're gonna have to work on. Next time, let's talk. We'll have a conversation. If I still decide that my decision is in your best interest, we can talk about how that might change in the future and steps we can take to get there, if whatever the thing is, is something you really want."

"Even if it's Drew?"

Emily takes a moment, but nods. "Even if it's Drew. Someday. But not today. Fair?"

"Fair."

"Okay. Um…" Emily chokes on the lump in her throat. "There's something else we need to talk about."

Fear gathers on Liam's face. "No."

"I'm sorry," Emily whispers.

"No!" Liam crumbles and bawls.

Emily pulls him into a hug.

Emily takes a deep breath and stiffens her lips. "She passed this afternoon."

Liam wails until he's got nothing left. He pulls away from Emily, just enough to speak. "Can I say goodbye?"

"Do you want to?" Emily asks. She searches his eyes for the answer.

"Yes. Please."

"Okay. Come on."

* * *

Nurse Hernandez leads Emily and Liam down the hall. He puts his hand on the doorknob to Sarah's bedroom, but before he opens says, "I'll be just outside if you need anything."

"Thank you," Emily says.

The door opens and Nurse Hernandez steps aside. Emily holds Liam's shoulders from behind, his support, but lets him lead. Liam's feet stay stuck to the floor.

"You don't have to do this, buddy. We can find another way to say goodbye. We can find another time. It's okay." Emily rubs his shoulders as she encourages him to make the choice for himself.

Liam breathes in. "I want to. But, come with me?"

"Of course."

Liam's left foot moves half a step forward. His right follows. Left. Right. Left. Right. One half step at a time, he inches closer and leads Emily into the soft light of the bedroom.

Sarah's body rests in the hospice bed. The I.V. tubes and tapes have been removed. The machines and monitors are off and pushed away to make space for the family. Liam and Emily step in to fill it.

Liam is silent for a moment. Emily holds her breath and waits.

"I love you, Mom." Liam's voice breaks as he speaks. It's all he can do to not fall to the floor as his knees buckle and his weight pulls him down. But Emily is there to hold him up. She doesn't let him go. "Bye, momma."

He shifts his weight back into Emily, who grabs on tight and holds him from behind in a hug. Liam and Emily pour their grief out in tears as they cry next to Sarah's hospice bed.

* * *

Emily and Liam stand on the front porch and watch as Nurse Hernandez and an EMT load Sarah's covered body into an ambulance. Once she's secure, Nurse Hernandez approaches and offers support with a bowed head and a hand on Emily's shoulder.

"Ms. Cassius, Liam. Thank you for letting me be a part of this journey for you. The best of luck to you in your healing. Please know that we are here to offer counseling at any time in the future," Nurse Hernandez says.

"I have one more thing for you. Ms. Kenneth made me promise not to give this to you until after she was gone." Nurse Hernandez hands over a sealed envelope addressed to my baby, Liam and my friend, Emily.

Emily feels a strange rush of excitement that mixes with her grief. It's uncomfortable and anxious. She accepts the letter. Liam stares at Emily with anticipation. They rush back inside their home.

sixty-nine

TO MY DEAR friend Emily and my baby boy,

If you're reading this letter, it's probably the worst day of your lives, because it means it's the last day of mine. Please don't be too sad. We had so much fun in our short years together, and that's what I want you to remember. The fun stuff.

Liam, I want you to know you'll never be alone. Emily is your family now, and I trust she loves you and has promised to care for you as her own. Emily will give you more than I ever could, but remember to stay humble. It's not the things we gain in life that make us special. Listen to her and know that her actions and choices in raising you are me still living through her.

I owe you an apology for Drew. I never asked more of him. I never expected him to change to be your father, and that haunts me as my greatest failing as your mother. I should have demanded more, and it's okay to ask for more from people who are expected to be there for you in life. If one day Drew decides he can be that for you and will prove he is safe to be in your life, I encourage you and Emily to explore that with him. But until then, never feel ashamed for expecting more of the people in your life. You're worth it.

As far as an excuse for him, the best I can come up with is, sometimes in life people make choices that pull them away from those they love, not because they want to, but because the circumstances of their own life and trauma have forced it upon them. It doesn't mean that person doesn't love us or want to be around us. It just means they need help, they need patience, and they need our compassion. It also means the people who do stick around are the ones who are our real family and they don't have to be blood to be so.

To Emily, I see the sacrifice you've made for me and my son. You gave up a life you didn't have to, and I am eternally grateful. I've loved watching you grow and learn over these past few years. To see you use your birth right to fortune as a force for good in this world has been heartwarming to watch. I can rest in peace now knowing we made a difference in the world and added a nice pop of pink.

I wish you both the best this life offers, and I know you won't let this single day dampen the rest of them. Enjoy every sunset and sunrise. Say hello to the people around you and excite in learning about their lives. Collect your moments and remember those are what make life wonderful. Squeeze out every drop of every day you have left.

Lastly, I hope you'll grant my final wish, which is to have one last moment of me with the two of you. This is how I want you to remember me. Not that I fought against cancer, and lost, but that I fought for every single moment and won, because I have given and received love, and that's all I ever wanted. To fight for what I love, and win.

Because today marks the day I'm finally free from cancer. I'm gonna need you to go ahead and smash that cup for me. And you better celebrate the win!

Love eternally,
Your mom and friend,
Sarah.

seventy

EMILY FOLDS THE LETTER.

"What do you think? Should we do it?" Emily asks as tears trickle down both their cheeks.

Liam smiles, at peace. "Yeah. We should."

Emily and Liam jump up from the couch and race to the kitchen. Emily rummages through cabinets and searches for the original pink cup. Excitement flows through Liam as he jumps up and down, shouting at Emily.

"Hurry! Hurry! Let's do this!"

"Got it! Let's go!"

The two run from the kitchen to the backyard, to Sarah's clay-stained oasis—surrounded by her art, her memory, her turntable, and her clutter. Here they feel close to her.

"Ready?" Emily holds out the pink cancer cup.

Liam grasps the other side of the mug. "Ready."

Holding on to either side of the cup, Liam and Emily brace themselves.

"Smash..." Emily starts the chant.

"Smash... smash... smash..." Liam gives it life.

"Three more!" Emily shouts.

Together in unison, "SMASH..." their arms pump. "SMASH!" Their teeth grit and their smiles go wide. "SMASH!" Their arms raise... and release!

The cup hurls to the concrete. Pieces of pink ceramic scatter on the ground. Emily and Liam jump up in celebration! They laugh, they hug, they relish in the last moment they've collected, together, with Sarah.